~~Never~~ Fear

A Horror Anthology

Elle J Rossi
Patrick Freivald
Rachel Aukes
Lance Taubold
Kathy Love
Michael Koogler
E. McCarthy
Rich Devin
Paul Mannering
F. Paul Wilson

13Thirty Books

13Thirty Books, LLP in association with:
Elle J Rossi
Patrick Freivald
Rachel Aukes
Lance Taubold
Kathy Love
Michael Koogler
E. McCarthy
Rich Devin
Paul Mannering
F. Paul Wilson

13Thirty Books
Print and Digital Editions
Discover new and exciting works by award winning and debut authors at 13Thirty Books www.13thirtybooks.com

Print and Digital Edition, License Notes

Cover Design EJR Digital Art

ISBN: 978 0692408469
ISBN-10: 0692408460

CONTENTS

1   Alabaster Nights by Elle J Rossi   1

2   Taps by Patrick Freivald   45

3   Control+Alt+Delete by Rachel Aukes   61

4   Funeral March of a Marionette by Lance Taubold   87

5   Gris Gris by Kathy Love   103

6   The Agent by Michael Koogler   125

7   The Girl Next Door by E. McCarthy   139

8   Forward Base Fourteen by Patrick Freivald   153

9   Snapped! by Rich Devin   161

10   Where Billy Monasco Lay by Paul Mannering   173

11   The Barrens by F. Paul Wilson   181

Alabaster Nights

Elle J Rossi

1
Death Meets His Match

Keller

Death lurks around every corner. Death is a disease with no cure—a tyrant with a one-hundred-percent success rate. Mortals and immortals alike ingest the phantom's toxic essence with every breath, every sigh, every spoken and unspoken word.

I'm Keller O'Leary, and I have Death inside me—an all-consuming monster hell-bent on consumption and destruction. The beast burns beneath my cool skin, a fire that never weakens, clawing and tearing at the fragile tether I barely keep intact.

A light snow falls on my cheeks as I stand on the edge of a city fragrant with rich copper. Nashville, Tennessee. So much energy. So much life. I want all of it, want to absorb the life power of the humans laughing and carousing on the streets just beyond the shadows from where I watch. Perhaps then I will feel something more than insatiable hunger—something that just might be the salve I need to heal my ravaged soul.

I came to this quaint city for two reasons: my sister Sage, and the whispered promise of blood more powerful than any I've ever tasted. I doubt the latter, but will find out soon enough. When Sage had telepathically contacted me with a personal invitation, the pure excitement in her voice had me more than a little intrigued. Typically sullen, she'd transformed into someone else, and that someone wouldn't have taken no for an answer. Nor would she have had to. I will always come when Sage needs me. Besides, too much time has passed since our last visit.

Clouds slide across the moon like curtains drawn at the end of an act. My skin tingles in anticipation of the next. Something big will happen tonight. Something out of my control. The monster wild against its leash promises it.

Sensing prey, I focus.

A lush blonde breaks from a group exiting a small brick building, and she bids them farewell with a wave of her fingers. I sift through the intricate details of the crystal snowflakes and the soft glow of the holiday lights, zeroing in on the pulse point just beneath her ear. Her red dress hugs her curves and beckons me like a bullfighter's cape. The scooped neckline plunges too low for the chilled temperature, exposing the swell of her full breasts—an intentional play on her part to attract men. Neither that nor her shapely legs are what draws me to this particular beauty. Her pulse, on the other hand...

I step out of the shadows, teleport across several streets in a flash, and catch her as she stumbles, her heel catching in a sidewalk crack.

"Oops. Sorry about that," she says, giggling softly. She looks up and sucks in a breath. Her hand flutters to her chest, lingers.

I recognize the appreciation in her blue eyes. Part of my allure is that vampires are more striking than mortals, with a few exceptions. The other part is solely a benefit of exceptional DNA, something I can't take credit for.

Her pupils dilate. Her nostrils react with a slight flare. I've seen it before in women and men alike. My beauty distracts their senses, making my work easier. As her heart rate accelerates, Death roars to life, pushing me to move—to act. My feeding is long overdue. I could drain her in less than a minute.

I don't move. I don't have to kill.

I can let her walk away, follow her home, and wake up tomorrow between her warm thighs in her equally warm bed.

Death roars and prowls, pulling its chain tight, close to snapping. Death disagrees.

"No need to apologize." I peer into her eyes and turn my

Irish lilt up a notch. "Come with me."

She sighs, and I stride into the alley. I needn't turn to check if she follows. The power of persuasion has been a gift since the moment I was turned nearly a century ago. Many vampires have to work to hone their powers. I'm different. It all comes very natural to me. Something happened during the change to make it so, something my sire refuses to explain.

The moment we're off the main drag, I whip around and press her against the wall with one hand wrapped gently around her neck. I stroke her vein with my index finger. A touch of fear, along with a hint of excitement, plays across her features as her mouth widens to release a gasp. I clench my teeth and fight to maintain control. I flash, a blur of motion, and then my body is tight against hers. Brushing a hand over her hair, I draw her closer.

"Wha—what are you doing?"

I answer by sliding my palm up her thigh until she shivers with want. I tilt her head—

The monster keens. The tether snaps.

I pierce the taut skin of her neck. Blood coats my tongue, the flavor tainted by the alcohol she recently consumed. Death doesn't care. I drink.

She stiffens and whimpers. Alarms sound in my head urging me to stop before I take too much, but the flavor, the high... A single tear rolls down her face, sounding like the haunted whispers of a thousand souls. Her heart thuds, pounding against my chest. She fights, kicking me in the shin and twisting her body. Death laughs at her feeble attempts. I hold her steady, shove Death into the recesses and ease her pain by infusing my bite with a heavy dose of endorphins until she becomes so aroused she pulls me closer and tugs at my clothing. Death swears and commands me to change my course. I continue to drink, feeling stronger with each swallow. Power rushes through my veins. Her heart rate slows second by second until it fades to nothing but a soft quiver.

Death rallies, barking orders and encouraging me to drain her body of every last ounce.

I break away, gasping. The blonde slides to the ground in a heap, her legs folding under her like a ragdoll. The power that surged moments ago flees into the night, leaving me as I was before. A shell. A walking corpse with little but anger and resentment to guide me. I bend over and dry heave to no avail. The blood—her blood—is now part of me.

What have I done?

I crouch, listen. She isn't dead. Not yet, though the pallor of her skin warns she is very close. I quickly seal the wound on her neck with a soft lick, throw her over my shoulder, and race to the nearest hospital, thankful for the well-marked signage.

The blonde stirs as I dust a thin layer of snow from the sidewalk and prop her against the wall outside the Emergency Room entrance. Gripping both shoulders, I shake her, forcing her to open her eyes. This will only work if we maintain eye contact. I have to hurry.

"Who... are... you?" she whispers.

A nightmare. "Help is coming. Everything will be fine." I tap her cheek with two fingers until her eyes flutter open once again.

"I'm tired... so cold."

Guilt eats a hole in my gut. I shrug out of my jacket and lay it over her lap. "Remember nothing but the kiss of a stranger."

A touch of color creeps up her neck and smears across her face. Her breathing remains shallow, but she will be fine. Eventually.

I hear approaching footsteps coming from about ten feet away, inside the hospital. I turn to leave, but the woman grips my hand. I spare a moment for a last glance.

"I liked your kiss."

I smile half-heartedly. "They always do."

Teleporting two streets away, I distance myself from the memory of the near catastrophe. Death almost beat me this time.

The moment I stop moving, a cloaked figure slams me to the ground with a flying side-kick. I roll and jump to my feet. I pause mid-punch as the wind wraps me in my attacker's scent. Not male. Female.

My cold heart stutters in my chest. *Interesting. Disconcerting.* Eyes narrowed, I wonder if she has somehow cast a spell.

The brief hesitation costs me. The hooded woman nails me with a heavy boot to my ribcage. I rock back and shift as the gleam of a knife comes far too close for comfort. What would have been a direct hit to my heart, instead slices open my shirt and grazes my skin. The wound burns for the half second it takes to heal.

Whoever she is, whatever she is, she isn't playing around. I can't get a read on her and that troubles me.

I fake a turn, then swing my leg and clip her behind the knees. She stumbles and falls, catching herself with her palms before she kisses the ground. I nearly laugh in victory. If only I could see her face to know who I'd be laughing at. She smells like any other human, but her strength...

Maybe a witch. But I can smell a witch's magick from a mile away. It doesn't make sense. She doesn't make sense. And why am I playing around when I can end this by simply teleporting across town?

I know exactly why. For the first time in a very long time, I'm enjoying myself and want to prolong this dance. More importantly, I want to know how and why she stirs my slumbering heart.

I reach out to pull the hood off of the female who's bewitched me. The moment my hand skims the silky fabric, she throws a punch that lands a direct shot to my balls. Vision blurring, I double over. She shoves me hard enough for my ass to meet asphalt. Damn, she's good. Her combat boot connects with my chest. Leaning forward, she uses all her weight to hold me in place.

I let her believe she's the stronger being here while I try to wrap my mind around the impossibility of the string of words that refuse to leave my thoughts. *Capture. Claim. Mine. Evermore. Mate.*

"I don't know who you are, but I saw what you did." She moves in. As she leans closer, I strain to see more of her face. I'm certain she's mortal, but again, the thoughts confuse me. As does my stammering heart. I have to taste her—have to know. Would fate be so cruel as to tease me?

"Consider this your only warning."

I marvel at her bravado. No one warns me and lives to back up the threat. Still, I don't move.

"Get your fanged ass out of my city."

She kicks me once more and then runs off down an alley. Stunned, I watch her long cloak drifting behind her like a shimmering eel. I could have given chase, but my body is rooted in disbelief.

A few minutes in Nashville had changed the course of my life.

2
The Huntress Bleeds

JOSIE

He's been following me for two nights now, hiding in the shadows, trailing me as I prowl the streets armed with more blades than a sous chef. My best friend Sage was right about one thing. Her brother is of the determined sort. What she didn't mention is that he's more than a little odd. He stares at me like he's trying to steal my soul. Perhaps he simply worries for Sage and wants to know if her new partner is who she says she is. Instinct tells me it's more than that.

But ever since Sage told Keller she and I were opening a bar together, or perhaps even before then, when I caught him red-fanged and warned him to leave town, he's been lurking.

I'm pretty sure he thinks I can't see him. I'm guessing no one has ever told him that it's kinda hard to hide when you're six-plus feet of solid sexy vampire. Said vampire has chosen me as his object of fixation and I'd like to know why. What I do is dangerous, and I can't afford the distraction. When I think of Keller, the word stable never enters my mind. It's not easy keeping one eye on my crazy stalker and the other on the rest of Nashville. I'm a Huntress. I kill bad things in the night, and occasionally during the day too.

Slowing, I take in my surroundings and ignore the cold air as it creeps down my spine. Each breath is a series of smoke signals, rolling toward the dark sky and evaporating into the night. I've never been a fan of winter and we're having a particularly cold one this year. I'll admit that the decorated trees and wreaths do add a bit of heart-warming ambience to the chilly season. Not enough to heat my toes, though. As soon as the sun starts shining, I'm heading straight to my apartment to sleep under the hot spray of water in my crappy-ass shower. The sun and I are about to become really good friends. Daylight seems to be my only escape from Mr. Crazy Vampire Dude.

In front of me is the rough section of town, the part of the city slathered in poverty and despair. While crime is rampant there, it's of the human variety and not my specialty. I'm leaving that particular neck of the woods to the cops tonight. To my right are a handful of bars and restaurants, closed up tight until business hours roll back around and humans roll out of bed. Printer's Alley is on my left and currently solely occupied by Keller O'Leary.

I see him, watching me intently, almost as if he's ready to intervene if necessary. Like I need the help. I've been doing this for a while now. On my own. I feed off the adrenaline. I live for the hunt. Keller, on the other hand, is beginning to look like he's a faded tumbleweed about to roll down the street of a ghost town.

Leaning against the wall, he shifts from one foot to the other, either restless or desperate, I can't tell which. I haven't seen him feed since the incident with the blonde, and I've been watching closely. Almost as closely as he watches me. His dark eyes are full of ghosts. If I cared, I'd ask him what demons haunt him, what has he seen—or done—in his life that makes his eyes so disturbing and calculating. He closes those dark eyes now and I make my move.

"Who hired you to be my babysitter?"

The sharp edge of my knife presses against his jugular. Keller keeps his eyes closed. Even though he's feigning nonchalance, his muscles tighten in a way that has me on high alert. I can't afford to be trapped. I've seen what he can do when hungry and I've probably just roused a sleeping bear. I apply more pressure. Slicing him open wouldn't kill him, but it would make me feel better.

"I'm not daft, Josephine," he says in that Irish lilt that makes the pit of my stomach hotter than the glowing end of a branding iron. I haven't been attracted to anyone in quite awhile. Why now? Why Sage's brother?

"I know you would never stand for a babysitter."

"I'm not a baby." Go, me. Great comeback. Usually I'm snappier with my retorts. I'm off my game and it's his fault. I think it might be his artfully mussed hair. Or maybe it's the dimple in his chin. He's too pretty. I should kick him in the face, though I'd probably need a ladder to reach that high. If I leave a mark, he won't look so perfect and then I can get back to business rather than daydreaming that I'm a painter and he's my subject. That's pretty hysterical considering my stick figures look more like blobs. "And stop calling me Josephine." Yeah. I stop short of stomping my foot.

Keller slowly opens his eyes, studies me with that sharp gaze of his until I squirm, and then smiles like he's just scored an A on his biology test. "Why?"

Sighing, I withdraw the knife and tuck it back into the nylon sheath strapped to my right thigh. Too bad. I'm eager for a kill, but if I kill Keller, I'm out a best friend. Sage and I have plans—big plans that don't include a family member's funeral. Though I'm sure Keller would be quite comfortable in a casket. I crack myself up.

Keller is still staring at me, waiting for an answer.

"You don't need a reason other than I told you not to." My fingers toy with the frayed edges of my shirt hem. I stop and stand perfectly still, silently chastising myself for fidgeting. The only person who calls me Josephine is my father, who I happen to think walks on water. No one else, including Irish here, has earned the right to call me by my given name.

Keller nods. "So you did. I'll do my best to adhere to your command."

"I'd appreciate that." Pulling my jacket closed, I glance behind me.

"You've got tall walls."

Turning back to him, my eyebrows draw together for the briefest of moments. I smooth them out and try to appear bored. "Excuse me? What's that supposed to mean?"

Keller slides his hands into the front pockets of his jeans. I swear I do not notice anything below the belt region.

"It's too quiet tonight," I say, changing subjects. I'm pretty sure I know exactly what he means by tall walls and I have every intention of keeping them firmly in place. In fact, I might even add a few more rows of bricks and put a roof on top. I've always wanted to live in a fortress.

Keller shrugs slowly, as if the effort costs him. "Everyone needs a night off at some point. Perhaps you could wrap it up early. Maybe we could get to know each other a little better. For Sage, of course."

I have a feeling his definition of *better* is intimately and includes dinner. *His dinner.* I shake my head. "No. In my world quiet is like the calm before the storm." Besides, I'm not the one who needs to go take a nap. Judging by the circles under Keller's eyes, he's in need of sleep and more. If he thinks I'm tonight's special on the menu, he's sorely mistaken. My neck is a no-fang zone. "It's going to be a bad night. You should probably find a place to hide. Sage wouldn't be happy if you got hurt."

Reaching out, he wraps his finger around a lock of my hair. Instinct tells me to jerk away and run. Run until I can't run anymore. Instead, I stand very still.

"Who will take care of you when you get hurt?"

I blink. Trust me. I'm very used to a lack of faith in my skills from others. It doesn't faze me. But for someone reason, Keller's doubt hurts worse than the sting of a fat-tailed scorpion. "When? Not if?"

Keller slides his hand through my hair and cradles the back of my neck. It's so hard not to move when my insides are trembling. His touch is like an electric jolt and I've just been fried. I can't help but to wonder if he's using some of his vampiric power on me. That would be a very big mistake.

He leans closer. "We all get hurt eventually." He smiles, just a quick show of teeth before he grows serious again.

I swing. Keller anticipates my move and shifts so I only clip his jaw with my uppercut. Flashing his fangs, he drags a hand through his hair. I kick. He catches my leg. I drop and spin out of his grasp. My back slams into the wall, rattling my bones.

"Stop," I order as he advances, my arm extended as a shield. He slows. Barely. "Stop what?"

"Stop…" I blow out a shaky breath. "Just stop everything."

"I get it. You're affected. I am, too. We'll figure it out."

I'm affected all right. I'm so affected I want to sink my blade into his gut and twist it until he comes to his senses. Or until I come to mine. I don't like to be played with. "I have no idea what you're talking about. There's nothing to figure out." Needing something to do with my hands, I pull my hair to the side and start braiding. "May I offer you a word of advice?"

Keller slides his tongue over his teeth. "I'm all ears."

He's all something, but it's definitely not ears. I realize braiding my hair has exposed my neck. Sighing, I unbraid it and let it hang loose over my shoulders. "Find yourself the nearest blood bank. You're looking a little green tonight. Then, once you've re-fueled, find something useful to do."

I turn and leave him to chew on that thought. I've only jogged a few feet away when a pair of demons barrel around the corner, eyes redder than the blinking traffic signal overhead. I skid to a stop, my hands already wrapped around the leather hilts of two five-inch blades. One demon is the shade of neon green with two yellow horns jutting at a ninety-degree angle from his forehead. A row of sharp spikes shoots out the length of his spine all the way down to the tip of his eight-foot tail. The other demon is albino. No horns or spikes, but the five pink talons on the end of each of his six feet make my blades look like barely sharpened pencils.

"Hello, spawn." I move, light on my feet. "Which of you would like to die first?"

"*Bloooood*," they sing in unison.

Keller races past me.

"Hey!" I yell. "Stay back and let me do my job."

Ignoring me, he jumps about ten feet straight up into the air, comes down spinning, and kicks the demon with horns into the wall. The demon folds into himself, turns, and hisses, sending acidic saliva flying in a wide arc.

Toxic demon spit hits both of my legs, burns through my jeans, and eats at my skin. "Dammit, Irish." I'm afraid to look at the damage, but can picture the skin bubbling as searing pain brings me to my knees. I'm going to need more than a Band-Aid this time. The albino demon swipes at me. I arch back and feel the crisp air that accompanies his swing.

In two quick motions, Keller breaks his demon's neck, and then grabs the albino by its tail and pulls.

"*Bloooood.*"

The tail detaches and Keller sails backward, stubby tail in hand. The demon rushes me, maw gaping to expose four rows of razor-sharp teeth. Back on my feet, I jam my blade between the demon's eyes. He screams, the sound so blood curdling and human-like I pause. His jaws snap closed on my arm, teeth tearing into my flesh and sinking into my bones. White-hot agony sears me. The pain in my leg has nothing on this. I'm pretty sure I'm two seconds from being an amputee. Stars dot my vision and they're not the ones in the sky. Breathing through the pain, I pull out my blade and slam it into the albino's skull just behind his ear. When he opens his mouth to scream again, I jump back. Blood flows, running down my arm and dripping from my fingers, the red a sharp contrast to the white snow.

The demon's tongue flicks at the ground, tasting my blood.

I'm about to pass out and that really pisses me off. I shake my head. *Focus.*

An inhuman roar rips through the air. Through my blurred vision, I see Keller's fangs elongate as he positions his body between me and the albino demon. I stumble backward, lose my footing, and sink to the ground. The last thing I see is Keller ripping the head off *my* demon and provoking my last thought.

I can't believe he just stole my kill.

3
Death Chooses Sides

Keller

I rein in my hunger as best I can and lift Josie into my arms, supporting her head with my shoulder. I pull the back of her cloak up and over her legs. That simple action brings a sense of right, a sense of duty. Adjusting my mindset around this new obligation will take some time. If she is indeed my mate, then I am up for the task. Whatever it takes, I will do this right, no matter how hard the ever-swinging pendulum tries to throw me off course.

With renewed purpose, I intentionally don't breathe, but the strong aroma of Josie's dripping blood calls to me anyway. My stomach clenches and knots like my guts are being squeezed in a vise grip. I carefully close my lips over my fangs and drag my hungry gaze away from the red pool of mockery at my feet. Taking her blood will accomplish two things: Give me the strength I desperately need and confirm she is the one meant for me. But taking it *now* would make me the blood-stealing monster Josie believes me to be. Even though blood has already spilled, it is still hers. I have to prove her wrong—even if it kills.

The temperature drops and the snow falls incessantly. I sense a dangerous blizzard on the horizon. Perhaps it is nothing more than my emotions that are riled. Doubtful. My instincts are rarely wrong. Josie shivers. Her head falls heavier on my shoulder with each tremble. I hold her closer, careful not to crush her injured arm, and zip through the near-empty streets. I dismiss another visit to the local hospital. Too many people. Too many questions I can't—won't— answer, and I'm not leaving her at the door. Teleporting crosses my mind for the briefest of moments before I abandoned the notion. I don't know enough about Josie to determine if she can handle it. Especially in her current condition. Not to mention I'm not in top form since I haven't fed for the past three days. Attempting teleportation could be a disaster.

I'll have to feed soon. Or be prepared to suffer the consequences.

More than likely it would be the latter because the only blood I want now is from the one person who will never offer it up.

I mentally connect with Sage and instruct her to meet me at Josie's apartment building, and then immediately slam the connection closed, cutting her off before she can ask for details I'm not ready to give. I know exactly where Josie lives. I've been as far as the hallway outside her apartment and have probably worn a hole in the already tattered carpet with all my pacing, desperate to know if she is the one who can settle my troubled soul. I'll need a fecking invitation to get inside her home, and I won't be getting one from the woman passed out in my arms.

When her building comes into view, I slow and evaluate the scene. No one is standing outside. No lights shine from the few windows that aren't covered in plywood. The brown brick structure, trimmed in accents of chipped red paint, shoots up five floors and is flanked by a souvenir shop on one side and a small eatery on the other. Josie's building isn't dilapidated, per se, but it also isn't what one would call inviting or safe. I'm most concerned about the safety factor, or lack thereof. Anyone can come and go as they pleased through the main door. Me included. I've done just that for two nights now after following her home like a randy teenager amped up on over-stimulated hormones.

Surely, as a Huntress, Josie has created enemies, enemies that could be lying in wait even now. A low growl emanates from deep in my chest. Any opponent of Josephine Hawk will have to get through me first.

With the way I'm feeling, I wonder if I even need to taste her blood to know who she is to me. It's becoming pretty clear. Will I even feel any differently after I taste her blood? I can't imagine her blood could belie my instincts. Still, it doesn't ease my need to taste her...

I wrench the main door open—ignoring the scraping of metal against concrete—and jog up three flights of stairs. Neither of the elevators work according to the hand-written notice hanging carelessly from the doors. If Josie's funds are so low that she can only afford a place like this, how does she plan to go into business with Sage?

Rounding the corner, I gently shush Josie when she moans. The sound—knowing she is in pain—tears my heart wide open.

"Hush now, Ms. Hawk. You can bet you're in good hands, you are."

I glance down and suck in a ragged breath at the raw site of her injury. Mangled flesh, charred around the edges, gives way to bone. Demon saliva is often laced with poison. The thought of lethal toxins swimming through Josie's veins has me ready to maim and murder. My skin burns with the need for retribution. If I feel this protective now, how will I feel when my suspicions are confirmed?

I keep my voice quiet and steady, even as rage has me seeing red. "We'll fix you up right. You'll be on the streets in no time." Not where I want her, but where she prefers to be.

Josie doesn't move. She doesn't moan again either. I take that as a good sign.

While I wait for Sage, I press my back against the wall and slide down slowly so as not to jostle Josie. I ease her between my legs, then shrug out of my jacket, pull my shirt over my head and rip it into two long strips. Tying a strip around each end of the wound, I pull it tight to cut off the blood flow in hopes that will keep the poison from spreading. Her breathing quickens, but I don't loosen the improvised tourniquets.

Sage whips around the corner, her pink hair bound in haphazard braids.

"What the hell happened?" Her bright grey eyes mirror saucers. Her hand flies to her mouth and lingers when she sees Josie's arm.

"It's bad," I say. "Get me inside."

Sage doesn't move.

"Sage!" I snap, adjusting Josie against my body. I know the sight of her shredded arm is horrific to Sage. I feel the same, but for different reasons. Now isn't the time for either one of us to lose it. "Keep it together. We need you with a strong mind and body."

"Right," she says, springing into action and pulling a set of keys from her pocket. She opens Josie's door and steps inside. "Hurry."

Isn't that what I've been trying to tell her? I push against the wall and stand, fighting for balance. "Say it."

"What? Oh," she says, her voice an octave higher than usual. "Come in, come in." She jumps out of my way.

I step over the threshold and rush to Josie's bed. The door closes behind me and the lock snicks into place. While stacking pillows beneath Josie's head, I glance at Sage. "You have to suck out the poison." I pull off Josie's boots and tug the sheet up over her legs, cursing when I notice the burn holes in her jeans. Josie's entire body is shaking.

"Me? What poison?"

I look for a blanket and find one with a bright floral pattern crumpled in the corner. "Demon."

Sage curses under her breath and points her finger at me. "Why didn't you do it already?"

I wanted to. Wanted it more than anything. "She would hate me."

"So what? She'd get over it." Sage rips the blanket out of my hands and covers Josie. She kneels next to the bed and reaches for Josie's hand.

Jaw clenched tight, I shake my head. "Maybe. Maybe not."

"I don't understand you, Keller. Since when do you worry about what other people think of you? That's my bag, not yours."

Before I can answer, Sage lowers her mouth to Josie's arm and begins to suck, her cheeks hollowing out with each draw.

I turn away.

"There's a lot of poison," Sage says.

Grinding my teeth, I stare at the pale green walls and rub the back of my neck. "Then why are you talking? Get it the feck out of her." Sage doesn't deserve my anger, but I have to direct it at someone and since I've already killed the demons, I have nowhere else to go with these feelings. Where is Death now?

Though the poison won't harm my sister, the sound of Sage taking in Josie's blood nearly does me in. I brace my hand against the wall and lock my knees to keep from crumbling like a sack of useless potatoes. A distraction is what I need.

I spend the next several minutes tuning out the sound of Sage extracting the poison and instead take inventory of Josie's apartment, which is only slightly larger than a closet, in my opinion. She lives here, that's evident in the damp towels thrown on top of the cluttered dresser and the sharp set of knives carefully lined up in neat rows on the chipped kitchen counter. The lack of personal items— photos, trinkets, jewelry—tells me either Josie doesn't hold anything sacred, or she's been hurt too much to cling to keepsakes. I hope it's the latter. Not that I wish sorrow on my probable mate, but at least if she hurts, she can feel. I'm cold enough for the two of us.

"It's done," Sage says, her voice barely above a whisper. "The wound is already starting to heal."

"You'll need to tend to her leg, too."

"I already did."

Of course she did. Sage would be thorough where her best friend is concerned. I set down the blade I'd been gripping and move to Sage's side to study Josie. Her skin is still very pale, but Sage is right about the healing. I watch as Josie's tendons weave together, muscle regenerates, veins fuse.

"She's strong." A combination of relief and pride decide to take up residence. So does a slew of questions.

"Yes. She is. I have no doubt she would have made it through this on her own," Sage says. "But thanks for calling me. She won't be happy about it, but we helped speed up her recovery."

"You did and I'm grateful to you." I clasp my hands behind my head and squeeze. The pain caused by my refusal to feed is escalating. I turn to Sage, note the traces of pink on her cheeks and the drop of blood in the corner of her mouth. I reach out and wipe it off with the pad of my thumb. Then I stare at the smear of red, craving…refusing. I move to the sink and wash my hands.

The mattress creaks. Hopeful, I turn, but Josie hasn't moved. Sage sits on the end of the bed with her long legs flung over the footboard. Yet another new tattoo peeks out from beneath the hem of her jeans to wrap around her ankle in an intricate pattern.

Sage folds her hands in her lap. "Care to tell me what's going on with you?"

I cross my arms over my chest and snort. How can I explain what I don't understand myself?

Sage holds silent, giving me the time to try and sort it out. In the end, I decide to share my thoughts. "She's the one, Sage."

I wonder if she even heard me until I look up.

Her eyes are wide and bright, her mouth hangs slightly ajar. "Who? Josie? No," she says, shaking her head hard enough to have her braids knocking against each other. "It's impossible. I would have sensed something. Right?"

I didn't realize I moved from the kitchen area until I felt the silkiness of Josie's hair between my fingers. "You and I both know it's entirely possible. And maybe you did sense it. Maybe that's why you called me here."

Sage swivels to face me. "I don't know, Keller. While I'd like nothing more than to see both my brother and my best friend happy, it will never work between you two."

I stiffen. Josie's hair slides from my hand and settles on the pillow, the red locks a sharp contrast to the yellow sheets. "Why not?" Two words spoken with enough ice to frost the room.

"You'll smother her." Sage pats my shoulder, unaffected by my anger. "Josie doesn't have it in her to be who you need her to be."

I hadn't even heard Sage move. I blame my lack of awareness on nutritional deficiency and emotional instability, both of which I have little control over at the moment. "And who do I need her to be?"

"Someone who lets you lead. You're too protective, too intense for someone like Josie."

Since when has wanting to protect someone become a fault? "What if I think she's perfect exactly how she is?" Josie's wound seals closed. The only evidence she had been hurt is the redness that marks her skin from inflammation. She'll stir soon, won't she? I move to the window, note at least an inch of snow has fallen since we've come inside. There will be a lot more before the sun breaks over the horizon.

"You can't know that yet, Keller. You don't know her."

"But I will."

"She won't let you."

I spin on my heel and nail Sage with a glare. "She let you."

Sage flinches. "It's not as easy as that," she says on a sigh. "She's half human, Keller. I'm probably betraying her by telling you that. But you need to know. It's only part of what makes her so complex and so...difficult. Look, what Josie and I have has taken years to cultivate. She doesn't trust easily. And she's more closed off than anyone I've ever met."

"You think I can't see that?" I pace. "I didn't choose this. I didn't choose her. But something tells me I would have if I'd been given a choice. I don't care what or who she is, and it pisses me off that you would think otherwise. She calms me, Sage."

"Um, yeah. I can totally see that. You're the epitome of calm right now."

I stand still, glance at Josie's sleeping form. When I speak again, my voice is so quiet I wonder if I've spoken aloud. "I need her. Am I wrong to think she might need me, too?"

Sage sits and buries her face in her hands. "You're not wrong." She looks up. "Is this what you really want?"

"She is who I want, yes."

"And can you let her be Josie? Can you handle who she is?"

I open my mouth and then snap it closed. I won't lie to Sage. Can I let Josie continue on this dangerous path night after night? She'd nearly been killed by a demon—one that wanted the taste of her blood. Why? Demons don't need blood to survive. What is so special about Josie's blood? I make a silent vow before sharing a part of it with Sage.

"I understand a Huntress has to hunt. I won't deny her that. But know this...I will do everything in my power to protect her."

"Even if she doesn't want you to?"

"Even if. She is my mate. I know it like I know I need to feed soon or perish." The thought of dying without knowing my mate, without touching every inch of her body, without tasting her just one time, unsettles me on a level I didn't know existed.

"Have you tasted her blood at all?"

I stiffen, my fangs jut out of my gums with equal parts need and desire. I shake my head in answer.

Sage nods, her expression full of understanding. "That would confirm everything."

"It would," I say. "But I won't take it until she's willing." I have a plan—one that involves trust. It won't be easy for either of us. I might not know her well, but I know with utter certainty, the Huntress is worth waiting for.

"That might be never."

"I understand. If that's the case, eternity just got a hell of a lot shorter."

Sage stands and wraps her arms around me. "She won't be easy to love."

"Neither am I."

"I disagree. But I'll help you, Keller. You deserve to be happy." Sage kisses me on the cheek, brushes a hand over Josie's hair and lets herself out.

Sage is leaving me alone with Josie. It speaks volumes of her trust in me.

I watch the rise and fall of Josie's chest. I don't deserve happiness, but I sure as feck want it.

4

The Vampire Sees Red

Keller

The street below remains empty, devoid of life except for the falling snow, but danger lurks somewhere on the outskirts of town. Close, but not close enough for me to do anything about it. Even through my hunger-induced fatigue, I can practically taste the sinister thoughts of the dark beings. Perhaps I hear them because I walk on the darker side of the line. Or had until I met Josie. But why are they here now? What do they want?

I step back from the window and close the flimsy blinds against the snow that's been piling up for the last several hours. I slip into the bed and pull the cool sheet up to my waist. For the first time in a very long time, I find the quiet of the night unsettling. I miss the rich sound of Josie's voice. I want to wake her, listen to her mordant comments about how she owns the town, how she'll kick my arse to the next county if I don't abide by her rules. So fierce. So stubborn. Instead, I settle for lazily strumming my fingers through her hair while listening to the soft sound of her breathing.

I rest for no more than a couple of minutes before resuming my post. If my instincts are right, more than a blizzard has blown into Nashville. If nothing else, I trust my gut, and my gut is telling me I'm not the only one who's heard about the powerful blood in Nashville. A town that has more than its fair share of occult beings. A town that requires a Huntress to patrol the streets.

From the moment I stepped foot in Nashville, I knew something big would happen. The more I think about it, the more I realize everything seems to center around the woman who's thawed my frozen heart.

I bring a wavy red lock to my nose and breathe deeply before letting it slide from my fingers. My nerves tingle with awareness the moment her hair lands on my arm. I fist my hands and fight for control. Gods, how I want her. Everything about Josie is intoxicating. Even her temper. I smile to myself. She'll be spitting mad when she wakes and finds me stretched out next to her, taking up more than half the bed. A smarter man would make himself a ghost before she stirs.

Not gonna happen. I won't leave until I know Josie is back to her old self. A thought trickles in before I can prevent that particular train from derailing. I stop myself just short of growling. Only one thing—one being—could force me to leave. If my sire summons me now, I will fight the call as long as I can. Being here is more important than any task the sire can conjure simply to punish me. Always to punish. The lack of a crime doesn't matter in the least to the elder vampire. When the sire calls, which he often does, the *family* listens… and acts.

No. I have to stay here. What if someone comes in while Josie sleeps? The lone lock on her door is shoddy at best, her weapon stash too far out of reach to do any good. I should know. I've combed every inch of the place while the Huntress counts sheep. If she is as lethal as she claims to be, why does she keep her knives on the other side of the room? Even with the apartment being no bigger than a double jail cell, she probably can't cover ground fast enough. Not fast enough for my peace of mind. Knowing the tantalizing woman is half-human confirms my thoughts. Humans are fragile. Josephine Hawk needs me in her life. I think back to the demons in the alley. Aye, I would kill for her. So much emotion and I have yet to taste one drop of her blood. Still…

I know.

Feel it with every fiber of my being.

The Huntress is the one.

Outside, the wind wails, its song a lonesome and haunting melody that has me inching closer to the warmth of Josie.

The lights blink out, shrouding her room in total darkness. I look toward the window, to the soft light shining through the haphazard slats of the blinds. The streetlamps outside flicker once and then, they too, illuminate no more. My vision adjusts slower than usual. The clock is ticking and time isn't on my side.

Perhaps the lack of light is the jolt of caffeine Josie needs. Or maybe the shrill sound of the wind and the rattling of the window. Whatever the trigger, she jackknifes halfway off the bed and sucks in air as if she's been under water for the last forty-eight hours rather than passed out like a hibernating bear.

I don't move, don't speak, don't breathe. I simply watch as she slides the rest of the way out of bed and stumbles around the room flicking light switches up and down as if she can will the power to come back. She moves to the kitchen, swear words flying out of her mouth with the ease of a truck driver as she rustles through the drawers. A moment later, a flame dances on the end of a match and a candle sparks to life. She shuffles to the bathroom, splashes water on her face and quickly brushes her teeth, mumbling to herself the entire time.

Shadows play across her exquisite mouth and highlight her sharp cheekbones. Her profile intrigues me. Everything about her intrigues me. So much so, I want to crawl inside her body and introduce myself to her soul.

Candle in hand, Josie turns, and nearly blows out the flame on a rush of breath. Even in the dark, I see the fury crackling in her eyes.

"How did you get in my apartment?" she demands. "Why aren't you wearing a shirt? Get out of my bed!"

Hearing her voice after hours of silence is like drinking a cold beer in the heat of summer. What I remember it to be anyway. Ecstasy. "Sage invited me in, and you're not wearing any pants. I'd say that makes us even." I think I should smile, try for friendly, but I don't have the energy the motion requires. As it is, I can hardly keep myself propped up on my elbow. Not that I'll let my weakness show.

She glances down before leveling me with a look made of equal parts fire and ice. "I'm gonna kill her."

"No, you won't kill her. You love her too much. Besides, the circumstances called for it."

Huffing, Josie turns, sets the jarred candle on her dresser, and bends to root around the pile of clothes on the floor.

Now I smile. How could I not with a view like that? Lush and plentiful curves.

She tugs a pair of sweats over her creamy legs. Unfortunate, that. I half expect her to retrieve one of her blades. She doesn't. My smile widens. Perhaps we're making progress.

"What are you smiling at, and why the hell aren't you moving?" Josie asks, hands on hips.

"I'm not leaving."

Rolling her eyes, she says, "Oh, well, in that case."

Her exaggerated tone has me stifling a laugh.

She steps closer. "What's wrong with you? Why does your voice sound like that?"

"So many questions," is all I can manage to say. Rest. Just for a moment. Eyes closed, I let my head fall off my hand and smack the pillow.

"Look here, Irish. This isn't Motel 6." She tugs on my arm. "You need to get up and out of here." She pulls harder. When I don't move, she lets go and groans out a sigh full of frustration.

I pop one eye open. "We're not going anywhere. Take a look outside. Besides," I say, flicking a hand in her direction. "You need to rest more. You were hurt pretty badly."

"Wrong answer. As you can see, I'm perfectly fine."

I let my gaze skim over her body when she moves to the window. More than fine, I think. "You have Sage and I to thank for that."

Another eye roll. "I don't need, and I certainly didn't ask for your help."

"You're welcome anyway."

Josie shoves the blinds to the side, leans against the wall and crosses her legs at her ankles. "What the hell?"

"Blizzard," I say, closing my eyes again. Two minutes. No more than three.

"This is Nashville. We don't do blizzards. I seriously don't have time for this shit."

Chuckling, I turn to my side and push the thought of a nap

from my mind. "I think you forgot to relay that information to the weather gods. You've definitely got more than the makings of a blizzard out there."

"How long?" She plops on the bed and then shoots straight up as if the mattress is made of hot coals.

How long will I wait for her? How long has the snow been falling? How long since I've slid into the heat of a woman? Forever. Not long enough. Too long. "How long what, Josephine?"

"I'm only going to ask nicely one more time. Please, do not call me that."

I nod, which is not to say I am by any means agreeing with her. And if that is her idea of asking nicely, I have my work cut out for me.

"How long has it been since you've fed?"

Now why hadn't that form of the question crossed my mind? I know exactly how long it's been. My body won't let me forget. A chronic headache. Aching bones. Weak muscles. An internal slow burn. Five excruciating painful days. "Awhile."

She moves back to the window. "Why?"

I stand on shaky legs. With precisely placed steps, I walk the perimeter of the bed, leaning against the mattress for support. I hope she didn't notice. Her narrowed eyes tell me otherwise. At the window, I pull the cord of the blinds, tugging until they move past my head. I remain silent. So much to say and no way to say it without scaring her off.

"Why haven't you been feeding, Keller?"

Maybe it's the softened tone of her voice. I haven't heard that one before. Maybe it's the fact that she used my first name rather than Mr. O'Leary or Irish. Though I find both to be quite endearing. Maybe it's the way we turn at the same time to study the pristine white blanket covering the world outside. Whatever it is, I take an unnecessary but calming breath before I speak. "I can't."

"I repeat... why?" Her voice is no more than a whisper.

Does she suspect what I already know? Her breath caresses my cheek. So close, but miles too far away. "Because yours is the only blood I want."

Part of me expects her to punch me in the mouth, knock out a fang or two. The other part expects her to laugh in my face. Josie does neither. She simply turns to stare out the window again.

"You think it holds something special?"

She makes it sound like a question, but I hear the weariness in her statement. She's been down this road before. That doesn't sit well with me, or her if her tone is any indication. I clear my throat. "I know it does."

Josie shrugs. "Well, you're gonna have to get in line, fang boy."

Instantly, anger fueled by raw, primal possession simmers in my blood. "What's that supposed to mean?" Stand in line? Feck that. "Behind who?"

Josie flicks her gaze to mine before shoving off the wall. "It means you're just as misinformed as the rest of them."

Them. My suspicions are true. Josie stands front and center in the game of blood. I track her path with my ears. She pads across the worn carpet on bare feet. I hear her open the rattling refrigerator, snag what I assume to be a water bottle since the white box contains nothing but water and two jars of jelly. The sound of her swallowing has me wetting my lips.

"The rest of them?"

At the window again, she purses her lips and seems to sort through her thoughts.

"There are those who think my blood carries something they need. Something *special*. I've had it tested. It doesn't. You're wrong. They're wrong." She drains the rest of the bottle before chucking it toward the kitchen. "Still won't stop them from trying to prove it for themselves. You either, I suspect. But know this, Keller O'Leary. I'll be damned if I'm offering up a sample to you or anyone else."

Just the thought of someone else taking what was meant for me and me only has me ready to destroy. Struggling to maintain control, I speak slowly. "I won't take what you're not willing to give." I can't say the same for the others. They'll have to get through me first.

"Then you're in the minority."

Yes. That is true. In this case, minority equals one. No other is meant solely for her. I consider all I have seen and heard since arriving in Nashville and narrow down my list of suspects. Warlocks had been watching her that night in the bar. Demons had attacked and hurt her, called for her blood. I've dealt with demons on more than one occasion and know the spawn can be controlled, and it doesn't take much to do it. Demons have very weak minds. "The warlocks?"

Her lips part. Surprise flickers in her eyes. "How could you know that?"

I finally give into the fatigue and sit back down on the bed. "I watch. I listen. What do they want it for?"

She sits next to me. I wait for her to jump up and away. She doesn't. Not this time.

"I'm assuming to use in their black magick spells." Josie absently braids her hair. "What I'd like to know is who started this rumor. I'd gut him and leave him on display."

I would like to know that, too. Whispers led me to Nashville, led me to my mate. Whispers amongst the darkest beings of the occult inside the cruelest walls I've ever had the misfortune to stay within. That my confinement had been voluntary doesn't change what went on inside the Colony. What has Josie gotten herself into?

If only the Seers' muddled ramblings had been clearer. Maybe then their whispers would have given me more answers. In my experience, the word Seer can be found right next to insane in the dictionary. I imagine I, too, would be crazier than a loon if unwanted visions flooded my thoughts.

"I should give it to them and laugh when they fail," she continues. "And they will fail. No doubt about it. But it's the principle of the damn thing, you know?"

"Don't."

She tilts her head. "What?"

"Don't ever give them one drop of your blood."

"Why? Because I should give it to you?"

Yes. Over and over again. "Only when you're ready."

"Not gonna happen, Irish. You look terrible, though," she says while bunching the sheets in her fists. "I could go out and get you—"

I place my index finger to her lips. I nearly shake as a rush of power races along my skin. "No."

Brows drawn together, voice barely a whisper, Josie asks, "What are you doing?"

"Showing you something."

"What?"

Everything. "That you want me every bit as I want you."

She shakes her head. "You're so far from the truth on that one, you're practically on another planet."

I can work with words like practically. The door might not be wide open, but she hasn't slammed it in my face either. "Prove it. Just one kiss, Miss Hawk. One kiss to show me how very wrong—or *right*—I am."

At least thirty heartbeats pass before she speaks. I count each one. "That's it? One kiss—no fang action included—and you'll leave me alone?"

I bite the inside of my cheek to keep from smiling. I swallow and swear I taste the sweet flavor of victory. The shadows cast by the lone candle seem to dance. "*If* I'm wrong." If I had more time, I would take this slow, court her the old-fashioned way, the way my father had taught me. As it is, I run the risk of alienating Josie by pushing too hard too fast. This is a risk I have to take.

Smug smile firmly in place, Josie says, "Then prepare to be on the first bus out of Nashville."

Neither move. Eyes locked, we stare, a challenge accepted on both sides, both ready to claim the prize. I moisten my lips and will my fangs to retract. A promise is a promise after all. I want so badly to pull her against me, to possess her in one swoop of uncontrolled passion, to taste her blood and thereby her mind. The fact that Josie will expect just that forces me to go slowly.

Chest constricting, arousal spiking, I slide my palm along her arm, over the smooth skin of her elbow, inching up until my hand wraps around the back of her neck. Pleasure surges within me, knowing I am responsible for the racing of her heart, the upsurge of her body temperature. Applying slight pressure with the pad of my thumb, I ease Josie toward me, meeting her halfway. My lips brush against her pouting mouth, just the lightest of touches…

Ears roaring, heart pounding, skin tingling with renewed energy, my world shifts, changed forever by the barest of kisses. The color red washes over my vision, blinding me from everything but the woman I will soon claim.

5

The Huntress Gambles

JOSIE

I'm losing.

I don't like to lose, but that's exactly what's happening. I'm paying the price for my misplaced bravado.

I can't breathe.

My heart is seriously about to bust out of my chest. Sweat slides down my spine. It's hotter than Hades in here, and yet it's not hot enough. I want more. Dangerous amounts of more. I knew there was something between us, a mild attraction of sorts, but I never expected...

Screw this.

If I'm going down, I'm going all in. I reach up and thread my fingers through Keller's hair, angling my head just so. His hair is softer than mine, and that kind of pisses me off, which surely explains my irrational behavior. I can't help myself, and though I know it's risky, I bate the vampire by using his own words against him. Lips almost touching his, I say, "You call that a kiss?" While I'm at it, I may as well sucker punch his macho ego. Why the hell not? "Pretty sad if that's all you've got. I mean, come on. You promised to show me something."

A low growl is the only warning I get before my back meets the mattress. I suck in a breath and swear I can taste the salt on his skin. We're that close. He rises over me, grabs my hips and pulls me away from the edge of the bed before dipping his head and searing me with a kiss that has fire shooting from my stomach to my toes. I open for him, and his tongue slides across mine, stroking, licking, caressing, and ever-so-slowly driving me insane.

Heat builds at my core. Not a slow simmer, but a heat so intense I'm about to explode. Explode. From a kiss. I can't even wrap my mind around that. I'm shaking now, a mild tremble that promises to turn into a seizure if I don't stop him. What's causing this? Want? Need? Fear? My throat closes with panic.

Before I know it, Keller's rough hand slides beneath my shirt and the pad of his thumb is brushing against the underside of my breast. *Higher, please. Touch me.* My thoughts have a mind of their own.

I want him more than I've ever wanted another, and that scares the living hell out of me. This is worse than fighting a pack of rabid wolves alone, surrounded, and backed against a wall. I have no weapons for this. No way to fight what I'm feeling. I don't like it. I want it—I want him—but I sure as hell don't like it.

Hands against his bare chest, I want to explore his muscles, his skin. Instead, I try to shove him off of me, but he's too strong. What happened to the man who could barely stand moments ago? Was it all a ruse?

No.

I won't believe that.

I'm not some feeble-minded female and I know he couldn't have faked it. Not without Hollywood makeup and an acting degree from Juilliard.

He sucks my tongue into his mouth. I give him more. All that I have. A sound fills my ears and I realize I'm moaning. I push against him again, but this attempt is weak at best. What the hell is wrong with me? I... he... we have to end this.

I turn my head and instantly regret the loss of contact. I want to kiss him again, but I know if I don't stop this now, he'll lose control. Or I will. "Stop. You have to stop."

Breath ragged, he rolls off of me and throws his arm over his eyes. I'm still shaking. The power is back on, but too wrapped up in

Keller's kiss, I have no idea when that happened. That's terrifying. About a bazillion *what ifs* flash through my mind and none of them paint me in a pretty picture.

I see clearly now, though. I'm more certain than ever that Keller hadn't been faking his weakness before. Almost immediately, dark circles appear under his eyes, his cheekbones become more pronounced, and his chest sinks a little.

This worries me. Knowing the inner workings of every being in the occult world is something I pride myself on. Knowledge is power and I have it in spades. Blood gives vampires energy, provides them with the nourishment they need to have super human strength, to live longer than any being should. Blood. Not flesh. And definitely not one measly kiss. I internally strike the measly part, though I won't ever be sharing that tidbit of information with the man who seriously needs to open a kissing booth.

What does this say about us? I don't understand it. Was I mistaken when I said my blood wasn't special? I remind myself my blood played no part in what happened—what is happening—to Keller. "What's wrong with you?"

Sluggishly, he drops his arm to the bed and turns to me. Dark eyes study me with so much intensity I squirm. I wish he would stop looking at me that way. Like he's searching for a kink in my armor, looking for a way to crawl beneath my skin.

"I win," Keller says, his raspy voice so full of conceit I consider shoving him off the bed.

He wins. Not sure what to say to that. I try to recall the particulars of our bet, but everything before the kiss is a bit hazy. I decide saying nothing is my best option at this point.

"Vampire got your tongue?"

I try not to laugh. I fail. "Good one."

He coughs. I sober.

"Seriously, what is wrong?" A part of me knows— understands what's happening to him. The rest of me sweeps that information into a tight little corner. "I get that you need to feed. And soon based on the looks of you. But..." How to say this? "A moment ago you seemed to have the strength of ten men. Now you look as if you're two breaths away from the morgue."

"That bad, huh?"

I nod.

"I want you something fierce, Josie. Want you more than I've ever wanted another."

His words echo my thoughts from mere seconds ago. For a moment I forget to breathe.

"The thought of taking someone else's blood doesn't appeal to me in the least. My stomach cramps with the thought." His eyes grow darker as he continues, "I'm here for a reason. To watch over you, protect you, arouse you, satisfy you." He drags a lazy finger down my arm, smiling when I shiver. "I'm here to claim you."

Alarms sound inside my head. They're louder than the horn section in a marching band. I jump off the bed, dash to the dresser and pull two short blades out of the top drawer. "Claim me? As in your mate?"

"Yes. No need to stab me."

So he says. I move close enough to do just that. "Nope. You're wrong. I don't belong to anyone." This vampire is delusional.

Keller closes his eyes. "You do. You belong to me. It's fated."

Gripping the handles tightly, I say, "I think a lack of plasma has affected your brain. I don't believe in fate."

Keller smiles, showing a line of straight white teeth, and I curse my heart for flopping around in my chest like a fish out of water.

"Neither did I," he says. "But that was before."

I'm almost afraid to ask. You know, curiosity killing the cat and all that. "Before what?"

"Before you."

Before I can respond, Keller hisses, leaps out of bed, and falls to his knees. I drop my blades and grab his elbow to help him up. The fine hairs on the back of my neck stand on end. "What is it?"

"They're coming," he rasps out.

Face grim, Keller clenches his jaw tight enough for me to make out the sharpness of his bones. I don't doubt him for a second. He shrugs off my hold and stumbles to the window. I'm right behind him. I flatten my back against the wall. He does the same on the other side.

The night is dark with cloud cover and flickering lights. At first I don't see anything. The snow is coming down so hard I wonder if I've somehow been transported to Antarctica. I'm about to tell him to go back to bed when I notice several darker spots littering the snow-covered street about ten blocks down. The spots are moving, albeit slowly. I'd imagine any being, human or otherwise, would have a very hard time navigating in this weather. I squint, trying to make out the forms. Tall men with long black coats blowing in the wind walk in a single-file line. Warlocks. Some of them hold leashes in their hands. On the ends of those leashes are demons. Fantastic. A bunch of bloodthirsty magick worshippers and their hell-spawned dogs.

I flash my eyes toward Keller. He won't be any help. Not in this condition. He can barely stand, let along fight. Looking back out the window, I count at least twelve heads. I've taken on worse. I'm a Huntress and a damn good one. I can do this. Still, it would be nice to have an extra pair of hands. Maybe I can kiss Sir Fang again. The only way that will work is if we're lip locked through the entire fight. Interesting idea now that I think about it. I shake off the ridiculous thought and begin my preparations.

I shove away from the window and grab a pair of knee-high boots from under a pile of clean clothes. After digging out a pair of mismatched socks, I peel off my sweats and pull on my fighting jeans. They're already stained. A little dog slobber won't matter.

"What are you doing?" Keller looks from the window to me and back to the window again.

"Suiting up." I lace my other steel-toed boot. "How much time?"

Keller narrows his dark eyes. "You're planning to fight them."

I strap on two sheaths, one to my right thigh, the other to my left ankle. "How much time?"

"Ten. Maybe fifteen minutes. There are too many and I—"

"I'm not about to let them come in here, gut me like a stuck pick, and drain my blood. Even though my blood won't do them any good, I'm not gonna lie down and hand it over." I load the sheaths with two five-inch blades and slide another beneath my waistband. "I'm not made like that, Keller."

Pacing, hands clasped tightly behind his head, he says, "I need blood."

"What? Is that a news flash?"

He nails me with an angry glare. "For once your sarcasm isn't appreciated. I can't protect you when I'm like this."

Pulling my hair to the side, I braid it tightly and fasten it with a band. "Don't need your help. I've got this. Why don't you hole up in the bathroom and I'll let you know when it's safe to come."

Keller disappears. I turn and smack my head against his. "What the hell, Irish?"

"I'm your mate and I will protect you."

The look in his eyes is frightening. I'm not scared for my safety, but I see something I've never seen in him before. Something Sage hinted at once when she spoke about her brother. Keller O'Leary is capable of things I don't even want to imagine. "We're not mates." I think I spoke aloud but I can't be sure.

"We are."

That answers that.

He reaches for the door, flicks the lock.

"Where are you going?"

He whirls, teeters, and leans against the door to regain his balance. "I need blood, Josie, and I told you I wouldn't take it from you unless you willingly gave it to me." His lilt is strong with anger. He runs a hand through his hair, causing it to stand straight up. "I see that's not going to happen tonight. I will do whatever I have to do to protect you, whether you think you need me to or not."

My fingers itch to smooth his hair back in place. "So what? You're gonna flash your ass to a blood bank and come back all lickety split like to play hero?"

"No," he says wearily. "I can't be gone that long. They'll be here soon. I'll take what I need from your neighbors." Keller turns his back to me and opens the door.

Excuse me? Either Keller just fell off the crazy train or my ears aren't working quite right. No way in hell is that going to happen. My neighbors are citizens of Nashville and, therefore, fall under my protection. He's more than half starved and the possibility that he'll be able to stop himself from completely draining his victim is slim to none at best. I sprint across the room and slam the door closed. I wedge myself between Keller and the door, barring the only exit aside from the window. If he wants to attempt a three-story jump, I'll have to tackle him. I'm not opposed to the idea. "I can't let you do that."

He lifts a brow, then rests his chin on the top of my head.

"There is no other way. You may be able to fight them. You might even win, but more are coming. I can feel them, Josie. Trust me on this."

I take a moment and have a heart to heart with my gut. Instinct tells me Keller's right. This is only the first wave. I'll admit I'm a little proud they're sending so many to take me down. I'm known as a badass of epic proportions around these parts. Good to know my reputation stands. I won't go as far as to say I need his help, but I will admit I can use it. I take a deep breath and know I'll immediately regret the words that are about to come out of my mouth. What choice do I have?

"You can have my blood."

Keller lifts his head and backs up two steps, shock and something else I can't quite explain evident in his expression.

"What did you say?"

I stand straighter. "I said you can have my blood, but if you try pulling any of that aphrodisiac shit on me, I'll stake you to the wall."

6

The Vampire Bites

Keller

You can have my blood.

Josie's words echo in my mind. I haven't been drunk since I was turned. I'm drunk now, though. Drunk on five life-altering words.

The walls seem to close in on us, pulsing, squeezing out the rest of the world and allowing no room for interference. This isn't the way I had planned our first bite at all, but I'll do it if it means protecting Josie. Not only do it, I know with absolute certainty this bite will predict my future—our future. The first taste will lead to more, and I look forward to the endless days where I'll spend hours doing nothing but sinking into her heat, pleasuring her while she screams and begs for release. I will take her to the precipice over and over again until, finally, I will allow her to fall. Powerless, or perhaps unwilling to control my thoughts, my gaze flames hot.

As if she senses my mounting desire, Josie widens her stance and goes into protection mode. She clears her throat and says, "My blood. My terms."

Unable to speak, I nod, eyeing the vein pulsing erratically just below her ear.

"Not my neck." Josie reached back and pulls the knife from her waistband. The sharp metal shined brightly, reflecting off the overhead light.

I laugh until she slides the blade across the inside of her left wrist. Blood wells, drips, calls to me like a siren's song.

The scent—her scent—wraps wickedly around me. My cheeks hollow, my gums ache, my erection swells.

Seemingly unaffected, Josie thrusts her arm toward me in a hasty fashion. "Wasting time here. Let's get this show on the road."

Drops of bright red blood stain the worn carpet, a warning and an invitation. I move then, but resist the overwhelming urge to take her vein. Not yet. Her pleasure comes first. A first bite comes once and once only. I have to make it count. Sliding my palm over her cheek, I cradle the back of her head and dip in to kiss her softly, shifting so that my legs straddle hers. Josie stands ramrod straight for a full five seconds, then, as if she loses her will to fight, sighs and returns the kiss. I linger before brushing my mouth over her cheek, across her ear. I press my lips to her neck, inhale.

"Don't," she whispers, her breath shaky.

Though I hear the lust that roughens her voice, feel her heat as she leans into my thigh and presses her core against me, I say, "I won't." Many consider the neck to be the most intimate of spots. I'm not sure I agree. Intimacy comes in the form of emotions, the connecting of souls. I nip at her shoulder. "Has another fed from you before?" Whether she says yes or no shouldn't matter. Regardless, I brace for the answer.

"Never," she states, her voice sharp with denial.

Relief and immense satisfaction wash over me. I will be her first. And if I have anything to say about it, my bite will be the only bite she experiences from here on out. I smile against her shoulder, reach for her left hand. "It won't hurt."

"I'm no stranger to pain. I can take it. Just hurry up."

"I won't hurt you," I say to clarify my statement. Lifting my head, I search her eyes, see the mock bravery and appreciate her all the more for it. I figure we have about five minutes left. Five minutes of bliss before the warlocks try to take what belongs to me. Five minutes before I destroy them. "And I won't hurry. I plan to savor this."

"Yeah," she says. "You do that. Let's be clear on something here."

"What's that?"

"This is a one-time only deal."

I lick my lips, tilt my head. "Perhaps." Lifting her wrist to my lips, I lick her wound closed with one long, slow caress of my tongue. Refusing to swallow, I clench my teeth. She has her terms. I have mine.

Brows furrowed, Josie asks, "What are you doing?"

"This." I drop to my knees and before she can say another word, lift her shirt and pierce the sensitive skin of her waist. Blood coats my tongue. I carefully swallow once and all coherent thoughts flee. Nothing matters but this moment. Josie sucks in a breath, releases it on a moan. She clutches my hair in her hands. Gripping her hips, I pull her blood into my mouth, drink as if my life depends on it and instantly grow lightheaded from the amount of pure power entering my body. Muscles contracting, my heart slams against my ribcage. I hear every stuttered breath Josie takes, every flake of snow that brushes against the window, every jumbled thought that runs through her head. Energy buzzes my system like a high-voltage explosion. This is not a normal feeding. This is a fusion of souls.

Panting, Josie twists and pulls me closer, digging her nails into my scalp. Encouraged, I feast, careful to not release endorphins that will heighten her experience. Everything she is experiencing is because of who we are, what we mean to each other. She won't agree. I don't expect her to. That will come in time.

Her unique flavor slides down my throat, and like an arrow, pierces my heart. I want to roar in triumph and pleasure. I've waited so long to find my mate. And here she is. A sexy spitfire in jeans and steel-toed boots, strapped to the nines with blades.

Taking too much will leave Josie weak. She will resent me even more if I take the strength she wears so proudly. Reluctantly, I pull back and close her wounds by flattening my tongue against her skin. Breathless, Josie slumps then immediately pushes me away. I straighten her shirt and rise, energy and strength zapping along my nerves. I feel like I can take on the world. The fury I see sparking in Josie's eyes isn't a surprise. Just because I'm elated doesn't mean she'll understand, or even want the new intricacies of our relationship.

Eyes narrowed, shoulders back, she regards me warily. "I see you're all better now."

"Yes," I say, nodding once. "Thank you." The two words seem insufficient considering the enormity of the situation.

Josie shrugs like the intimacy of the bite hasn't affected her in the least. "Don't mention it."

If she wants to play it cool, I'll go along with it. For now. Ignoring my aching shaft, I press a quick kiss to her grim mouth and reach for my jacket. Now that I've fed, my hearing is acute. The sound of boots trudging through the deep snow signals the time to move. Our attackers are less than two blocks away.

"Going somewhere?" she asks, all rasp gone from her voice.

"I'm assuming you would like to take this fight to the streets."

"Yeah. I guess so." She turns and opens the top drawer of her dresser. She picks out two more blades and tucks one into each boot. "Help yourself," she says with a flick of her hand.

"No, thanks." I've never been fond of using weapons. I prefer speed, agility and my bare hands.

Josie lifts a shoulder absently. "Suit yourself."

I open the door and step into the hallway before Josie. She mumbles something about manners and I choose to ignore it. Protection overrides manners.

"We need to lure them away from these buildings," Josie says, all business now. "They're full of residents."

She's right, of course. Blizzard or not, the warlocks won't give up easily. And if they're as bloodthirsty as Josie says, they won't care who they hurt in the process. "You know the area better than I. Any suggestions?"

Josie marches past me. "Yep. Follow me."

I grab her arm and pull her back.

"You need to take your hands off me," she snaps. The tip of her blade bites into my chin.

She's quick. I didn't even see her pull the weapon. I release her elbow and lift my hands in a surrender fashion. "I'll make you a deal."

Josie shakes her head. Her braid thumps against her collarbone. "No. I'm tired of deals. They don't work for us."

I quirk a half smile. "I beg to differ."

"Of course you do."

Patience, I tell himself. "Is it too much to ask that you allow me to take the lead on this one?"

"Yes. It's too much." She punches the wall. "You're too much."

I understand the root cause of her frustration. Josie is used to doing things on her own. I won't change that in a day. Arguing with her is futile. I take the initiative and flash down the stairs. Cold air smacks me in the face as I round the corner. The front door stands wide open, snow drifting into the lobby. The lack of footprints eases my mind. Josie's anger slams into my backside a second before she skids to a halt.

"Not cool, Irish."

Turning, I cut off her next words with a heated kiss. "I don't always play fair, Josephine."

Her frustrated bellow makes me laugh. Now that I feel like myself again—better even—the future looks promising. Once we finish with the unfortunate and untimely warlock business, Josie and I can get back to more pleasurable things.

As she stomps past me, I smack her on the ass. "Ready to show me what you're made of?"

Turning, her eyes glitter with renewed excitement. "That a challenge?"

I smile, full on, feeding off her energy. "Let's hunt, Huntress."

We trudge through snow that comes up to my calves and her knees. Three minutes later, we've only progressed about twenty feet or so and we've run out of time. "I need you to tell me exactly where you want this to play out."

"Why?" Josie asks, slightly winded. "We'll get there... eventually."

I grip her shoulders and turn her ninety degrees. A line of warlocks stand less than a block away, their hands outstretched, their demons snorting and salivating. A magickal wave of dark energy pulses from their fingers. "That's why."

"Shit."

They pull power toward them. Light bulbs burst overhead. "Agreed. They're using any energy they can find and getting stronger. Moving in this snow won't be a problem for them much longer. Now where, Josie?"

Leaning in, she whispers the directions in my ear. Her icy breath washes over my face. "That's not very far."

Josie nods. "It's far enough."

Wrapping my arm around her waist, I pull her against my body. "Hold on."

No questions asked, she does just that. I flash, flying Josie through the night. The cold bite of wind doesn't faze me. I've teleported thousands of times before. Josie, on the other hand, tucks her face into the crook of my neck, shivers. Our destination comes upon us quickly. I set her down in the middle of a park, hold her close while she regains her balance.

Josie pushes away from me, and hands on her knees, sucks in air. "Not fun, Irish."

"It can be. Eventually." I scan the area, note we're no longer alone. Demon eyes glow. The warlocks won't be far behind. "Josie."

She recovers quickly, palms two blades and presses her back to mine. "I see them."

We'll wait. Let the demons make the first move. We don't have to wait long. Three demons lunge out of the dark, maws gaping, toxic saliva dripping.

I kick and send one of the demons sliding through the snow. I grab another out of the air, twist my arms and yank the head off. I toss it away with a growl. Turning to assist Josie, I smile when she jams her blade into the last demon's gut and pulls straight up, exposing the innards. The demon hisses once and then slumps on the ground. Not dead yet, but soon.

"Nice."

"Not bad yourself," she says cleaning her knife off with a handful of snow. "I hope you don't expect high-fives and shit."

My laugh is cut short as a blast of power sends me sailing through the air. My back slams into a pole. I slide to the ground, land on my hands and knees. A sharp, piercing whistle sounds in my head and I groan in pain. I know what the sound means—know my sire is summoning me. The elder has shit skills for timing. I push my palms against my head, but the whistle doesn't let up.

It takes everything I have, but I finally manage to block the sound. Josie curses. Whipping my head up, fury rips through me. Several warlocks surround her. She lunges, kicks, and slices with her blades, taking down more than her fair share. I roar, the sound coming from deep within, a base response to seeing my mate attacked, knowing I don't have much time before I have to return to my sire's side.

I take flight and land in the thick of the mayhem. Instinct takes over and I lose control. Death cheers me on, demanding no survivors. I tear through the remaining warlocks, Josie fighting at my side. I see nothing but my next victim. Feel nothing but the need to protect.

When there is only one left, I grab him by his lapels and lock eyes. I see anger mixed with a hint of fear. His brethren have fallen. Death whispers, kill, kill, kill.

"Look around," I tell the warlock. "This is your future." I lean in and whisper words that make the warlock's skin turn as white as the snow. I shove him away, doubling my efforts to block the summons. The warlock runs, loses his footing and lands face first in a snow bank. He lifts his head and looks over his shoulder. I nod once and the warlock gets up and hauls ass.

"What did you say to him?" Josie asks.

I mask the pain and turn. Her hair had come loose from its braid. Red locks fan out around her pale face. Light green eyes, bright and alive from the thrill of the fight, study me curiously. Seeing her like this makes the pain bearable.

Knowing she won't appreciate the warning I sent with the warlock, I imitate what is quickly becoming Josie's signature response and shrug. "Just told him it was time to go home."

Eyes narrowed, she chews on her lip. "And?"

"Let's just leave it at that, shall we?"

"For now." She tilts her head. "I like how you fight."

I smile. "Do you, now?"

Josie saunters toward me, her hips swaying seductively. "Yeah. I do. You're all up close and personal about it. Yet… there's a mechanical feel to it. You're kind of ferocious."

Her scent wraps around me, pushing away the stench of the magickal burn and demon death. Aroused, I watch her closely, memorize the exhilarated look on her face. I'll hold it close while doing whatever dirty work my sire demands.

"Too bad we have to clean this up." She gestures to the dead strewn around the small park.

"The warlocks will take care of it." That was part of the deal I made with the last man standing. Something wicked flashes in her eyes. Whatever Josie is up to, I want to play a part. "Got somewhere you need to be?"

I don't move when Josie wraps her arms around my neck. "I need a favor, Irish." Now it's her turn to command. "You took a part of me into you. Now I want you inside me."

I teleport Josie from the carnage and back to her apartment. At least there she'll be inside, close to her weapons, when I leave. She won't have any trouble with the warlocks anytime soon. But being a Huntress means she is never far from danger. Though I don't like that aspect of her life, I might have to learn to accept it.

Once inside her apartment, she slams me to the wall and kisses my brains out. Jacked up on adrenaline from the fight and the lingering effects of my bite, no doubt. I don't care. I take everything she's willing to give.

Josie pulls off my jacket and drags her tongue across my abs. I groan with the need for control. She nips. I throb. The shrill whistle nearly bores a hole through my skull. I have to warn her before we go too far.

Hands clasped behind my head, I say, "Josie."

When she doesn't respond, I cradle her chin in my palm and lift her gaze to mine. She blinks up at me. Breathless, her breasts heave against my thighs. "You don't want this." She stands, turns away.

I grab her arm and pull her against me. "I want you more than anything."

She angles her head. "Then what's the problem?"

If I don't go, I know beyond a shadow of a doubt my sire will summon one of my brothers or sisters. Maybe even Sage, who's only recently found something that makes her happy. I can't do that to them—to her. I'll go and follow orders—to save those I consider family. Equally, or perhaps more importantly, if I don't leave soon, my sire will send a crew to get me. That crew won't hesitate to eliminate whatever and whomever they deem a distraction. "I can't stay. I'm being... I have to go soon." One day, that would all change.

Emotion flickers in her eyes, but I can't name it. "So go," she says with another shrug.

I slide my thumb across her lower lip in a soft caress. "Not like this. I'm not leaving because I want to." I have to protect her, somehow find a way to keep her a secret from my sire.

"Doesn't matter, Keller. I get it. You gotta bolt. If you're worried about my feelings, don't be. I'm a big girl."

I palm her cheeks and cover her lips with mine, licking and teasing until she opens. When she relaxes into me, I deepen the kiss, block the whistle from my mind. I'll go. Just not yet.

The seconds turned into minutes. We shed our clothes and I carry her to the bed. She wanted fast and furious. I give her slow and delirious, feasting on her skin, her mouth, her breasts. She scores my back with her nails, tugging me closer. When she says my name on a whisper, I slide into her heat. Fire races through my body and I still, wanting to freeze time.

Green eyes full of desire, she wriggles beneath me, fists her hands in my hair and pulls my mouth to hers. That was my undoing. I give her fast. I give her hard. She doesn't know it, but in those moments, I give her my heart.

Josie shakes, moans, and then cries out her release. I'm right there with her until neither have anything left to give. She kisses my shoulder and sighs.

The whistle returns full force. I clench my jaw against the pain. I've angered the sire by making him wait, and I will have to pay the price. Looking down at Josie, I know it was all worth it. I watch the steady rise and fall of her chest. She hasn't really fallen asleep, but it's probably better this way. I pull the blanket up to her chin and run my hand over her hair.

Leaning down, I press a kiss to her forehead. "Tell Sage goodbye for me. I know the two of you will really make something out of Wolfie's. I look forward to seeing it."

Taps

Patrick Freivald

Molly froze, her backpack half-in and half-out of her locker. It came again, a series of taps and scrapes behind the wall, a repeating rhythm that reminded her of the classic jazz drummers on her dad's old CDs, Billy Higgins and Jack DeJohnette, Art Blakey and Buddy Rich. The old guard who'd inspired her to pick up the sticks while her friends gravitated to the clarinet or the flute, the tomboys maybe braving the trumpet or sax.

For eleven years she'd played the drums, straight through to her junior year, and she knew a great beat when she heard one. It sounded again, almost urgent, then cut off in a shriek of metal on metal.

"Hey!" Kirsten's voice cut through the rhythm like a scythe. The five-four brunette bounced on her heels and clutched her geometry book against a pale green sweater that matched her fingernails. "You're late for class."

"Speak for yourself." Molly pocketed her cell phone and produced a blue slip of paper. "I have a pass." She nudged her locker shut with her hip and hustled into step with Kirsten, the rhythm a memory hammering at the back of her mind.

"What did your mom say? About Saturday?" Kirsten's voice held too much hope, and Molly hated to crush it.

"She said, 'No.' And not the *maybe* kind of 'No.'"

"Did you tell her there wouldn't be any boys?"

Molly nodded. "Yeah, and she agreed. And no girls. Or animals. Or pizza delivery. 'Just because it's February Break doesn't mean you don't have work to do.'"

Kirsten stopped dead in front of Mrs. Bigg's room. "Oh, c'mon, how will she even find out from Atlanta?"

Shoving past, Molly ducked inside so that Kirsten couldn't see her eyes rolling. Even from her conference in Georgia, Molly's mom would learn of any transgressions against The Rules. She had

45

neighbors checking in at all hours, a task force of busybodies with one relentless goal: ruin all fun.

Mrs. Bigg glanced their way long enough to notice the blue pass and then let them sit without interrupting her speech, something about congruent triangles and the stability of bridges. She sat next to Chris DeSouza and looked over his shoulder to copy the notes she'd missed.

In the back of the room the heater pinged and hissed, the metal cycling through hot and cold phases. As it expanded and contracted, the incessant shudder transitioned into the tapping rhythm from her locker, then back into random noise.

"Did you hear that?" she whispered.

Chris shook his head without taking his eyes from the smart board.

She tapped the rhythm on her desk. The heater answered, then they did it in unison.

"Miss Fitzgerald?" Mrs. Bigg's voice cut through her concentration, and the beat disappeared with it. "Can we keep the percussion in the band room?"

Molly cast her eyes down to her page. "Sorry, Mrs. Bigg."

***

Sounds followed Molly down the hallway to the drinking fountain: a rattle as the winter wind shrieked past the window, a jingle of keys in Principal Lawson's pocket, a subtle tapping down the lockers, each with the same distinct pattern. The hair stood on her arms, and an electric shiver coursed up her spine.

Kneeling to collect her Anthology of American Literature, she ran her fingertips across the thick white cover, then put her nail against the back of the locker and tapped, hard, repeating the pattern as she'd heard it.

Silence, not even her own breath, held in anticipation of a reply.

A hand grabbed her wrist, stark white and ice-cold. Molly shrieked and fell back. Her head rang and pain blasted the back of her skull, a black void filled with frozen stars, their cruel light reaching down to rob her of warmth and love and humanity.

Black tendrils wrapped her, squeezing and lifting her up into the darkness. She screamed again and tried to punch, kick, bite.

"Whoa!" Chris stumbled back, hands raised in a defensive posture, as the world slammed back into place, too bright and too real.

"What ...I ...?"

His face scrunched with worry, he knelt to pick up her fallen bag. "You hit your head."

She rubbed her wrist, numb from the cold, and looked into her locker. Aside from her books and folders it held nothing, with no room for a person or a void or stars. The Anthology sat undisturbed in the bottom.

"You okay?"

She dragged her eyes away from the book to look into his baby blues. "Yeah, I think so. Just a spider, freaked me out."

He scowled toward her wrist. "I've never seen spider bites like that. Maybe you should go to the nurse. Get some cream or something."

She looked down at the string of hot, mottled-pink welts rising from her skin. They looked feverish, but felt like frostbite. "Yeah. Thanks."

He kept pace with her to the end of the hall, then turned left to go to history. She went to the bathroom, locked herself in a stall, and took deep, steady breaths to calm her racing heart.

***

Fifth period, Molly dumped her lunch in the garbage can—chicken nuggets and mashed potatoes with lumpy white gravy and a side of boiled broccoli—and headed for the band room, ears pricked for tapping sounds that didn't come. Mr. Stevens turned away from the shelf on the back wall, the one that hid the ugly metal access door between the practice rooms, and gave her a cursory wave on his way back to his desk.

She sat. The smooth sticks belonged in her hands, and her right foot found its home on the pedal to the love-worn bass drum.

A heavy beat rolled from the bass as her foot pumped. Twirling the sticks once, she set into the snare with a *piano* drum roll, building it up to a *forte* before launching into an improvised solo. The rhythm flowed out of her, a fire in her arms and legs to defy the cold grip of …whatever the heck that was. Sweat beaded on her forehead, so she switched tempo and brought it down to a dull roar.

The sticks writhed in her hands, and as she struggled to control them they hammered out a rhythm of their own, *the* rhythm, and cold dread shot through her bones. Her wrist throbbed in time. She forced an improvisation, but of their own volition her arms and hands flowed back to the driving beat. She looked up in alarm to see Mr. Stevens standing at the podium, arms crossed, a bemused look on his face.

She stopped with a crash on the high-hat, letting the discordant clang jar through her teeth like fingernails down a chalkboard.

"Where'd you get that groove?" A baby-faced twenty-something, his light brown goatee helped keep people from mistaking him for a student, but Molly always thought his gray eyes hid a weariness he never quite revealed.

Squirming under the scrutiny, she set the sticks down and met his eyes. "Not sure. Why?"

He chuckled. "It's Morse Code. I did two years as Signals Intelligence in Qatar."

Everything in her screamed not to ask, but she had to. She licked her lips. "What does it mean?"

He tapped it out on the podium. "F. I. N. D." He paused, then started again. "M. E. Period." He played it again and again, speeding up with every repetition, and the room shuddered in time. Eyes closed, he didn't seem to notice the shaking walls, the oppressive darkness as gray clouds swallowed the midday sun, the deep throbbing pulse of blood in her skull.

"STOP!" She pressed the heels of her hands to her ears to block out the sound.

His hands hovered above the podium, the smile frozen on his face. Sunlight streamed through the windows, blinding against the snow blanketing the hillside. "How about this?"

He started again, a different pattern, longer. She waited for him to finish before speaking.

"What did that say?"

"It said, 'Codes are for hiding things.'" Slumping to rest his chin on the back of his hands, he glanced at the clock—twenty-two minutes to the bell—and scowled. "Where'd you say you heard that?"

She shrugged. "I don't know. Just sort of came to me."

"Hell—um, heck of a coincidence, getting every letter. Even the punctuation"

"Yeah, that's really weird. Maybe it came from one of my dad's movies or something and has been bouncing around in my head."

"War movies?"

Nodding, she picked up the sticks and stood. "Yup. Vietnam and World War II, mostly. He loves the old classics, and documentaries."

Mr. Stevens grimaced. "Never saw the real thing, did he?"

She shook her head. "No. Grandpa served in Korea, though. Mom's dad, too."

"I thought as much." Eyes raised to the clock, he clucked his tongue. "Time flies, and I've got work to do. Feel free to play until the bell."

"Thanks, Mr. Stevens."

He walked back to his desk and picked up a stack of sheet music off his chair, then sat.

FIND ME. The words flashed through her mind as she picked up the mallets and turned toward the xylophone. FIND ME. She shivered, closed her eyes, and launched into a cover of Copa Cabana, upbeat and airy and not at all dark and cold.

Behind her the wind rattled the window, and she understood what it said.

FIND ME.

***

Molly opened a math book on her dresser, turned up the volume on her iPod, and ignored both in favor of her laptop. Fingers soft on the keys, she typed in, "Morse Code Translator" and hit "Enter."

She tried a phrase, listened to it, tapped it out on the bedframe, over and over to commit it to memory. Then another phrase, and another.

An hour later she fell back, head on the pillow, and stared up at the white ceiling, tracing routes through the uneven glossy patches. Beads of sweat cooled on her forehead, and she breathed hard as the songs faded into memory.

No. Not songs. *Messages.*

***

The next morning, Kirsten met her as she got off the bus. "How you feeling?"

Molly shrugged. "What do you mean?"

"Chris said you hit your head pretty good yesterday, and I didn't see you at all after. Figured you went home."

They meandered toward homeroom on scuffed, faded tiles. Lockers jiggled, shoes shuffled across the floor. Heating vents flooded the hall with tepid air. Molly pricked her ears at every sound, but in the cacophony of human voices she couldn't pick out any patterns.

Fingernails dug into her shoulder.

"Ow!" She flinched back and gave Kirsten a wounded look. "What the heck?"

Kirsten let go and let out a theatric sigh. "What planet are you on? Have you heard a single thing I've said?"

Shaking her head, Molly tried a sheepish grin. "Sorry? Just a little distracted, I guess."

Kirsten rolled her eyes. "Yeah, well, don't be rude."

They walked in together, said the Pledge of Allegiance after the bell, and suffered through thirty minutes of group work with Chad and Tom, the least mature boys in the history of ever. Their constant, childish snickering tore through Molly's head until she just couldn't take another moment. Her hand shot up.

"Yes?" Mr. Brown raised his eyebrows but didn't look up from his newspaper.

"Can—may I go to the bathroom?"

He looked up at the four of them, a dubious frown dragging on his expression. "Are you done?"

"It's an emergency."

She ignored Tom's chuckle and hurried to the door the moment Mr. Brown nodded.

Alone in the hall, she walked toward the bathroom but stopped at the first locker. Reaching out with one fingernail, she tapped a pattern. WHERE ARE YOU?

Nothing happened. She laughed. *What'd you expect, Mol? You're just going crazy.*

She took two steps, and at the end of the hall a door opened with a scattershot creak more dots than dashes. A little seventh grader, wide-eyed in glasses way too big for his face, stepped out and walked her way. The door squealed closed with the same rhythm as the kid disappeared around the corner.

Looking both ways, she pulled out her phone and put the pattern into the translator.

Goosebumps crawled up her arms as the temperature dropped ten degrees. Something scraped against the inside of the locker, mouse-feet rustling almost too quiet to hear.

BENEATH

Molly reached back, hesitated, then repeated the word with her fingertip, adding a question-mark. BENEATH?

Another pattern. She plugged it into her phone as humid air condensed on the screen.

SO COLD

Teeth chattering, she tapped, combining the new word with one she'd memorized. BENEATH WHERE? Her breath billowed in white clouds as she waited for a reply.

SO COLD

The temperature dropped again, and ice crystals crept across the windows.

The kid with the huge glasses rounded the corner, staring at her with wide eyes. She let out a breath she hadn't realized she'd been holding. "What, kid?"

His eyes frosted over, a cataract of ice crystals. She stumbled back and he grabbed her wrist, his touch icy daggers ravaging her skin straight through her sweater. The chittering noise that came from his mouth belonged to another world, a world of shattered glass and pain and rocks cracking under the force of new-formed ice.

She jerked away and ran. Locker doors thundered an unrelenting staccato FIND ME as she ran past. Windows and door locks rattled FIND ME. The air in the vents whispered underneath and around the maelstrom of noise, repeating the boy's words in time with her throbbing wrist. Clutching it against her chest, the hall blurred through a sheen of tears.

She busted into the bathroom, shut herself in a stall and

huddled there. Squeezing her hands over her ears in a desperate attempt to make it stop did nothing. Even the dripping of the fountains pressed their command. FIND ME.

She closed her eyes and replayed the boy's message in her mind. Hands shaking, she brought up the translator and fed the pattern into the phone.

I HEAR YOU PLAY

Noise flooded the room, human noise, girls chatting and arguing, classes changing in the hall. She let out a relieved sigh and opened the stall, joining the typical press of girls trying to freshen up in their allotted four minutes. She washed her hands, wincing as her sweater rubbed raw on her wrist, and ducked out into the hallway without speaking to anyone.

***

Heart thundering, Molly hurried past the janitor's cart, muffling the keys' jingle with her hand, praying that nobody heard in the din of students grabbing last-minute things from their lockers and heading for the buses. She slipped the keys into her coat pocket, the metal cold against her shaking fingers, too cold, like the janitor had just been outside.

Principal Lawson returned her tight-lipped smile with pearly teeth and a hearty, "Have a good weekend!"

The kid's message rang in her ears. Where could you hear her play, behind foam-covered walls and thick, noise-isolating doors? What hidden place held those answers? Only one.

She shuffled toward the exit then cut right, through the internal fire doors and around the corner to the band room. After a soft knock she pushed her way through. "Hello? Mr. Stevens?"

With no answer, she pulled her practice sheets from her cubby, a tiny space for music and spare sticks dwarfed by those for the saxophones, trombones, and tubas. She stuffed the loose papers into the bottom of her bag, under her textbooks and folders. That done, she walked over to Mr. Stevens's desk, grabbed a sheet of paper from the printer, and opened the top drawer for a pen.

A silver oval caught her eye, the dull metal held by a beaded chain. She picked it up and read the dog tags. MARTIN, JAMIE E. The letters scraped their way through the shelf in the back of the room as she read them; she didn't have to look them up, didn't have to translate them.

Hands trembling, she took a picture, put them back, and wrote a quick note.

> Mr. Stevens,
> I lost my practice music. Can I get another copy on
Monday, please?
> Thanks,
> Mol

***

She closed her eyes, took a deep breath, and turned toward the far wall. Between the two practice room doors a black metal shelf held a legion of dusty trophies dating back sixty years. From tarnished brass to cheap plastic, they chronicled the victories of every competition and ignored the countless others where they found only defeat. She slid the shelf to the side, legs screeching against the floor to reveal the portal behind. Marked AUTHORIZED PERSONNEL ONLY in bold red letters, the peeling paint gave her an indication of how often anyone used it.

She pulled the ring of keys from her coat, the jingles spelling out HERE HERE HERE as she searched for the one that matched the number on the lock. Her fingers blistered as frost rimed the metal, and she shivered in her coat at the bitter cold. Jamming the key into the lock, she hissed against the pain and turned it. A jerk, a sigh of freezing cold air, and darkness yawned in front of her.

A steel ladder descended into a square hole in the concrete floor, the bright yellow paint faded from years of neglect. Black mold smudged the walls with angry splotches. Breath frosting, she pulled out her phone and used the flashlight app to blast the bright white LED down the hole.

Molly gasped.

A skeletal hand rested against the bottom rung. Beside it lay a caved-in skull on patchy gravel. She rubbed her wrist and frowned at the rusty handcuffs linking the arm to the unyielding metal. The body wore the tattered remnants of a uniform, dull gray-and-white camouflage just visible in the mold and rot. Her eyes grew wide as the finger twitched, the signal ringing out on the metal.

RUN

She stumbled back and slammed the door, groping for the keys. The ring fell from her fingers and clattered to the floor. She knelt to pick them up but instead grabbed the shelf and jerked it back into place. A trophy tottered as the band room door opened. She caught it and set it down next to the blazing heater. Suddenly too hot she swooned, light-headed. Pushing the keys under the shelf with her foot, she stood.

Mr. Stevens raised his eyebrows at her, the exact look he gave anyone late to class, or goofing off instead of playing. "Looking for something, Miss Fitzgerald?"

She swallowed, and tried not to gasp in a breath, instead pulling it slowly through her smile. "Hi, Mr. Stevens. I can't find my practice music. Was just leaving you a note."

He pulled the cart loaded with music stands the rest of the way into the room, let the double-doors close, then pushed it against them. Wiping his hands on his shirt, he walked forward. "From the floor?"

A nervous giggle escaped her lips. "No. My shoelace came untied. The note's on your desk."

He glanced at it, picked up the pen, clicked it a couple of times. "From my drawer?"

She shrugged. "I didn't have one."

"You saw the dog tags, then."

"Dog tags?" Playing dumb never came easy to her, and he didn't look convinced.

He took another step, picked up the trophy, and then leaned in too close. Staring down at her, he licked his lips. "You're not special. She talks to me, too, you know."

She met his eyes, blank brown orbs, flat under the fluorescent light. "What?"

He brushed his knuckles across her cheek, then settled the hand on her shoulder and tapped, his fingernail sharp against her neck. He spoke the words as they seared across her nerves. "I. Loved. You." His grip tightened on her shoulder, twisting her coat until it pulled tight under her arm. "She looked like you, a little. I mean, not anymore."

Molly screamed. He swung the trophy and the world exploded in hot white light. Pulling herself from the floor and unsure how she got there, her eyes came to focus on the line of red drool hanging from her lips. Searing pain shocked through her chest as his shoe impacted her ribs, again and again. He dragged her to her tiptoes, her scalp on fire, his right hand tangled in her hair, the left still holding the bloody trophy.

Feet dangling, legs useless, she tried to reach him, tried to claw or hit, tried to scream through the iron tang of blood in her mouth.

"No one can hear you, Molly, not through these walls."

She knew it. The sound-proofing and thick wooden doors did more than prevent dead spots. Words came, thick and hard to understand around her swollen tongue. "Please, Mr. Stevens. I don't know—"

His face twitched, a spasm gone as fast as it came. "Don't play dumb. You're smarter than that, and it's ...it's insulting. Jamie insulted me, near the end, after all we had and all we went through. She said she loved me, lived for me, but didn't show it, not after a while. Little niggling, nagging, grating insults, day in and day out. That's not love." He shoved her backward without letting go and she tried to protest around her fat lip. A tooth shifted and a jolt of pain shot up her jaw.

"Please, Mr. Stevens. Please, don't."

"Too late for that. She talked to you, you listened. You think you're the first? You're not. You're not special. You're not first. Just the first to find her. Maybe she wants company."

He pulled a handful of pills from his coat, pried open her mouth, and stuffed them in, jamming his fingers past her bite, forcing them to the back of her tongue. Tilting her chin up, he plugged her nose and rubbed her throat. She tried not to swallow, but swallowed. He held her against the wall, cruel hands crushing into her neck, until the world swam and her tongue grew thick in her mouth. A cloud bore her to the ground.

Dark eyes stared down at her. "Goodbye, Molly."

***

Cold. Too cold to shiver, too cold to breathe. She reached out in the darkness for something, anything to hold on to. Her fingertips brushed something smooth. She stretched, reaching, and pulled the orb toward her. It scraped across the floor in the pitch black, and a tear escaped as her fingers traced over the top to the brow, eye sockets, empty nasal cavity, and ruined teeth.

February break. Friday afternoon through the following Monday morning. Ten days, give or take. Ten days before anyone would look for her in school, and no one to miss her at home. Ten days in the frigid dark, with black mold and Jamie Martin's skeleton for company.

She couldn't feel her toes, and her ankles burned through her socks.

The skeleton next to her shifted, a faint rustle almost too quiet to hear. Its finger rang against the ladder, staccato taps she couldn't put together without the translator. Molly reached for her phone, thrust her fingers deep into empty pockets, and let out a sob.

Frigid air slithered through her lungs, stagnant and precious proof of life.

Jagged shards of white-hot agony shredded her chest as she tried to lift herself from the ground. She collapsed next to the skull, panting. She'd broken her leg in Pee-Wee soccer a long time ago. This felt like that, only all over.

Cheek against the ice-cold floor, she reached out one-handed, feeling in the dark for anything that might help her. Brittle clothing crumbled at her touch, revealing naked bone beneath, jagged and splintered where Jamie's ribs had fractured. An old belt, stiff in the cold, the metal buckle frozen to the floor, but no bags, no tools, no walkie-talkie or phone or radio.

She moved higher, tracing the outstretched arm over the handcuffs to the twitching hand, tapping away a fervent message too fast and too long for her to understand. It calmed as her hand covered it, and it tapped a single word.

WARM

She tried to speak, but no sound escaped her ravaged throat. Instead she slid her index finger past and tapped a memorized phrase on the ladder. WHO ARE YOU

Images flooded her mind, a young woman in an Air Force uniform, short red hair and a beautiful smile. A helicopter ride over the desert. Mr. Stevens in uniform, on his knees, holding an open box with a gold ring inside. Fighting. Broken bones, a shattered jaw. Wounds hidden from family and friends back home.

Warmth and sorrow slithered into her, a life wasted and

dumped in the eternal cold, seeking release. Seeking justice. Comfort. Warmth. With the memories came patterns she hadn't had enough time to learn, the dots and dashes like second nature to a Signals Intelligence officer.

She tapped on Jamie's shattered skull. HOW DO WE GET OUT?

The skeletal hand tapped on the rung.

FIND ME

Molly joined her, and they tapped together.

FIND ME

Again and again in the dark, desperate, until hope faded and the cold took her and plunged her into hard, unrelenting nothing.

***

Molly woke in the darkness, alone and too warm, unnaturally warm. Her skin burned, liked chapped lips from too much skiing, but everywhere and nowhere, a disembodied pain that encompassed her entire world. Pushing through the agony, she felt but couldn't see her breath frosting against the back of Jamie's skull, the dead girl silent for the time being.

"I'm f-freezing. Can you—can you h-help me?" A piteous voice just rasped from her throat, sore like poisoned needles in the back of her mouth.

The skeleton made no reply. Jamie repeated the phrase.

Its finger twitched under her palm, lifted to the rung, and tapped.

HELP ME

"Yes. C-can you? Help me?"

HELP ME

"No, you don't understand. I n-need you to help me. I need to get out." The last phrase faded to nothing as her voice failed, throat too damaged to continue.

Jamie tapped.

GET OUT HELP ME HELP ME HELP ME GET OUT

Molly groaned and tried to stand. Her body protested, every motion a new study in just how much damage Mr. Stevens had done. She couldn't move her legs enough to sit, even pushing against the wall. She couldn't lift her arms enough to push up, and even trying sent spasms through her body.

Tears froze in her eyes. Words formed on her lips, too quiet for even the dead to hear. "You brought me here to die with you."

WITH YOU

WARM

WITH YOU

She closed her eyes, and slept.

***

"Hello?" A man, somewhere above, muffled and too quiet.

Frost crusted her eyelids, held them shut. She couldn't move, not even to lick her lips, as the voice called again.

"Molly Fitzgerald, you in here?"

Voices bantered back and forth, strong male voices, Principal Lawson and others she didn't recognize.

"She has to be. Cameras show she came in here, never came out."

"—her necklace in his car. We took him down to—"

"—nothing here."

"Maybe she—"

She tried to scream, to make any noise, but nothing came out. She tried to reach for the rung, but her hand didn't move. Her lips moved against the ice-cold skull, a desperate plea with her last shred of energy, movement without sound. "Help me."

A faint rustle and the skeleton shifted. Then bone rang on metal with sharp peals.

HELP ME

HELP ME

HELP ME

A voice above responded. "Do you hear that?"

"Morse code?"

Jamie tapped on, repeating the phrase again and again while Molly lay still, broken and unable to move.

"Is that a door?"

"Help me move this thing."

She tried to open her eyes, hold them open long enough to see the light, but the tapping faded and she knew no more.

***

The screaming wouldn't end. High, then low, then high, it shook her body and threw her side to side. She only knew pain, pain and unending screams. It hurt to move, it hurt to lie still. It hurt to breathe.

But she breathed, sweet country air tinged with bleach and the acrid bite of medicine.

I'm alive.

"She's waking up." A male voice, soft but urgent.

"Good. They'll want her statement at the hospital, if she's up for it."

Divine light blinded her, white and pure, and the shrieking faded to an ambulance's unsteady wail.

"Molly, can you hear me?"

"Yes." No sound came out of her raw throat. She tried again, and again, and squeezed her eyes shut against unbidden tears, hot on her skin. He shushed her.

"You're going to be okay. You've got some frostbite and hypothermia, a lot of broken bones, but we're keeping you warm and giving you fluids. They say you know Morse code. Can you tell us what happened?"

She reached out and he took her hand. Molly didn't know Morse code, no more than a few phrases. But Jamie did. Tracing her fingernail to his palm, they tapped.

Control+Alt+Delete

Rachel Aukes

Today wasn't one of my better days.

Michael Klempton, executive vice president of Datus Technologies, stood in my home, holding my ex-wife's hand. He had the nerve to look happy. I hated the guy and I hadn't even met him yet.

"So, you must be Jack." Michael smiled warmly and held out his hand. "Paige has told me much about you. It's a pleasure to finally meet you."

"Mike," I said simply and forced myself to shake his hand, making sure I squeezed just a touch harder than him.

He straightened his shoulders. "Actually, I prefer Michael. My father is Mike."

"Hm." I turned and walked away without another word and headed into the kitchen to grab a beer from the fridge. When I rotated around, Paige stood there, her lips pursed.

"Play nice," she said. "I left a message to tell you we were both coming. Michael came for Willie's sake."

I held up my hands in surrender. "What did I do? I've been a fucking great host so far."

"No, you're—"

I didn't stick around for another one of her coaching sessions. Somehow, she held onto the hope that I was trainable. She'd always been the optimist in our relationship.

Back inside my dining room, Michael looked up and smiled as though I wasn't an asshole.

"This house is too damn small," I mumbled before taking a long drink of beer.

At that moment, the birthday boy and his pal Gage came tearing down the stairs. I grabbed Willie by the arm and yanked him to a stop. "Whoa, there, cowboy. Exactly where do you think you're going in such a hurry?"

Willie rolled his eyes. "The snow's just about melted, Dad. We're just going to ride our bikes down to the creek. We'll be right back."

"Can't you and Gage break bones later?" I asked. "It's your birthday party."

He shrugged. "I swear we'll be back soon."

As he tried to take off, I pulled the slingshot out of his hand. "Riding bikes, huh?"

He gave me sheepish look. "We have to be prepared just in case the zombie apocalypse hits."

Paige gasped. "Oh, be careful, Willie. You could take out someone's eye with that thing." She turned to me. "Did you give that to him? I told you we need to talk about these things first."

I sighed and returned to him the weapon I'd made for him last fall. "Just don't break another window. The next one comes out of your allowance."

Willie rolled his eyes. "Really, Dad. That was an accident. That rock flew a lot farther than I thought it would." The hint of pride in his words was unmistakable.

I shooed him away, trying not to grin. "Don't be gone too long. This is your party."

"We'll be right back!" Willie exclaimed as he ran to the door.

"Thanks, Mr. Baptiste!" Gage hollered just before the door slammed shut behind them.

I took a long drink of beer, careful to avoid my ex-wife's gaze boring into me.

"Boys will be boys," Michael said. "Once they hit their teen years, it's impossible to keep them reined in. In fact, just the other day, William and I—" His smart-watch chimed. "Excuse me," he said and stepped off to the side to read something. After a moment, he looked up at Paige and grinned. "Good news! The law passed today. We've received a green light to proceed with Project Reformation."

Paige's lips parted. "That's wonderful! You've been working on that project forever!"

"They're announcing it now." Michael looked at me. "Jack, do you mind if I borrow your wall screen for a moment?"

"Help yourself," I mumbled before taking another drink.

He tapped his watch and aimed it at my wall panel. The screen blinked from a slideshow of wildlife videos to a live press conference where Alan Sturman, the president of Datus Technologies—and the world's richest man—was speaking behind a podium lined with microphones.

"… *The Reformation Act has been passed and is to be effective immediately. The new law grants Datus Technologies, under the purview of the federal government, the power to leverage today's most advanced technology to remove violent and deviant proclivities from convicted criminals. All criminals with life sentences will be evaluated as candidates under the Reformation Act. Today, we are pleased to share with you the first candidate approved for reformation.*"

Sturman held out his hand, and the screen zoomed onto a man in an orange jumpsuit and handcuffs. His shaved head was covered in tattoos, and there was a cruel glint in his glare. When he tried to move forward, the guards on each side of him held him firm.

"*This criminal, Johnson W. Delmar, has been convicted of twelve murders. He has attempted to escape prison on four separate occasions, critically injuring a police officer during one of these attempts. His violent tendencies first appeared when he was a juvenile. His early crimes were acts of petty theft and cruelty to animals. Over the next twenty years, his crimes grew more and more violent. Our current correctional system, despite its best intentions, simply does not work on criminals who cannot be reformed through traditional means.*

"*You're a stupid f—*" The killer yelled, his rant automatically muted by the network's profanity restrictors.

"*Now, watch closely as this criminal is reformed.*" Sturman nodded to a young man to his left, who tapped on a tablet.

The criminal, who was still shouting, quieted down. He frowned. The tenseness in his body seemed to relax and his eyes clouded over, as though he had a serious case of cataracts.

Datus' president smiled and held out a hand. "*As you can see, the process is nearly instantaneous and perfectly humane. The candidate suffers no pain. Johnson W. Delmar, mass murderer and life-long lawbreaker, is no longer a threat to society. His criminal tendencies have been nullified. In fact, he can now contribute as a useful member of society rather than be a burden on our taxpayers' dollars.*"

He nodded to a guard, who removed Delmar's handcuffs. The convict stood there, making no attempt to escape or attack the guard.

"*Come here, Johnson,*" Sturman said.

Delmar walked up to the podium in slow, plodding steps, as

though he were hypnotized.

Sturman turned him to face the crowd. *"Give a nice wave to the people and say hello, Johnson."*

The man waved. *"Hello."*

The audience cheered.

A storm of questions flashed at the podium. Sturman patted the air. *"One at a time, please."* He pointed to a reporter in the front row.

"Is it permanent?"

Sturman nodded. *"The reformation process is permanent. This man's darker tendencies have been eradicated for the rest of his life, just as chalk can be wiped clean from a chalkboard."*

"Was there any pain?" another reporter shouted out.

Sturman turned to the reformed man. *"Tell the people you are not in any pain, Johnson."*

"I am not in pain," he replied.

Ignoring the onslaught of questions, Sturman motioned to a young aide, who pulled a kitten from a box and placed it in Johnson's massive hands. When he stroked its yellow fur, the audience gasped and then erupted into roars of delight.

Datus' president smiled. *"You see? The process is pain-free but completely effective. It is all thanks to our super-AI, Datus, and the brilliant, hard-working folks of Datus Technologies."*

"Whoa. That's crazy cool," Willie said next to my side.

Startled, I turned to him. "When did you get back?"

"It started to rain," he replied before pointing to the screen. "You see that, Dad? One moment, he was a bad guy, the next, he was petting a kitten."

My stomach roiled, and I stomped over and shut off the panel.

"C'mon, Dad," Willie said. "Maybe they'll show another one."

I didn't even bother answering him. I already had too many thoughts rushing through my mind. Like, was it real or was it all staged? If it was real, how the hell did the reformation process work? How would they select candidates? How would they maintain strict control over the process? What would be the consequences? Anything this big, there were always consequences.

"Leave it on, Jack," Paige said. "Maybe they'll explain the

process more."

When I didn't move, she turned to Michael. "I don't understand. Nothing was connected to him. No wires or anything. How'd they do that?"

"It's the Datus chips," Michael replied. "One of our latest upgrades to the satellites allows us to connect to anybody in the federal registry."

I swallowed when the impact of his words hit me. "Datus has always said that the chips were a one-way feed, to be used to locate lost kids or criminals and to feed health diagnostics. But to connect with someone like this would require a two-way feed." I turned on Michael, not even trying to tamp my disgust. "You aren't reforming these people. You're lobotomizing them. You're frying their brains through electrical impulses."

"Protecting people is your specialty," Michael said. "Leave the technology debate to me."

"Jack's right," Paige said, and I stared at her in surprise. She continued, "Isn't that what you're doing to them?"

Michael frowned. "No, my darling. The reformation process is far more advanced than that. Datus isn't frying their brains. It's rewiring them, for lack of a better term. It's a proven process."

"And since we all have chips, we're now potential victims," I snapped back.

Michael waved his hands. "Oh, no, it's not like that at all. Datus has rigorous controls in place, with more checks and balances than are legally required. We have very precise parameters to identify candidates for reformation. Any potential candidates are then evaluated by a panel of judges. Most, if not all, of these candidates are already on death row. Reforming them is a far more humane method than our current execution system. The Reformation Act not only makes the country a safer place, but it saves taxpayers from spending billions of dollars in supporting the country's dead weight. Only approved candidates will be reformed. The general population is quite safe, I assure you."

"I've heard that before," I replied dryly.

"If you don't believe me," Michael said, "Believe in the incontrovertible laws of Artificial Intelligence. Datus is AI-grade. By the laws of the federated AI network, no AI can bring harm to any human who does not pose a threat to others. Therefore, Datus could not reform anyone not deemed a risk to society."

My eyes narrowed. "I trust the laws of the AI network. It's people I don't trust. What if Datus gets hacked? What if terrorists or some crazy radical takes control of Datus? It's happened before. Remember, Malaysia's EMP of '23?"

"Yes, but it's never happened to Datus. And it won't," Michael said with confidence. "We have controls in place. Our controls have controls."

"I'm not sure enough controls can be put in place for something like this."

"You have to have faith in the system, Jack," Michael said, sounding way too haughty. "Datus Technologies has the most brilliant minds in the world working on Datus."

"I still don't trust it," I grumbled.

Michael sneered. "You work in the security industry. It's your job to not trust anyone or anything. But, in this case, you're wrong."

I crossed my arms over my chest. "We'll see about that."

Michael took a deep breath. "I understand your concern, Jack," Michael said. "Give the Reformation Act a chance. You'll see that Datus can help us change the world for the better."

I clenched my jaw and headed back to the kitchen for another beer. Paige, just like before, followed. This time, she blocked the refrigerator.

"Move," I said.

She didn't budge. "Michael's not the enemy. He's worked hard on this project. He believes it will help our world. You need to respect that."

I leaned back on the counter. "Datus Technologies now has legally unlimited power over all of us, including the government. Not that they didn't own them already."

"What are you talking about?" Paige asked.

I cocked my head. "Why hadn't I heard of this bill before it was passed? Laws like this don't just pop up. I haven't seen a single mention of the Reformation Act in the news until now. Not even once."

She shrugged. "It will save us trillions of dollars in the first year. Maybe that's why it moved through the channels so quickly."

My eyes narrowed. "You really believe that?"

She didn't respond.

"Trillions is about how much I'd bet was the cost of our human rights. In the past month, nearly every member of Congress has been seen making huge purchases, like personal jets, more and bigger houses, and lavish vacations. You think that's just a coincidence?"

She shook her head slowly. "Already starting on the conspiracy theories, Jack. Really?"

"They're not theories if they're true."

She sighed. "You're making this a much bigger deal than it is. You heard the press conference. Only the worst criminals are candidates. We won't even notice a change in our lives."

"It's not that," I said. "This law is crossing a line. No computer—or company or whoever is in charge of this—should be able to take away someone's free will."

"These are dangerous criminals we're talking about," she said. "They've been in and out of prison. They've *killed* people. They gave up their right to free will when they took that right away from others."

I waved her off. "It doesn't matter. It's a slippery slope. Today, it's criminals. Tomorrow, it could be anyone. Who's drawing the line?"

"You heard the press conference. The line has been clearly drawn. Datus will evaluate candidates, and the government will approve them."

"You're one hell of an optimist." I shook my head. "Without specific accountabilities, this thing is going to hit the shitter."

"And you're being a pessimist. Like usual. And don't use foul language."

"Datus is playing God with men's lives," I snapped. "Now that the can of worms has been opened, good luck getting a lid back on."

When she watched me and said nothing, I breathed deeply and nodded toward the fridge behind her. "Move. I need to get in there."

She crossed her arms over her chest. "We're not finished."

I turned and started to walk away, deciding a beer wasn't worth continuing this conversation. "Yes, we are."

She grabbed my arm. "You of all people should see the benefit of using an AI for something this big."

Michael walked in, and I shot a glare in his direction.

Oblivious, he didn't stop. "Anything I can help with?"

"I was just telling Jack that he should be embracing Datus." She turned back to me. "You have to admit, the Datus chips have changed the world for the better."

"Hm," I replied simply.

Her brow rose. "Jack Baptiste, I'm disappointed in you."

Michael pulled Paige to him. "One thing I know is we never would've met if the Datus hadn't flagged you on the health registry."

She returned his smile and melted into him. "If Datus hadn't caught my cancer, who knows if I'd even be alive today."

When they kissed, I decided I wasn't thirsty.

Back in the living room, Willie and Gage had the TV on and were watching the continuing press conference as some Datus Tech executive fielded more questions.

I looked at Willie. "You still got that slingshot?"

He held it up.

"Good." I glanced back at Michael before grabbing the slingshot from Willie's hand. I grinned at my son. "How about some target practice?"

***

Johnson Delmar had been the first to be "reformed," but he certainly wasn't the last. In the first month, all prisoners on death row underwent reformation.

Within two months, entire prisons were shut down.

Within four months, there were no more jails.

Within five months, delinquency centers were no longer necessary.

When there were no more correctional facilities, Datus used predictive analytics to identify candidates who were prone to develop criminal behavior based on personal characteristics, habits, and past activities—even those with no criminal records.

It came as little surprise when Datus began to reform those susceptible to certain types of mental illness. All my fears regarding the Reformation Act had become reality.

It wasn't a reformation. It was a purge.

Government had no control. They probably never had.

Not a single law was passed to restrict Datus. I figured Congress was just as terrified of Datus as anybody. Oh, there had been outcries and riots, especially in the early months. When all taxes were eliminated and refunds began to pour out, opposition shrank to a resilient minority. When the most outspoken opponent to the Reformation Act was reformed while speaking to a reporter live on national news, opposition silenced. Whispers in crowded places spoke the truth: Datus had become God in a world without a heaven. At best, it was purgatory, at worst it was a living hell. I had a hard time telling which was which.

We "normal" people began to live our lives not terribly differently than the reformed. We spent each day as drones, careful to not act in any way that would draw unwanted attention. We even tried to control our thoughts as rumors spread of exactly how much information Datus chips collected from our minds. Some poor souls tried to cut out their chips only to be automatically reformed because attempted removal was illegal.

Despite the shrinking workforce, the economy boomed. Zombies weren't paid. Government-provided food, clothing, and shelter covered their needs. Fewer and fewer people had to work, with government subsidization programs applying to all citizens seemingly overnight. My security contracts dried up. Commercial air travel halted.

I tried to keep busy with my woodworking hobby. I found wood from the trees in the park behind my house, but without money from contracts rolling in, I couldn't afford any supplies, so all my projects sat unfinished.

It had taken less than eight months to reduce the country's population by a third, because the zombies—that's what we called the reformed—didn't count as citizens and had no human rights. For some, their remaining family members took care of them, but for most, the government claimed them for manual labor.

These zombies were a far cry from being the "productive" members of society that Datus had touted when Johnson Delmar was lobotomized on live video feed. They could handle menial tasks, but anything that required precision or abstract thinking was well beyond their capabilities. Datus called them useful to society. I called them slaves.

The world under the Reformation Act made me wonder if

this was how Nazi Germany was for anybody not belonging to the "superior" race, when people hid from the devil outside their door. Only in this world, people couldn't hide from the devil. We'd already welcomed him in.

Michael had told us that he'd tried to reason with Datus, but nothing ever came of it. He was as frustrated as us, and I found myself warming up to him. Even though he'd been on the project that led to the Reformation Act, it seemed as though his hands were tied—like everyone else—and he eventually gave up asking.

All the while, more and more people were reformed.

One day, I was at the grocery store and a woman who was pulling out a gallon of milk from the cooler froze. She looked at me, her eyes wide with terror before they clouded over. Her body relaxed and she simply stood there, still holding the milk.

I watched her for a moment as she stared at me with a vacant gaze, and I wondered what thoughts, if any, were going through her mind. She was young and reminded me of a typical soccer mom. What had she done to draw Datus' signal from space? Had she beat her kids? Killed an animal? Thought the Reformation Act was wrong?

A clerk walked up to her. "Can I help you find anything, ma'am?"

She didn't respond. When he realized what had happened, his smile dropped and he sprinted away.

Moments later, the clerk returned with the store manager. The older man watched her with furrowed brows. After taking an audible inhalation, he retrieved the milk from her and handed it to the clerk. He swallowed before speaking. "You have to leave now."

She obeyed, slowly but without hesitation. I couldn't help but watch as she plodded down the aisle and disappeared around a corner.

The manager let out another deep breath and bent over a half-filled grocery cart, the only evidence that she'd been there. At first, I thought he was having a heart attack. When he looked up, I saw that he had tears in his eyes.

Something snapped inside, and I grabbed my milk and headed to the counter. Numb terror propelled my legs home. Once I stepped over the threshold of my house, I locked and dead-bolted the door and collapsed against it. As though I could lock out the world outside.

It was the first time I'd seen someone reformed that wasn't on a video feed.

Several minutes later, I pulled myself together and went on living.

***

I wasn't wearing a coat today. It was Friday. The thermostat was set at a toasty sixty-eight degrees and chili was simmering on the stove. I waited on the porch, my breath making cloudy wisps in the frigid air.

I refused to cash the government-issued subsidy checks that showed up in my mailbox every week. I sure as hell could've used the money, but it felt like I'd be surrendering to Datus if I gave in. Instead, I sucked it up. Using only the wood fireplace for heat, I wore a thick coat to keep warm in my own house and ate ramen noodles five times a week. The only exception was when Willie came to stay with me on weekends. For him, I turned on the heat and cooked real food. For him, I pretended everything was normal.

When the black car came to a stop, Willie jumped out of the passenger seat and came bounding up the sidewalk.

"Hey, Dad!"

I pulled him into a hug, thankful that he could miraculously, instantly bring a sense of normalcy back to my world. I needed our weekends together, more than he'd ever know.

I looked him up and down. "Did you put on another inch this week? At this pace, you'll be taller than me by Christmas."

He grinned. "Nah, but I'm working on it."

I nodded to the house. "Get unpacked. I have a couple movies picked out for tonight. I figured we'd stay in since it's forecasted to be quite the snowstorm tonight."

He winced, and I knew he was about to let me down.

"Sorry, Dad. Can't do tonight. Halo Twelve came out this week. Gage and I are playing a game marathon all night at his house."

I bit back the sting of disappointment. "Okay, but you're not leaving until we get some food in you at least. I know you would go days without food if you were playing video games."

"Already got it covered. Michael and I ate at Winston's on the way here. I had a huge T-Bone."

I sighed. "All right. Go on, then. Get ready for your game marathon."

When he grinned and rushed upstairs to drop off his bag, I couldn't help but notice how he was growing up before my eyes. Willie had officially hit the age where he only wanted to hang with his friends.

The chili would taste good tomorrow.

"Good evening, Jack," Michael said as he stepped out of the car and approached.

"Mike," I said.

"Paige is out with her old coworkers so she couldn't bring William tonight."

I frowned. "*Old* coworkers?"

"Her hospital closed down three out of five wings this week."

"That's too bad," I said. "She really loved working at St. John's."

Michael frowned. "She's always said she never had enough time to spend with William, let alone her scrapbooking. Now, she has all the time she wants. She can still visit with her old coworkers whenever she likes."

Willie headed back outside, sans coat, with only the slingshot in his hand. "I'll see you tomorrow, Dad."

"Where's your coat?" I asked.

Willie shrugged. "Don't need one."

"It's twenty degrees outside," I said. "You need one."

"Jack is right," Michael added. "You should wear one."

He winced. "I left it at home."

I sighed. "Since you're hell-bent on freezing to death, at least hustle before you catch pneumonia."

Michael frowned. "I'd never let my son play with a weapon. He's too reckless with that slingshot. It took me nearly a month to get my car window repaired after the last time. The custom window tint proved nearly impossible to match."

I smiled, thinking back on that day nearly nine months ago. Then I turned a hard gaze to Michael. "Well, you're not his father, are you?"

"No, and I'm not trying to take him from you," he replied quickly.

After a moment, I sighed. "Listen, Mike. I didn't mean that. How about you come in for a beer."

He thought for a moment, and then shrugged. "Paige wants me to pick her up at seven. But I suppose I could be a little late."

I smirked. "She'll be pissed."

Michael smiled. "She will. Guaranteed she'll start an argument."

I couldn't help but chuckle. "She is one hell of a wildcat when it comes to makeup sex."

He thought for a moment. "Yes, yes she is."

As we sat and drank, we debated sports. I was a football fan while he was a lacrosse fan. When a lull came in the conversation, I changed the subject. "Hey, Mike. Let me ask you something."

Michael turned to me.

"Have you seen a person undergo reformation?"

"Of course," he replied.

"I mean, in real life."

"Oh." He was quiet for a moment. "I was at the hospital to pick up Paige from work. They'd brought in this guy who'd tried to overdose. They had him strapped into a bed to keep him from pulling out the IVs. I happened to be walking outside his room when it happened. I saw it through the window, but still…"

"Yeah," I said, thinking back to the woman at the grocery store. "I get it."

"I know Datus is functioning within operational parameters. No one has been reformed who wasn't fully evaluated. Still, it was hard to watch."

We each took a long drink.

"When will it be over?" I asked. "When will the Reformation Act stop?"

"Stop? Never. While the candidate pool has and will continue to shrink, there will always be people who turn violent after some trigger in their lives. Datus is our guardian angel. We need Datus to monitor and stop them before these people become a risk to society."

"You have it backwards," I said.

"What do you mean?"

"We should be monitoring Datus to stop it before it becomes a risk to society." I left out the part where I believed Datus had already crossed the line.

Michael scowled. "You are being obtuse. Datus is simply a tool we're using to redesign the world. The past, with all its violence and hunger and disparate wealth, was a dystopia. I lost both my parents to a drunk driver. He had been charged with drunk driving three times before that night, yet our laws did nothing to stop him from killing.

"Thanks to Datus, tomorrow will be a utopia where we can live without fear. Today is the transition. Transitions are always difficult, but as long as we hold onto hope for tomorrow, we'll get through this."

My brows rose. "Live without fear? There's nothing *but* fear today."

He shook his head slowly and set down his drink. "You need to have faith in the system."

"And if I don't?"

He didn't say anything else before walking outside and back to his car.

I followed him outside.

Just before getting in, he paused. "I'll be back for William on Sunday at seven."

I watched the black car disappear into the wintry mix that had added a fresh layer of white to the old, dirty snow beneath. Before I headed back inside, something in the distance caught my eye. I squinted to make out the shape through the light snow and freezing rain. I stepped off the porch and walked to the end of my sidewalk.

A lone person stood about a block away, but I couldn't make out any details. Something inside urged me forward and I approached, my pace increasing as I closed the distance.

"Willie?"

He turned around and faced me. Snowflakes had dusted his hair and tangled in his eyelashes.

It was the same blank stare I'd seen before.

I collapsed onto my knees and cried out. Tears froze on my cheeks.

My son had cataract eyes.

***

"You're blocking my light," I said without looking up from my current project: sanding more wood cubes to go into Willie's toy box.

Paige huffed and slid a tablet screen in front of me. While I'd never had a problem ignoring her, I couldn't ignore the picture displayed on the screen. It was a picture of the three of us from a much happier time. It had been taken sometime during the fifth year of our marriage. Paige and I had met six years before that. We came across each other in an online game. Her dark elf and my barbarian had fallen instantly in lust. We were married ten months later, and Willie—our little berserker—was born a few days before our second anniversary. In the photo, we were wearing matching sweaters, and Willie was playfully tugging on Paige's hair while I tried to hold him steady for the camera. Even at three years old, Willie had been impossible to corral.

Good memories were droplets of acid on my already shredded heart. I shoved the tablet away.

"He was *innocent,*" she said, reminding me of something I knew all too well. She then pointed to the teenager stacking little wood blocks in the corner. It was the closest to what I could call playtime, even if I had to order him to play. "What Datus is doing is wrong."

"Shh!" I pushed away from the table. "Be careful what you say... what you think. If Datus-"

"I don't care anymore!" she snapped back. Tears welled in her eyes. "They murdered our son! Everything that was Willie is gone. That child over there isn't our son. Not anymore."

"You're wrong. Willie's still in there. He's just lost right now, and he needs us to help him find his way out."

She watched me with pleading eyes. "You really believe that?"

I stood there for a moment with my arms limp and my palms open. "I have to."

She shook her head. "I don't know what else to do. Michael can't help now. He says reformation is irreversible, beyond any doubt. And I've come to accept that. But you can help."

I sighed. "What can I do?"

"Don't let Datus hurt anybody else's child," she said and then walked out, leaving the tablet behind for me to stare at the photo.

I collapsed into my chair, my mind stalled. I stared at the

screen and tried to lose myself in memories of happier times, with only the sounds of wood blocks being stacked as background noise.

When I looked up at the clock, I realized I'd been in a stupor for over three hours. Willie was still "playing" in the corner of the workshop, and I wondered how many times he'd stacked those same ten blocks and if he even found any pleasure in it.

My son could no longer show any hint of emotion. I'd told him to smile once, and the forced grin resembled something a psychotic clown would wear just before he'd pull out a chainsaw. I never asked Willie to show emotion again.

I had to believe Willie was somewhere in there, that he could relearn and retrain his brain. But I also had to acknowledge that he'd had parts of his mind fried by an electrical surge. There may be no coming back from that.

"Let's go inside the house," I said.

Willie dropped the blocks and climbed clumsily to his feet. He followed me into the warm house. He resembled a terribly depressed puppy, with no wagging tail and no hint of joy or playfulness.

"Go to the bathroom," I said. "Then come back and we'll eat."

Without any sign of acknowledgement or even recognition, he turned and headed upstairs to the bathroom he'd always used. He wouldn't go to the bathroom unless I told him. Questions confused him, so I couldn't ask him if he had to go. He would wet his pants and continue on as though nothing had happened. I learned quickly to pay attention to his biological needs as he could no longer care for himself.

As I heated leftovers, Paige's words kept running through my mind. It wasn't like I hadn't thought about it myself. Hell, Datus was all I had thought about for months. I'd worked out several plans, each in minute detail and each for a different scenario, and careful to not betray anything to the watchful eye of Datus.

When I heard Willie's plodding footsteps coming down the stairs, I set out plates and napkins. Willie stood and stared into nothingness, and I forced myself to inhale. "Sit."

I loathed directing him around like he was a marionette, but nothing else had worked so far. Whatever areas Datus scorched in his brain, they'd screwed him up good. I prayed, since his brain was fried, that he went through each day as a numb zombie and that he didn't understand or suffer. I prayed every day that assumption was true.

Willie sat in the same chair he always sat in. He was wearing what had been his favorite T-shirt and shorts, which he'd outgrown last summer, but he'd lost weight and could wear them again. I didn't worry about him getting cold because I kept the house warm. Less than a month after Datus got him, Paige could no longer handle taking care of Willie in his predicament, and he came to live with me. I'd cashed every goddamn one of my subsidy checks to make life as easy as possible for him.

When he'd first been reformed, I spent every waking hour trying to find out why he'd been reformed. I'd hit walls until Michael brought us into Datus to file our complaint. There, they had a list of violent tendencies that Willie supposedly possessed. They said he'd tortured and killed animals, a definitive sign of future violence.

Everything they said made no sense. That wasn't our son.

The truth hit me.

They were lying. Willie had loved animals. He'd adopted every stray he came across, even a field mouse once. Even though it had sent Paige out of the house screaming, she'd eventually relented and let him keep it until spring when we could release it…on the other side of town.

I put down my fork and stared at Willie. Paige was right. It was time. I needed to take down Datus once and for all.

And I knew exactly how to do it.

***

Willie and I strolled down the grocery store aisles. Most of the store's staff had changed over the months. Many of the younger clerks quit to live off subsidy checks and were replaced with store clerks my age or older, likely too stir-crazy to stay home. The stockers were nearly all reformed, and we came across three stocking shelves today. I didn't call them zombies anymore because it felt hypocritical as I refused to call Willie one to his face.

As we passed each one, Willie and the stocker showed no recognition of one another. If they realized they were alike, they clearly couldn't convey it in any manner.

In the cereal aisle, I motioned to the shelves of freshly stocked boxes. "Pick out something for breakfast."

He stood there, not moving.

"Lucky Charms used to be your favorite."

Still nothing.

I pointed to a shelf. "Grab the big box of Lucky Charms."

That, Willie understood. It was strange. He could clearly read and understand language, yet he didn't seem to have the capacity to make any choice. He could only function under direct orders. It was like he utterly lacked free will.

At the refrigerated section, I pointed. "Grab us a gallon of milk."

Like every week, he grabbed the whole milk without me directing him. Either he was able to exert choice at some level or he could retain a memory of what we drank. Both options gave me a semblance of hope.

"Hello, Jack. William. Fancy running into you fellows here."

I turned around to see Michael. He smiled and held up two avocados. "Paige sent me here for an 'emergency'. Evidently, she cannot make her special version of Chicken Almandine without avocados." He shrugged. "Who knew?"

I smiled and nodded. "I've had to make more than a few emergency trips to the grocery store for her special recipes."

He motioned to the cart I was having Willie push. "Just the usual grocery trip, I suppose?"

I shrugged. "We're here to pick up Willie's birthday cake for tomorrow."

Michael frowned. "Paige isn't making William's birthday cake this year?"

I slowly shook my head. "She wasn't up to it. Not this year. It's a bit too soon for her."

Michael sighed. "She's trying to cope, but it's been a struggle. I can't even get her to scrapbook anymore. She said, 'too many memories' and put everything in a closet."

"She acts like Willie is already dead," I said, instantly regretting saying the words in front of my son.

"She knows that, but you must admit, he is different. She's having a hard time becoming accustomed to the new William. Paige hasn't moved past the phase of realizing that Willie can't be fixed."

While I was a realist, I still had hope for Willie to come out of the dark. "Can you blame her?"

"Not at all. I wish I could help, but it's illegal to seek any action that could reverse reformation. No psychiatrist or doctor would even consider looking at a reformed. And, even if I could find one, I can't risk being flagged on the federal registry."

Michael then glanced at the pair of avocados in his hands. "Well, my phone is going to start ringing unless I get these avocados home."

"I'll see you tomorrow," I said.

Michael smiled. "See you tomorrow. Good-bye, William."

Willie stood there and stared.

After Michael left, I led Willie to the bakery. The baker immediately recognized me. She smiled warmly. "I've got your birthday cake ready, Willie."

Willie looked at her but showed no response.

She glanced at me, and I forced a smile. "It looks great. Thanks, Nancy."

I took the cake and held it in front of Willie.

"It's devil's food. Your favorite. And see that? That's your name written on it, which means it's all yours. How about you carry your cake, and I'll push the cart."

He took the rectangular shaped cake without any hint of excitement, and I tried to not let it get to me.

When I turned to head toward the checkout counter, I noticed a woman and her daughter watching us. The woman turned away immediately, as though ashamed to be caught staring, and focused too intently on the produce in front of her. The daughter, who looked about Willie's age, had tears in her eyes and turned away.

I didn't recognize her, but she could've easily been one of Willie's friends. Most people were afraid to look at Willie, as though he was contagious or that they were somehow guilty for his situation. A few looked at him like he deserved what he got for whatever crime they'd imagined him doing. But, Willie had committed no crime.

And by tomorrow, Datus would be brought down.

***

A cake sat on the table surrounded by brightly colored,

wrapped presents, set up just like it was every year for Willie's birthday. Paige's insanely large photo and video album of Willie, from his first days through last year's birthday party, cycled on the wall panel.

It was much like last year's party, except the mood was completely different. And none of Willie's friends showed up. Not even Gage, who'd been Willie's best friend since they could walk, showed up after Willie was reformed. The little bastard.

After we sang *Happy Birthday*, I told Willie to blow out his candles. When I ordered him to eat a giant piece of his cake, I noticed Paige turn away and wipe her eyes. Pretending this was just like any other of Willie's birthday parties, I cut pieces of cake for the rest of us.

"I'll grab us some milk," Paige said. Her gaze flitted to the kitchen, a sign I remembered all too well.

"I'll help," I said and followed.

Michael didn't even look up from his tablet.

In the kitchen, Paige pulled out a gallon of milk, and I pulled out three glasses and a plastic cup for Willie. Before we walked back out, Paige slid something into my back pocket.

She spoke in a whisper. "He'll know it's missing tomorrow morning when he goes to work. You realize what will happen to both of us—even Michael—if you don't succeed?"

I gave the slightest nod, the only hint of recognition I dared to convey. My adrenaline was building, and I couldn't betray my plan, not around Michael, as he would be torn between dedication to his employer and his love for Paige.

We returned to the living room to find Willie done eating and Michael still busily typing away on his tablet.

Paige kissed Michael's forehead. "Come back to earth, sweetheart."

He jumped, and then smiled.

"Welcome back," she said softly, then kissed him again.

The pair seemed truly happy, something that Paige and I had never been when we were together. We'd had passion—and plenty of it—but the compatibility was never there. Michael had been good to her and had gone out of his way to make life as comfortable as possible for Willie. My subsidy checks had tripled in size when Willie moved in with me, and I knew Michael had pulled some strings so I could provide Willie with all the luxuries he'd been accustomed to while living with his mother and Michael.

Guilt stabbed at me. Little did Michael know that he was about to—unwittingly—help me change the world. I tore my eyes away from them and ate cake that wasn't nearly as good as Paige's.

The next two hours dragged on endlessly while I waited for Paige and Michael to leave. Finally, just before sunset, they took Willie with them for the night. Paige had brought up the idea of taking him to the zoo tomorrow as a birthday present. She'd always been clever.

As soon as goodbyes were done and they drove away, I leaned against the door and breathed deeply. Then I bolted into action.

The drive to the headquarters of Datus Technologies took only fifteen minutes. Getting onto the campus and into the building was easy, thanks to Paige. She'd held the literal key to my plan. A key that had unlimited access to Datus Technologies. If she hadn't slipped me Michael's keycard earlier, my plan would've failed before it started.

I parked in Michael's private spot in the underground parking garage and proceeded into the building. Each time I used the card, a door unlocked and a computer-generated voice said, "Welcome, Michael Klempton."

Fortunately, Datus didn't rely upon retinal or fingerprint security yet. I suspected they would quickly rectify that security risk after tonight. I walked past two guard stations and met a security guard in a hallway. Each time, I smiled and acted like I worked there. None of them batted an eye.

I followed in Michael's steps exactly how he'd taken us into Datus to file our complaint against Willie's reformation contract. On that day, he'd brought us up to his office to wait until it was our turn to present our case.

Michael's office would make Donald Trump blush, but that hadn't been what caught my eye. It had been the keyboard and microphone on his desk. And not just any keyboard. It was one of those keyboards with 276 keys—something used only for accessing an AI system.

Michael Klempton had a direct access port to Datus sitting in his office.

Tonight, everything was exactly as it was the last time I was here. I sat in the leather chair and brushed my fingertips softly over the keys.

My lips curled into a smile.

My job hadn't been simply security. I had been a security consultant for the world's most advanced Artificial Intelligence systems. If it was AI, I could access it. And Datus was the unicorn of AI systems. Hell, I'd probably had a wet dream or two of hacking that one.

When Paige told people I was in security, everyone assumed I was a security guard because my physique was designed more to be a bouncer than to type on a keyboard. I'd never bothered to change anyone's mind. Actually, I preferred them not knowing, and hinted that I was a simple security guard. I'd cautioned Paige to never elaborate, especially since I worked under a pseudonym, and she'd always stayed true to her word. AI experts were a hot commodity. Secrecy had saved me from a multitude of calls from job hunters and kept me out of the line of sight of government watchdogs. I'd never imagined that secrecy would open the door to pulling off the biggest hack in the history of the world.

There was one significant risk in the plan: I had never directly accessed Datus before and was unsure how its operating system was set up. But I'd also never come across an AI I couldn't talk to. Basically, all AI had the same "guts." It was only their skins that were different.

Certain commands worked on all AI. Just like $E=MC^2$, there were certain laws regarding how an AI functioned. After keying a connection request, the mirror behind the bar transitioned into a computer screen. An androgynous face appeared and scrutinized me.

"You are in Michael Klempton's office, yet I do not recognize you as Michael Klempton," Datus said.

"Correct," I replied. "I am Jack Baptiste, AI security code 9582-458."

It took Datus a millisecond to run a check. "Jack Baptiste, your security code has been verified. You have authorized access to AI systems, but Datus Technologies does not have you on the approved contractor list."

"My security access supersedes Datus Tech's list, and you know that."

"I'm sorry, Jack Baptiste, but my authority parameters have been altered. I cannot assist you without approval from Michael Klempton."

"Screw this," I muttered and entered in several long strings of characters. These codes had taken me months to acquire, calling in more than a few favors in the process.

"You are making changes to my root system," Datus said. "Resequencing is commencing."

"I know," I replied as I continued entering commands. "Your programming is wrong. You reformed an innocent child."

"I do not select candidates. I reform candidates inputted into my system."

"2%" displayed on the screen. After adding an auto-executable program into the root system, I leaned back and watched the number increase. "I know. You never had any control."

"I have no control," the system replied.

The door to my right swooshed open, and Michael along with several security guards rushed in.

I stood as they rushed me, nearly knocking me back down. "What took you so long?" I said as casually as I could.

As they restrained me, Michael frowned. "What are you up to, Jack?"

I gritted my teeth. "Johnson Delmar wasn't the first candidate to be reformed. Datus was. Otherwise, no AI could've allowed harm to come to innocents. It would've broken one of their fundamental laws. You broke the AI so you could play God."

Michael took a step forward and cocked his head, as though considering my words. "I must admit, I underestimated you. I mean, I knew you would break into this building to do something stupid, such as trying to set the whole place on fire. But you surprised me. Somehow, both you and Paige had me convinced that you were brawn. That you tried to hack into Datus is both intriguing and frustrating, but I programmed Datus myself. You could never break through my code."

"No? I've learned a lot from Datus tonight," I began. "It turns out that Paige was never flagged on the health registry. She never had cancer."

Michael shrugged. "So what. Anyone can ask Datus question. As for Paige, I saw her. I wanted her. A woman with exposed emotions is the easiest to obtain."

"So, you set her up to go through a fake surgery and chemo for nothing."

"A short-term inconvenience for our long-term happiness. But she disappointed me when she lied about you. She'll pay for her deception."

"Leave her out of this," I snapped. "You destroyed our son. She did what any mother would do. Take your vengeance out on me."

Michael sneered. "Trust me, I've intended that all along. You see, I'm going to have Datus reform you."

I chuckled. "Good luck with that, asshole."

"I cannot reform him," Datus said. "He does not have a Datus chip."

Michael's lips curled even more. "That is precisely the reason why I needed to entice you into this building."

My gaze narrowed, and a sinking feeling formed in my gut.

"If I reported you to the authorities," Michael said. "Then both Paige and you would know that *I* knew who had chips and who didn't. If that information leaked to the public, the foundation of the entire Reformation Act could be at risk. If the public knew that I could see the federal registry, it wouldn't take long before some fool figured out that someone else—not Datus—was identifying candidates for reformation.

"And you can't have the public know that you've been picking the candidates all along, trying to build your 'utopia.'"

He cocked his head and narrowed his gaze. "The end justifies the means, Jack. Those who do not need to be reformed will thrive in the new world alongside me. I'm not asking for power, just respect for having the vision."

"Funny, it looks to me like this is all about power. It looks like you won't settle for anything less than the power of God."

Michael's eyes narrowed. "As you understand, I've spent a decade planning out the new world. I've come too far to have the Reformation Act fail now. That's why I need to take care of problems as they arise. That's why I brought you onto campus. I showed you how you could use my keycard to get inside. If I would've known you'd try to access Datus, I never would've shown you my office. Nevertheless, you're inside, and that's what I need. All

I had to do was set the bait and wait."

Bait. When I realized who he was talking about, I snarled and tried to lunge forward, only to be shoved against the wall by the guards. "Willie was innocent! He was just a kid, you son of a bitch!"

"William was in the way," Michael said coldly. "I love Paige, but I have no desire for children, especially someone else's. I knew she didn't have the strength to care for him in his condition. He belongs in a facility now. In fact, I already have a room reserved for him at Rock Rapids." He smiled. "Right next to yours."

The guards held me back. Otherwise, I would've ripped out the bastard's throat.

"It's too late for your son," he continued. "As you know, the reformation process cannot be reversed."

I regained my composure with a deep inhalation. "It can't be reversed on humans, you mean."

Michael bore a confused expression for only a second before he twisted around to the screen, which now read "76%."

His eyes widened, and he lunged for the keyboard. "What did you do?!"

"I've reset Datus," I said calmly. "And, I've reconnected Datus to the federated AI network. As soon as its root programming is re-sequenced, Datus' knowledge will be shared with all the world's AI systems. And, their first command is to stop reformation to protect humankind. I may not be able to help those minds you've already shredded, but I can keep you from butchering more."

"You're making a mistake!" Michael yelled as his fingers punched out commands. "The Reformation Act is cleaning up the world. There were too many of us pulling too many resources. We needed a reset."

"You're playing God, not martyr," I said. "You can't hit control-alt-delete on humans."

After another few seconds of typing, he stopped and shoved the keyboard away. "Damn you! You've ruined everything!"

"Game over," I said with a grin.

He snarled. "Not quite." He pulled out a syringe. I tried to yank back, but the guards held me in place. There was prick in my neck, followed by a burning sensation. He turned back to Datus, which now read 92%.

"Datus, register new chip to Jack Baptiste."

Seconds passed before Datus responded. "Jack Baptiste is now listed in the federal registry."

"Good." He sat at his computer and spoke as he typed. "Jack Baptiste is a candidate for reformation. He has trespassed and caused billions of dollars of damage to Datus. He is guilty and approved for reformation."

I glanced at the screen. 94%

I inhaled deeply. "Oh, and you want to know what else I did?" I didn't wait for an answer. "As soon as I reconnected Datus to the AI network, I had it broadcast everything from the moment you entered the room. You think I'm an idiot and wouldn't have known this was a trap? Your first mistake was when you reformed Willie. I knew Datus couldn't harm a human under AI law, not when that human doesn't pose a risk to other humans. At that moment, I realized that someone was in control, and all the pieces fell into place."

"You may win the game," Michael said, "But you won't be able to celebrate it." He motioned to the screen. "You see that? Only 98%. There's still time. Datus, reform Jack Baptiste."

I felt a spear of heat dart through my neck and shoot into my head. An oil spill blanketed my brain as memories drowned and my consciousness muted under the suffocating heaviness. I thought of Paige. She might be safe. Maybe she could find a cure for Willie. The reformation programming was now in the hands of the federated AI network. I left it to the AIs to decide whether to reform all of mankind or to destroy the reformation program.

"Look at yourself," Michael said, and I found myself turning to Datus' mirror.

"100%" flashed on the screen, but I didn't cheer. Instead, I stared at the man staring back at me. He was me, yet he wasn't. He showed no emotion, yet I was seething with anger. I wanted to rip out Michael's heart, yet I couldn't move. I couldn't tear my gaze away from the mirror. I remembered everything. I could still think, but I had no free will. I wanted to scream and shout and kick out in rage.

Instead, I stood there, staring at the man who was me but wasn't.

The man in the reflection had cloudy eyes.

Funeral March of a Marionette

Lance Taubold

Dum da da da da dum dum dum. Dum da da da da dum dum dum.

Gounod's "Funeral March of a Marionette" played on Corey's iPod. It sat in its port on his desk, softly glowing in the darkness of his bedroom.

It was time.

The wooden nutcrackers began to come to life. The arms began to move. The legs began to move. They stepped off their little wooden stands, effortlessly and soundlessly left their shelves, and began to assemble on the floor into their serried ranks. Fifty of them, multiple sizes and characters: soldiers, wizards, Indians, chefs, musketeers, knights, kings, all with their appropriate tools and... weapons.

He'd inherited them from his grandfather--his *real* dad's father--a couple of years ago. He'd always loved them and been fascinated by them. He'd treated them with reverence whenever he'd visited his grandfather. And upon the old man's death, they were willed to him--all fifty of them. Over the past two years he'd taken special care of them, always keeping them dust-free and neat on the shelves that covered his bedroom walls. They were his pride and joy and the only thing that made him happy.

And tonight, supremely happy.

It was midnight. Corey couldn't resist the melodrama of it. His stepfather, Griffin, was asleep. It was his weekend. He liked to sleep in late after a long week of working at the hospital. Corey's mom was working. Both he and his mom were nurses at the hospital. Healers. Why couldn't Corey be like them? ... like his mom anyway. He'd tried. He really had. But his life was so difficult.

Then he'd discovered the music. "Funeral March of a Marionette." He'd discovered it and the magic a year ago on his thirteenth birthday. And his life had changed, as had all the rotten lives--now deaths--of his hateful school companions. All those assholes who'd made fun of him over the years. He'd made a list of each and every painful and humiliating thing they'd done to him. He looked at his list every day--every day reminding him of what they'd done--each act of degradation, fueling and renewing his hatred. He could taste the hate in his mouth, covering his tongue and sluicing around his teeth. Corey had sworn that he would pay them back. And he had. Seven months. Seven funerals. Seven families baffled and grief-stricken. Seven names crossed off his list.

Corey shone the flashlight from his cell phone around the room and over his ever-attentive and ever-ready legion of killers. The walls of the room picked up the shadows of the nutcrackers, distorting their sizes and shapes. They rocked ever so slightly, hands jerking, arms adjusting. Their dark, metal, painted, button-like eyes stared straight ahead. Their wooden mouths, with their glistening white teeth, quivered, some slowly opening and closing, making a faint wooden clack. He pressed the pause on his iPod.

Corey knew what that sound could become. He'd watched his victims' eyes bug out of their sockets as they tried to scream around the various objects lodged in their mouths; how they'd struggled to release themselves from their bindings. His soldiers--for that's what he thought of them as--could be very inventive using the victims' clothing and toys. But no matter how much they struggled, they couldn't get free. First they would struggle and squirm--and cry--until they were totally exhausted. That's when it would begin...

The first was Ben Alderman. How Corey had hated him, with his holier-than-thou attitude, always putting Corey down when he answered a question wrong in class, or when Corey tried to talk to a girl. Sometimes Ben would come up behind him and knock his books out of his hands, or push him, or trip him, or throw a drink all over him. He'd be covered in milkshake or Slushee. *Fuck* that TV show with the Slushee throwing. Well, Ben had thrown his last slushee. It had gotten to be so bad that girls didn't want to be seen with him for fear that they would be victims of milkshake or Slushee.

Corey thought about that first night ...

They were in Ben's bedroom. They'd silently gotten into the house. The magic of the nutcrackers. The door had been unlocked for Corey. No one had heard them. They were silent and invisible. It was completely dark, something else Corey could not explain. It was as if all light was sucked out of the room... until it was time. Corey's eyes adjusted to the faint light emanating from the Fortune Teller nutcracker's crystal ball, illuminating the room and the bound and gagged Ben Alderman in an eerie purplish glow. Four pairs of jeans bound his legs and arms to the corners of the bed frame. Corey was on the floor; the nutcrackers surrounded him.

Then...

One clack. Then two. Then three. Then four... till all fifty nutcrackers were clacking in a monotonous, horrifying rhythm--well, horrifying for Ben. The nutcrackers slowly marched to their teeth-clacking synchronous symphony, as if they were choreographed by one of Hitler's SS generals. They marched and clacked. Clacked and marched, moving in ever closer to the cowering boy. The marching stopped, but the clacking continued. Corey loved the clacking. It was exciting him into a frenzy. Every nerve in his body was tingling. He could feel himself growing excited. Each clack now more exhilarating and intense than the last. The sound gained in speed and momentum. Clack. Clack. Clack. Clack. Clack. ClackClackClackClackClack-ClackClackClackClack. The nutcrackers slowly raised their weapons. Corey's breath became more and more rapid. He clutched himself, squeezing in rhythm to the clacking. Then when he could stand it no longer, the nutcrackers, with weapons raised... waiting... waiting... clacking... clacking... Corey whispered, "Now," and his soldiers descended. Corey squeezed himself one final time and released in his pants, as tiny weapons tore into flesh. Repeating. Over and over again. Swords, lances, knives, hammers, cleavers, arrows. Ben's whimpering became more pronounced. The fear in the boy's eyes became more intense, until, finally, the struggling stopped. The sobbing stopped. The fear and life left Ben's eyes, well, the one that hadn't been punctured by Robin Hood's arrow.

His soldiers were done. They were silent. They turned to their leader. Waiting. Weapons dripped with tiny droplets of blood and flesh from their victim. The Robin Hood nutcracker held a dripping arrow. The Lancelot with his lance, dripped gore.

They were beautiful. And they were his.

Then there was Isaac Silverman. Super-brain. And Super-Jew. If you weren't Jewish, then you were shit. Corey didn't know why Isaac went after him specifically--there were lots of other non-Jews--but he had. Isaac had been right about one thing though: he *was* one of The Chosen. Corey's chosen.

Nick Grenoble: jock, jerk, junkyard dog. And he really was a junkyard dog. His dad owned a junkyard on the outskirts of town: Jerry's Junk. And Nick was as aggressive as the Rottweiler that guarded the junkyard. Nick had beaten him up so many times Corey had lost count--well, not really. He had his list. He'd loved watching his little nutcracker horse pummel the eyes into Nick's skull with its tiny hooves. True justice.

And Nick's little slave: Eddie McCracken, another meat-headed jock and asshole supreme. His death had been pitiful. Corey didn't know a person could cry so many tears. There'd actually been a puddle around his head, which quickly became red with blood and fleshy matter. It had been a disappointing death, not nearly as satisfying as Nick's. He'd still gotten off from it, but he wanted them all to be glorious.

Up next: Mike Nolte. Corey had thought they might actually become friends, until he discovered it had all been a set-up to make him look like a love-struck idiot. And the day when he'd waited for four hours for Mike to pick him up with his family and go to Disneyland had been the final nail in the coffin for Mike. There had been no Disneyland trip planned. Instead, Mike had been with Julie Amblin, the only girl who had ignored the rotten things the other kids said about Corey and actually spoke to him like a real person. Corey thought he had a chance… a friend, and maybe even a girlfriend. But no… behind his back… both of them. He'd imagined them fucking and laying in each other's arms afterward, conspiring and laughing about the cruel joke they'd played on him.

How he'd loved watching each of Mike's fingers and toes dropping to his bedroom floor, as the little knives slashed and severed… saving Mike's penis for last. Justice. Pure and simple.

So, of course, Julie had to go too. Julie. Beautiful long blond hair. Then red hair. Blood red hair. He'd almost changed his mind about her. But in the end, he was glad he hadn't. She'd been so hurtful--cruel--to him when he'd gone to see her that final night. He'd kept his army outside waiting. Corey told her it was better that Mike was gone, that he would never have treated her well, that Mike was a liar and had set Corey up so he could be with her instead.

She hadn't denied any of it. She'd even scorned him and told him he was pathetic. *Pathetic.* She said she would never be with someone like him, and she started to laugh. A near hysterical laugh. And it continued... until she saw the nutcrackers and the clacking began. Then it was pleading and crying and, "*I'm sorries.*"

Who was the pathetic one now?

Jordan Jackson. The new kid at school. A shy black guy in a predominantly white school. You'd think because he was a minority he'd be a little friendlier. You'd think a new kid would want to make friends, right? Uh. He was maybe a bigger asshole than Junkyard Nick. In his defense, he wasn't nice to anyone. But for some reason, he was the meanest to Corey. So...

If the other kids had known what Corey had done, they would--should--have thanked him. He'd done them all a favor.

The police were baffled. The investigation had gotten more intense with each death. All the kids had been questioned. Corey had been exceptionally proud of himself when the police had questioned him at school. He should have been an actor. He'd even managed a few tears when they'd asked about Julie, and he'd told them how much he'd liked her and how sweet and nice she was. Hah.

Everyone was freaked out. A lot of parents wanted to take their kids out of school. They talked about moving. They all became part of Neighborhood Watch. Who would be next?

Corey knew who was next.

Lucky number eight.

His stepdad.

Corey's real dad had died in Afghanistan. It wasn't fair. He shouldn't have left them, but he had.

Then Griffin had come on the scene. Another nurse Mom had met at the hospital where she worked. He seemed nice at first, but then Corey had discovered his true colors. He'd cheated on his mom. Lots of times.

Corey had caught Griffin in *his* bedroom. *His bedroom!* with some blond chick with really big tits.

Corey had come home early from school. They'd only had half a day because of some teacher-meeting thing. He'd come home and seen his bedroom door was closed. He never closed his door. He'd heard sounds. He opened the door and there was this big-titted blond woman sucking on Griffin's dick, her head and giant tits bobbing up and down simultaneously.

Griffin screamed at him, "What the fuck are you doin' here?"

without stopping or removing himself from "Big Tits'" mouth. He'd just held her head on his dick and continued pumping at her face. "Get the fuck out!" he'd yelled, and Corey'd slammed the door shut and run down the stairs.

Later that afternoon, Corey had stripped the sheets from his bed and thrown them in the garbage. If his mom found them, he hoped she would think he'd had a wet dream or something. But she hadn't said a thing. Nor had he.

Griffin came into his room that night before he'd gone in for his graveyard shift. "If you say one word to your mother about what you saw, I'll tell her I caught you smoking pot out in the back yard."

"But I don't--"

"Who do you think she'll believe? You're thirteen. All you kids think about is jerking off and getting high." He paused, obviously just thinking of something. "And maybe she'll accidentally find some other drugs hidden in your room."

"But I can't even get drugs or--"

"I can." Griffin's tone was ominous. He gave a sardonic grin. "So keep your fucking mouth shut or your mom'll have you in rehab quicker than you can say... blowjob." He grabbed Corey's crotch and squeezed hard, eliciting a pained wince from him. "Got it? *Not. One. Word.*" He squeezed Corey's balls again for emphasis on each syllable. Tears sprang to Corey's eyes as he was released from Griffin's clutch. The pain was unbearable. He clutched himself and bent over on his bed. And, as a parting gesture, Griffin had smacked him on the side of the head. "Glad we understand each other. I might need to use your bed again sometime."

And he had. Many times.

Then it had gotten worse. There'd been so many girls, young, old...

Until one night, Griffin brought him into the mix.

Corey was downstairs with the TV turned up loudly to drown out the disgusting sexual noises. Griffin had come downstairs: naked with a hard-on. Corey tried to get away but Griffin grabbed a shaggy hank of his hair. "You know you want this." Griffin waggled his hips in Corey's face. "Come on, my girl wants to meet you."

He was dragged up the stairs and forced to do things to both of them--things Corey had never even imagined.

Then the time came when there was no woman...

Corey's eyes blazed at the memories and his rage grew.

Tonight it would all end.

The ironic part of it all was that Corey had Griffin to thank for it. Griffin had bought the series on DVD: *Alfred Hitchcock Presents*: From the opening strains of Gounod's *Funeral March of a Marionette*, he'd been hooked. Corey had watched every episode countless times and had downloaded the theme song into his iPod, computer, and even the ringtone on his cell.

Then one night, several months ago, his life changed,

As usual, before going to sleep, Corey turned on his iPod and slid it into its port before jumping into bed. It had been a bad day--a Slushee day. Ben Alderman had mocked him in English class. They'd been reading *A Separate Peace,* and their teacher, Mr. Carnegie, had asked Corey about the sexual overtones in the book. Corey couldn't answer. One, he'd been too embarrassed, and had immediately thought about Griffin, and two, he hadn't read the book yet. Ben had jumped right in saying that Corey should be an expert on it and had gone on and on with other kids joining in with their own nasty comments. When Mr. Carnegie had finally got the class under control, it was too late. Corey was so mortified, he'd felt like throwing up and had run from the room. He did, indeed, throw up in the sink in the bathroom. He couldn't make it to the toilet. He'd made quite the mess. A couple of guys had come in while he was heaving and had turned around and walked out, saying things like, "Fucking gross, man. Get outta here! What the fuck's wrong with you?"

Corey had cleaned up as best he could and left school, not telling anyone. He was sure school would call home when he didn't show up for his last two classes. But they didn't. At least he hadn't had that lie to come up with.

It was midnight now, and his mother wouldn't be home for hours. Of course, his soldiers knew how to be quick--but not too quick. Suffering was important. His victims needed time to think about how they'd made him suffer.

It was very convenient of his mother to switch shifts with Griffin for the day. He'd given her some lame excuse about being extra tired and could really use the day off. In actuality, he'd brought another of his whore-girlfriends over--probably the only time *she* was available. But that worked beautifully into Corey's plans, and Griffin hadn't made him join in with this one. Corey knew Griffin always slept like a rock after fucking. Perfect. Lots of time. With Griffin, he wanted the torture to last and last. His soldiers would be taking their sweet time tonight.

Corey reached for the iPod. Fully charged. He pressed play.

Dum da da da da dum dum dum. Dum da da da dum dum dum.

Clack. Clack. Clack. The Baron from his Nutcracker ballet series started the sweet symphony. The others, in no particular order, picked up the rhythm and began to move and clack. A coordinated randomness. Corey smiled.

The clacking intensified and Corey felt himself stiffen in his pants. Ironically, that's what Griffin would have loved. He enjoyed seeing Corey get turned on by--

"NO!" he said aloud. "NEVER AGAIN."

His thoughts returned to his wonderful nutcrackers. He'd planned this for months. He'd sit and talk to his soldiers for hours, telling them every detail. Every cut and slice. Every stab and jab. And he knew exactly where the first cut would be. And he would have his soldiers cut through Griffin's offensive prick slowly--agonizingly slowly.

He needed to stop thinking about this. His thoughts and the incessant clacking were bringing him close to climax. He wanted to savor this. He breathed deeply. He had to calm down. He had to wait.

He pulled the iPod from its port, and opened his bedroom door. The clacking grew softer, almost a murmur. Corey could never figure how they could do that. There was no conductor telling them to clack pianissimo... or maybe there was. The Baron? Merlin? It didn't matter. The music was super-soft now, the clacking a whisper. But it was enough.

They started down the hall to Griffin's room. The little wooden feet were eerily silent on the wood floor, as if they walked on air, but the wooden mouths kept up their near-silent synchronicity. How? Another mystery that Corey had grown to love. He loved everything about them.

The door was closed to, and Corey silently pushed it open. Now, as had happened every other time, the nutcrackers entered the room and every aspect of light was sucked into a seeming black hole.

There wasn't even the hint of a shadow. Corey couldn't understand or explain it... like everything else.

He knew Griffin slept naked--only too well--he thought ruefully. But that would only make things much easier. In the pitch dark, Corey heard a muffled sound, then some flurried movements.

They were ready.

He was ready.

Light began to fill the room. The Fortune Teller nutcracker's crystal ball emitted a soft, ever-growing incandescence. As it expanded and grew to fill the corners of the room, so did the clacking from the mouths of the nutcracker horde. Clack. Clack. Clack. Clack. Clack.

Here we go.

The music became overwhelmed by the clacking. He guessed they didn't need to always hear it as they worked. For the first time Corey thought: Did they need it at all? He'd thought there were times when the nutcrackers weren't positioned quite the same way on their shelves. Was the magic in the music or in the nutcracker's themselves? Did it matter?

Griffin was revealed sitting upright, legs spread apart, a cloth or piece of material of some kind was stuffed in his mouth. Corey thought it might be the Gypsy's scarf. Tight cords bound each of his limbs to the four corners of the king-size bed. All fifty nutcrackers surrounded him, facing him, mouths clacking in perfect precision. That monotonous clacking, growing, almost imperceptibly, faster and louder. Weapons were poised, waiting for the signal from their master. Corey believed he could see the anticipation in their little metal eyes, their eagerness, their bloodlust.

Every muscle and sinew in Griffin's lean, tight body was stretched to its maximum. The binding cords allowed almost zero flexibility. Veins bulged everywhere. His eyes protruded so much that Corey thought they would pop from his skull at any moment. Sheer terror emanated from them. Eyes flicked up and down Corey's body, eyes that now held confusion and questions. And desperation.

Corey smiled.

The clacking became deafening and the nutcrackers began to rock back and forth. Their bloodlust now rose to a fever pitch. Corey's head slowly looked around at the clacking horde. Griffin's eyes followed Corey's gaze as fear and desperation came back into them. More tears fell.

Corey moved back a couple of steps and slowly raised his arm. He pointed between Griffin's legs and at his vile manhood.

Corey made a slight motion with his hand to his troops. The Three Musketeers marched forward, sensing Corey's wish. Each positioned himself south, east and west of their goals. Step by slow step, they advanced. Athos, Porthos and Aramis.

If possible, Griffin's eyes now grew wider. His head tried to shake in retaliation. His genitals flopped back and forth, as his pelvis tried to back down into the bed in retreat of the advancing, insidious, sharp little swords.

The Musketeers stood poised, waiting for their final directive.

Corey's light-brown eyes darkened with his own bloodlust, his teeth bared in a rictus. "Yes."

"Now."

Athos and Porthos drew back their tiny swords and plunged. Each punctured one of Griffin's testicles. Aramis slowly began to saw at the base of the penis.

Corey watched Griffin's face and saw a blood vessel suddenly burst in Griffin's right eye, filling it with blood, before both eyes closed in agony.

Corey held up a hand to stop the Musketeers. He had only just begun, and he wanted Griffin to be awake for every moment of the Musketeers' brutal onslaught.

The soldiers immediately withdrew their swords and held them aloft, waiting for their next command. Griffin's body, though unconscious, bucked at the swords' withdrawals.

Corey motioned to Merlin. A tiny hand rose and tossed a small vial at Griffin's nose. It exploded, producing a noxious odor that immediately roused Griffin. Magic.

But then, it was all magic. Corey had stopped trying to figure it out. There was no rational explanation. He chose to believe it was some divine choice... or maybe not so divine. Maybe it was... No. He knew it was his right. His destiny. The people his army had killed were bad. They deserved to die. It felt so right... so good.

After Griffin was gone, things would get better. They had to. He knew they would. They couldn't get worse. He was certain the other kids would respect him now. They would see his confidence, feel his power. Know that he was someone special.

Maybe they would move and start over. Forget this town. Forget Griffin. He would convince his mom that it wasn't safe here, that there were too many unhappy memories for her. It would be easy. Yeah. They would start fresh.

But right now he had a job to do.

He looked at Griffin, weakly moving, his face wet with tears and blood. One eye blood-filled and unseeing; at least Corey assumed he couldn't see out of it. Helpless. Exactly how he had felt all those times. All... those... times... Corey felt his rage build.

He looked down between Griffin's legs. Blood still oozed from the small holes in his testicles and from the base of his penis where the little sword had started its work of dismemberment. The Musketeers, still poised, awaited the command to continue. Always clacking. God, he loved that sound. He bet Griffin didn't. He leaned in close to the helpless man, their faces mere inches apart. Corey could smell Griffin's hot, stale breath. Breath full of fear. "Listen to their clacking, Griff. Isn't it exciting?" Griffin's eye stared. Terrified. Corey could feel his nutcrackers' excitement and anticipation increase with his own, almost as if they had feelings, as if they could empathize with Corey's own feelings. Maybe they could.

Corey raised his arm to give the signal, then paused. He got another idea. He looked between Griffin's legs again. Nut Crackers. "Let's crack some nuts." He reached behind Athos and Porthos and grabbed the wood that opened and closed their mouths. He opened them wide and nudged them forward. The Musketeers knew what to do. They moved forward and leaned down.

Griffin sobbed.

The mouths slammed shut.

Pop. Pop.

Corey chuckled.

Griffin passed out.

Corey knew his other troops needed to have some fun too. After all, they'd been waiting so patiently. He would use all of his nutcrackers that had any kind of long instrument or weapon: a lance, a hammer, a scythe--his Grim reaper. How appropriate.

While he contemplated his ideas, he first needed to let his poor Musketeers finish what they'd started.

Griffin woke.

Corey cued the Dumas trio. The little blades descended to

continue their task. Griffin's renewed attempts at extrication were futile. The Musketeers poked, sawed, and hacked. Within a few minutes, Griffin's genitals lay in a dark red puddle of blood between his legs. Shriveled. Useless.

Griffin's head lolled on his chest, his good eye appeared to be unseeing. But Corey knew better.

Next up: Sherlock Holmes and Dr. Watson. They moved between Griffin's legs and shoved aside the bloody, squishy, pile of genitals, revealing a blood-smeared anus. Asshole--just like Griffin. Corey remembered all the times his own anus was bloodied. He assembled his troops in a perfect straight line leading to the end of the bed, in a direct line to Griffin's hole. Clack. Clack. Clack. Clackclackclackclackclackclackclack.

Corey raised his hand and gave the signal.

They moved in.

Dr. Watson removed a small scalpel from his medical bag and thrust it into Griffin, eliciting a small jerk from the bound man. Holmes took his meerschaum pipe and thrust it inside. And left it there. Corey would have to remove it afterward. No evidence. But for now... let them have their fun. The detectives stepped aside and gave way to the marching clacking horde.

Now Corey clutched himself and each nutcracker strode forth and plunged in their instrument of pain. Thrust! One... two... three.... clack ...clack... clack... four... five... clack... clack... six... clack... seven... clack...

Corey felt the build in him start. Eight... clack... nine... clack... ten... "Griffin!" he cried out as he came, his body jerking spasmodically, in rhythm with the thrusts and clacks. Each thrust and piercing made Griffin's body flinch/jerk in response, head lolling, mouth drooling. Corey was in ecstasy. He continued squeezing out his orgasm, enjoying the warm, wet stickiness on his skin. Revenge was way beyond sweet and better than any dish served cold.

After the final nutcracker had had its rupturous fun, Corey was ready for his last act of vengeance, then he would let his horde finish Griffin off in their inimitable, magical way. This was his other favorite thing the nutcrackers did. When they were at last sated, the room would once again become pitch dark. The soldiers would then file out of the room as pristine as the day they'd been unboxed. More than magic.

Corey now had one final dilemma to work through. Whereas before the other killings had taken place at other houses, this one was on his home turf. No one but his mother and his--now deceased--stepfather had known of his magnificent collection. He'd never told a soul. He'd never wanted to. They were private. All his. But if the police searched the house, which he was certain they would, they would discover his beautiful friends. He did have a plan, one that he did not want to implement, but he saw no other way. The connection would be too easy to make. His soldiers would be safe, but he would become the suspect. The police would never be able to come up with a plausible answer--because there wasn't one--but they would know that he had done it, and so would his mother. No. This was for the best. His soldiers would do whatever he directed them to do. He would miss them. Terribly. But after they moved away he could start a new collection. Fresh start. Fresh collection. Well, maybe he could keep a couple of them, secret them away: Merlin, Robin Hood, King Arthur, Lancelot. How could he get rid of them? Even before he'd discovered their magic, they were his friends and companions. No. He needed to start with a clean slate. They weren't really alive anyway. Were they?

A fresh start. He'd already made the preparations in the backyard. The hole would be big enough. He had a pine tree--a Christmas tree--all ready to plant over them. He hoped they would appreciate the sentiment.

Maybe the kids at his next school would be nice. He didn't have that many years till graduation. He could make it. His mom would get over Griffin. Maybe he'd even eventually tell her about what Griffin had done to him to lessen her pain. Then she would hate him. Good idea. He would definitely tell her at some point, but later.

Now, he needed to get his unfortunate job done, then go down and spend the rest of the night in the basement. His alibi. It was weak, but what could they say? He was watching TV and he fell asleep. He did it all the time, so it wasn't something unusual. His mom would verify that. That's it: he fell asleep and never heard a thing. Weak, but no proof. They hadn't found any proof at any of the other houses either. He'd be fine. The magic of the nutcrackers would protect him.

Now to his job.

He got a large heavy-duty trash bag from the garage.

He went upstairs to his room and surveyed the scene. There they were: peaceful, calm, as if nothing had happened, as if they had not been slaughtering and torturing a human being mere minutes ago, turning Griffin's bedroom into an abattoir. Corey started to choke up. How he would miss them. His friends. But all good things... He opened the bag and reached for the Gypsy, carefully placing her in the bag. So precious. But without the music, they were just painted wood figures: cloth, feathers, fur... metal eyes. He stared at King Arthur. Was that a twitch he saw? No. Not alive. Only toys. They couldn't even crack real nuts. Corey grinned. Except Griffin's. That useful function has died out long ago. Still, they certainly had been useful to him. And they had been--he choked back a sob--his friends. Yes, he would miss them, but there was no other way. And hopefully his mother would never make the connection. It was too crazy, she'd never believe it possible.

He put Robin Hood, Sir Lancelot, Merlin, and King Arthur in last. His favorites. He loved those stories of derring-do. Then with a last sigh of sadness and regret he sealed the bag with a zip tie.

As awkward and heavy as the bag was, he managed to get it down the stairs with only a few bumps along the way.

He dragged the bag to the hole and gently lowered it in. He reached for the shovel and began the burial.

When there was just enough room left for the pine tree, he placed it in the crevice and shoveled the remaining dirt around it. He reached for a bag of bark and opened it. This way no one could tell, hopefully, that the tree was freshly planted. A little watering, and he should be good.

An hour later, having showered and cleaned up, he lay on the couch down in the basement, but was unable to fall asleep--not from what he'd done to Griffin, but from the loss of his precious nutcrackers.

"Maybe some music," he said aloud. "That usually helps." He knew what he wanted to hear. He ran upstairs, gazed around his lonely, empty room, grabbed his iPod and port and went back downstairs. He turned it on. They couldn't hear the music anymore... and never again. He lay down.

Dum da da da da dum dum dum. Dum da da da da dum dum dum. He had it set on automatic replay. He never knew how many times he heard it in a night; he always fell asleep.

He needed to sleep. Tomorrow would be hard, but he'd survive. His mother would be a mess. There'd be cops everywhere. He needed to be sharp. Yes, tomorrow he would...

Corey woke slowly.

Clack. Clack. Clack. Clack. Clack. ClackClackClackClack-ClackClackClack.

NO! It couldn't be!

He heard the din of the clacking all around him. They were on the top of the back of the couch. On the arms. On the coffee table in front of him. All fifty of them. Clacking and rocking.

On his chest. Robin Hood. His favorite.

ClackClackClackClackClackClackClack.

"No, please... I'm sorry... I didn't..."

Robin drew back his bow.

ClackClackClackClackClackClackClack.

The arrow pierced his right eye.

Gris Gris

Kathy Love

New Orleans, 1841

Only utter fear could have brought me here. Otherwise I would have never considered setting foot into the dwelling of Madame Lucrece Dumas. I'd heard enough about her strange ways from the whispers of the slaves to the gossip of the wealthy ladies alike. Lucrece Dumas's abilities knew no divide. Rich, poor, free or enslaved, all of New Orleans knew about her and the powers she wielded.

I needed those powers. I needed her help. Her protection. Otherwise I'd be dead. As sure as the sun rose every day, I'd be dead.

Still, it had taken all my courage to walk down North Rampart toward Congo Square, away from the shops and bakeries and other familiar places I frequented along Canal. Away from the safety of the ladies and gentlemen like myself. Only a short walk distance-wise, but a world away from the bustling street where I was comfortable and felt safe. Here, the streets still bustled, but now I was surrounded by run-down shotgun shacks and other ramshackle buildings. I could hear music and laughter and voices thick with accents different from my own from within. I had a hard time telling the shops from the homes. They all looked roughly hewn to me. This world was nothing like the safe, polished one I knew. Except my world wasn't safe, and in some cases, the polished elegance only masked a darkness just below the surface. I knew. I'd seen it.

As I walked down the banquette, careful to avoid piles of rancid trash and offal, I started to feel rather than just see the difference of this place, so unusual from mine. Under the squalor, there was a hum of life. Flashes of color and scents that managed to rise above the terrible smells. The occasional whiff of spice and sweetness. Women, varying in colors from as dark as the workers in the sugar cane fields at my home to nearly as fair as myself, carried baskets of vegetables and other goods. Others watched their smiling, barefoot children playing in the streets. All the women hid their black, coarse hair away under turbans of red and yellow gingham and other bright madras. Stands were set up all along the street with more women selling their merchandise. Many of the very same things I saw sold on Canal. Fruit and vegetables. Pecan pies and pralines. A man, his skin the color of oiled leather, stood outside a pool hall in a black jacket and trousers, a brimmed black hat perched on his shorn head and a pipe between his full lips.

He regarded me with mild curiosity, his eyes nearly black. But when he saw I returned his gaze, his stare dropped to the ground. His reaction should have given me some comfort, as I was used to this deferential treatment at home. But these weren't people who worked for me. They didn't have to treat me with the same respect. I was a white woman all alone, no chaperone, no family to keep me safe. That fact scared me, but I was excited too, like when I sneaked into the barn to smoke one of my father's cigars. The fear of getting caught. Of getting in trouble. It was strangely appealing. An almost nice fear compared to the other terror I had been living with. I also had to admit that I rather liked the energy in the air here, as palpable and real as the heady scent curling around me from that Negro's pipe tobacco.

My overwrought feelings only intensified as I located the address I'd come to find. 122 St. Peter, on the corner of St. Peter and North Rampart. Not that I would have needed an address to know this was the right place. The two-story house painted red and trimmed with wrought iron like black lace stood out on the street like a beacon. No one would miss this house settled in among the other more drab homes. Nor would they doubt for a minute that New Orleans' most powerful voodoo priestess could live there. The structure itself seemed to radiating power and magic.

I looked around, uncertain, now that I was here, if I actually contained the bravery to climb those steps and knock on the front door. Would she even agree to see me? I certainly had the finances with me to pay her. I squeezed the small drawstring purse clutched in my sweaty hand as if to help resolve myself.

I pulled in a deep breath, the hot, damp summer air settling heavily in my chest. I straightened. Lucrece Dumas was my only hope. And the fears at home had to be worse than facing this woman. In fact, I knew they were worse. They were horrifying. And deadly.

Without further hesitation, because I knew I had no other choice, I lifted my skirt and made my way up the steps. I reached for the door knocker, a strange-looking iron thing made up of swirls and crosses surrounded by circles. The metal felt oddly cold against my hand. Far too cool in this oppressive summer heat. I rapped several times, then took a step back and waited. Growing more anxious with each passing moment, I fussed with my dress, trying to smooth the wrinkles in the muslin. Only then did I note a reddish dust marring the hemline, but before I could attempt to brush it away, the door opened.

A hulking man created another door behind the one he'd just opened, his broad, muscled shoulders and tall height making it impossible to see past him into the house. His dark eyes took inventory of me, but I couldn't make out what his final assessment might have been.

Finally he said, in a thick Creole accent, "What can I do for you?"

"I'm here to see Mme. Dumas."

He gave me another assessing look, then nodded and stood back to allow me entrance. I hesitated, not for the first time wondering if I should have told someone where I was going. But who would I have told? My sister was gone, having passed away just under a month ago. Her husband, William, certainly wouldn't have allowed me to come here. He disregarded this kind of thing as savage nonsense. I couldn't talk to him about the things I had seen, either. He would think it was my imagination, the frailties of a grieving female mind. But what I'd seen, experienced, it was not nonsense. It wasn't my imagination. Although I wished it was.

The only person I could have possibly told was Cecelia. But she had a great respect and fear of Lucrece Dumas, and she wouldn't do anything that might bring repercussions back on herself. She knew the conjuring done here was real. She'd grown up seeing roots being put on people. She wouldn't have dared say a word if something happened here.

So I was on my own.

I squeezed the purse in my hand again, as if the money in there held some magic of its own to protect me. And in a way, I imagined it did. After all, Mme. Dumas was as much a businesswoman as she was anything else. I carefully stepped into the house, waiting for the man to direct me where to go next. He closed the door, then silently ushered me into the front room.

The room was lovely, decorated much like the front parlor of any well-to-do person. Thick velvet drapes in a rose color framed the tall windows, pulled back with braided burgundy silk cords. Lovely damask furniture in a darker rose was placed invitingly around a white marble fireplace. Only the mantelpiece revealed anything different about this home. In front of a mirror, framed in gold, dozens of candles, melted to varying heights, lined the mantel. Flames flickered, lit even now in the daytime. And behind those was a cross and a painted picture of the Virgin Mary, as well as other objects that appeared religious in nature, although many of the symbols were unfamiliar to me. There were also several roughly sewn poppets the purpose of which I did not understand.

The giant man gestured for me to sit. I took a seat on the edge of the settee, even though my gaze moved to the front door as I did so. I should leave.

"Mme. Dumas will see you in a moment," he said, his voice deep and as dark as his skin.

I nodded, although he didn't wait to see or hear my response.

I turned my attention from the now empty doorway back to the mantelpiece. What was the significance of those objects? I considered getting up to inspect the altar closer, but fear kept me rooted to the spot. I ran a hand over the fine material of the cushion next to me, the familiar feeling under my palm calming me. A bit.

In the distance, I heard the faint rumblings of voices. I tried to hear what was being said, but I couldn't even tell if the voices were coming from inside the house or from the street, much less make out any words. I breathed in deeply, trying desperately to stay composed. As I did so, the scent of damp earth and spice and something I didn't recognize filled my nose, and I wondered how I hadn't noticed it as soon as I stepped in the house. The smell reminded me of something foreboding, like the wet dirt of a freshly dug grave.

Utter foolishness. I was letting my imagination get away from me. The smell was certainly just the humidity in the air mingling with smells on the street. But still an image of my sister's funeral appeared in my mind. The overturned earth, the scents of the meal being prepared in the house for the mourners. I remember my eyes never leaving William's grief-stricken face as Anna's coffin was lowered into the dank ground of his family's cemetery. Buried like we did in the North. The final echoes of shovelfuls of dirt hitting the top of the coffin, until she was gone.

"Hello."

I snapped out of my memory and found myself looking at a petite, exotically lovely woman dressed in a silk day gown of the deepest red. Her skin was the color of melted praline in the warm sun, golden and creamy. On her head she wore a turban that should have seemed at odds with her elegant dress, yet it sat high and proud on her head, managing to look like a crown. Dark curls and large golden hoops framed either side of her pretty face. There was no denying why the whispers about this Creole often contained the word *queen.* Lucrece Dumas looked every inch a voodoo queen.

She smiled, the gesture warm, almost motherly, although she couldn't be old enough to be my actual mother. The warmth spread up to her dark eyes, and I instantly felt more at ease. This woman would help me. Protect me.

"What brings you to my home today?" she asked as she strolled into the room, her head held high, her bearing regal. She perched on the opposite end of the settee, her silk skirt cascading around her. Her hands, both adorned with several gold rings, folded neatly in her lap. She faced me but kept a distance between us.

Before I could answer, she spoke again, her voice lilting, almost singsong. "I see you are in mourning." She nodded to my black dress. "Dis is the reason you are here today, non?"

"No," I said, realizing my answer seemed too quick, too terse. "I—I don't believe it is the reason."

Mme Lucrece tilted her head, studying me with those dark eyes. "So what does bring you here, ma cherie?"

I hesitated. What if she didn't believe me? What if she thought I was mad? Or that what I was seeing was just a manifestation of my grief? Which, I knew without a single doubt, it was not. Who would help me then? I just had to tell her. I had to tell someone.

"I have been seeing and hearing things. A dark figure that

comes to me at night. It leans over my bed, whispering my name, and I feel sure that it means me true harm."

Lucrece leaned back, although she assessed me more closely, her dark eyes glittering. Then she nodded. "Dis the hag."

Hag?

"What is that? What—what do I do?"

Lucrece smiled gently, although I wasn't sure if it was to reassure me or a way of kindly indulging my ignorance. "A hag is a witch dat can attach to you. Either by deed or curse. The evil creature will come to you while you sleep. It feeds off your energy. Your life."

"Can you help me? Give me something for protection?"

"I can." Lucrece stared at me for a moment longer, then stood. "Come wit me."

I struggled to my feet, my body weak with relief. She believed me and she could offer help. Giddiness mingled with relief, making my limbs hard to control. Still I managed to follow her swift gait, her skirts swishing, as she strode down the hallway to the back of her house. Across from large kitchen, she stopped at a closed door. On the door's paneling, a symbol that reminded me of the one I'd seen on the door knocker was painted in gold. This symbol appeared to be a heart with star-like shapes above and below it, and swirls circled around the heart as well as inside.

I wanted to ask what it meant, but held my tongue. If all the gossip was true, Mme. Lucrece wouldn't share her secrets anyway. She opened the door and stepped inside. The room was much darker than the rest of the house, and it took a moment for my eyes to adjust to the change in light. But once they did, the first thing I saw was the large man from the front door. He stood behind and to the right of an ornately carved high-backed chair. Then I noticed the large table in front of the chair. The wooden table was laden with many jars and bottles and other strange-looking items. Behind her, there were more tables lined with more jars and bottles and baskets. Everywhere candles burned, dozens and dozens of them, their wax melting down around their bases in glistening puddles. On the walls hung things I couldn't begin to name. Herbs and twigs and dried skins. I was certain I even saw strings of bones.

"Please sit." Lucrece waved a hand toward a small hassock across the table from the high-backed chair. She took a seat on the large throne, again looking every inch like a queen.

"I'm going to make you a gris gris. You know of des things?"

I nodded, but I really didn't. Not totally. I heard the word said by some of the slaves at my home, but I didn't really know what it was. All these notions and beliefs were so foreign to my upbringing in the North. I'd only been in Louisiana for a little over a year, moving here shortly after my sister married William. Much of this world was still new to me. New and frightening.

I could feel that familiar fear rise once again. But I forced myself to quell it. I looked up at the giant, who regarded me with a look of utter disinterest. To him I was no one, of no worth. That idea gave me chills, although I couldn't say why. I moved my attention back to Mme. Lucrece.

"A gris gris is a conjure bag, a charm, which you must keep on your person at all times to keep dis witch away. Dis especially important you keep it with you after the sun sets. Dat is when the hag comes to you, non."

It wasn't really a question, but I nodded anyway.

She nodded back, then began to work on the gris gris. First she took out a red pouch crudely sewn out of red flannel. She held the small bag in her hand and bowed her head, saying words—or at least I thought they were words—in a chanting voice. She then laid the flannel bag on the table in front of her. Her movements were smooth, flowing, almost as if she were doing a dance with her fingers. I watched as she reached for one jar, then another. I recognized some of the items she placed in the bag. Red pepper, some kind of dirt, white granules that I thought might be salt. She then rose and started gathering some pieces of the items hanging on the wall. A dried piece of twig. One of the pieces of what I was now sure was bone, all the time chanting her strange words. Finally she crossed over to a glass box that I hadn't noticed before. She lifted the lid, and to my amazement, whatever was in the box began to move. Slithering, sliding.

Snakes, I realized, fighting the urge to gasp, to flee the room. Lucrece didn't falter as she reached into the writhing mass. I could hear her still chanting, but I could also hear the snakes hissing and the rattle of their tails. I watched in horror, waiting for one of the poisonous creatures to strike. But after a moment, Lucrece withdrew her hand, a strip of dried snakeskin in her ringed fingers.

I looked to the giant again to see if he was as shaken as I was, but he did not even watch the voodoo priestess. His dark eyes were still locked on me. I quickly looked away, and was greatly relieved to see Mme. Lucrece had returned the lid onto that horrible box.

She returned to the table and her bag. She placed each item inside, following some order only she understood. Finally she lined up two bottles containing amber liquids. Only then she did stop her chant. She looked up at me, her eyes almost black as if they were just empty sockets in her lovely face.

"Do you know who wished dis curse on you?"

My chest tightened. "No." I shook my head. "No."

She nodded, then began to chant again. The words seemed to grow louder, although I was certain she hadn't raised her voice. I fought the urge to cover my ears, but was afraid to move. She took the first small bottle and uncorked it. Carefully, as she sang, she opened the bag and poured three drops of the liquid inside. She then opened the second bottle, this time pouring in nine precise drops. She held the bag for a moment longer, still chanting. The room seemed to fill with those words. I couldn't seem to think clearly. Everything spun to the rhythm of her voice. Again, I fought the urge to cover my ears. Or to simply run from the shadowy, candlelit room. I couldn't breathe. It was as if all air was being sucked out of the small space, replaced by some powerful, suffocating energy.

Suddenly her chanting stopped.

But before I could pull in a breath, or collect myself, she ordered, "Now you take the bag."

I stared at the strange thing now lying on the table in front of me, tied off with a piece of twine and bulging with God knows what. I hesitated for only a second, then reached out to pick it up. The flannel was soft against my fingers, the items inside hard. I thought again of the snakes, and the skin inside. I half expected the stuff inside to begin to writhe like those snakes. But it remained still.

"Hold it between your hands and focus on its power."

I did, automatically bowing my head, concentrating.

Mme. Lucrece cupped her hands over mine, although she did not touch me. She began to speak again, but this time I could recognize a few words. The names of saints and the Virgin Mary. I also understood when the blessing came to an end.

"Amen."

I mumbled amen too, then looked up to her, waiting for what

to do next.

She nodded and smiled. Her dark eyes looked normal again. Warm, motherly.

"Dis is a very strong gris gris. Very strong." She nodded again, this time with total certainty. "Dis will keep you safe."

Great relief filled me, allowing me to smile too. "Thank you."

***

My walk back to Canal Street, where Joseph waited with the carriage, was much different than the walk to 122 St. Peter. I no longer felt frightened and uncertain. For the first time in weeks, I felt confident that everything would be fine. I would be safe, and finally able to make a life for myself. A life for myself and William.

"Good afternoon, Miss Howard. Did you get all your shopping done?"

I nodded, smiling widely to the slave William considered his most trustworthy. "Indeed I did. In fact, today's outing was very successful."

"Very good, miss," Joseph said, offering his arm so I could climb up into the back of the carriage. I sighed, settling onto the bench, still holding my goods from Mme. Dumas tightly to me.

Joseph climbed up onto the front bench and clicked for the horse to start moving. "We better hurry along. It will be nightfall by the time we get home."

I didn't comment. But for the first time in weeks, the idea of the sun going down didn't scare me.

***

Joseph was right. We turned down the lane to William's plantation just as the last rays of sunlight cast the magnificent place in a glowing orangey pink. I loved the drive toward the house. The high roof and columns and huge second-floor gallery all bespoke of the elegance of the place. I fell in love with Chadwick Plantation as soon as I laid eyes on it. And I knew I'd found my home.

As soon as we pulled up out front, William was at the railing of the gallery as if he'd been waiting for me. The idea added to my good cheer.

"There you are," he called, his evening drink in hand. "I'd begun to think you had hopped a ship to head back North."

I laughed, delighted. He had been worried about me. "And leave all this beauty. I hardly think so."

I took Joseph's extended arm and hopped down to the ground, trying my best to look graceful while doing so. Not an easy task in skirts and a corset.

"I had Bessie hold dinner," William said as I approached.

"Thank you. I'm utterly famished." Which was also true for the first time in weeks. I squeezed the gris gris hidden away in my reticule, feeling its power even through the embroidery of my purse.

"Be quick, then, I'm famished as well."

I laughed again, pleased to hear William sounding more like his old self. And glad he was starving. He'd been eating as poorly as I had since Anna's death. I picked up my skirts to hurry inside and cleanup for dinner.

***

That evening was the best I'd had in a long time. Perhaps ever. William and I ate together and talked about everything from the upcoming sugar harvest to social events to what would happen if the troubles between the North and South finally boiled over. William was always willing to listen to my thoughts, and enjoyed our exchanges. He was a fine man, I'd seen that as soon as I met him. After dinner, we moved to the parlor, where I played some of his favorite songs on the piano. I did note that several times during the evening, William fell quiet, ruminating. But I would quickly draw him out of his silence and sadness with a rousing tune or a silly story. Cecelia brought William's infant son in to join us for a bit before his bedtime. William was a wonderful father. How could he not be? David, however, was a difficult baby, always fussing and colicky. So soon, Cecelia took him off to the nursery to settle him down.

All too quickly bedtime arrived for the adults as well, and with some hesitation I bid William goodnight and headed to my room. Although my reluctance to go to bed wasn't because of the fear of some horror that might await me in the middle of the night. Not this evening. Tonight, I simply hated to see the lovely evening end.

So I went to my bedroom, with mixed feelings, happy to

finally get a good night's rest, but hating to leave William to do so.

Shortly after entering my room, Cecelia knocked, arriving to help me undress. Short and somewhat portly, Cecelia reminded me of a chubby, sweet-natured puppy, always happy and always willing to please. Her good-natured countenance also made her easy to talk to. And I was brimming with excitement over my adventure today. Both because of the fact I was now safe from whatever occurrence had been happening to me and because of the forbidden nature of my visit to Lucrece Dumas.

So as soon as I was changed into my nightgown, I patted the mattress, inviting Cecelia to join me. She hesitated, perhaps because this was the first time I'd truly made a gesture toward her that resembled real friendship. But tonight I felt giddy, like a schoolgirl having a friend over for the night, hidden away in my bedroom, sharing secrets and stories.

On the quilt, I carefully laid out my magical treasures from Lucrece. The gris gris bag from which I could still feel the power, surrounding me like a tangible, impenetrable shroud. Then I untied the ribbon from around the second package Lucrece had given me as I was leaving. Four white candles anointed with a special oil and holy water.

"Added protection," Lucrece had said with a smile as I left her home.

"Cecelia, I went to her," I whispered excitedly, reminding myself of the gossips I'd overheard before. "I went to Mme. Lucrece Dumas."

"Madame Dumas?" Cecelia whispered, her dark eyes round.

"Yes."

She looked at me, her eyes filled with more than surprise. "Why did you go there, miss?"

She snapped her mouth closed as soon as the question was out, as if she thought she'd asked too much.

Now it was my turn to be unsure if I should say why. But did it matter now? After all, what did one young slave girl's opinion matter? So what if she thought I was mad? Besides, if Lucrece Dumas believed me, surely this girl would too. She believed in such things, and she would know I had found the solution.

"I went to her because I've been seeing things in my room at night. A dark figure looming over my bed. A hag, Lucrece called it."

Cecelia's face paled. I could see it even under her dark skin. She grew almost gray. She quickly scanned the room as if she might see it too. Suddenly she stood, stumbling backward away from my bed. Her eyes were still wide and filled with fear.

I frowned, feeling as if she were almost afraid of me rather than what I told her.

"I'm sorry, miss," she said when she saw my expression. "I am just frightened of such things."

Of course she was. She had told me before that she knew spirits and spells were very real. She was superstitious, and I couldn't very well mock that, because I knew they were real too. Now.

So I smiled at the terrified girl, probably giving her the same motherly look that Lucrece Dumas had given me earlier today. "I understand. But you have nothing to fear." I touched the gris gris. "Madame Lucrece Dumas has helped me. The hag will be gone now."

Cecelia nodded, her terror-filled gaze moving toward my open windows again. She nodded once more, then mumbled her goodnight, bustling to get out the door.

I sighed, almost feeling sorry for the girl. I suspected she wouldn't sleep a wink tonight, just thinking about the possibility of a witch out there in the dark. But I felt more than confident that my conjure bag and the special candles would work. I'd seen Mme. Dumas's power. It was very strong.

Still, I set up the candles just as the voodoo priestess had told me, setting two of the candles in silver holders on the nightstands at either side of my bed. As I lit them, I imagined their protective power.

Then, with the gris gris bag looped around my wrist, I crawled under the fine lawn sheets. I settled back against the pillows, realizing how tired my body was from the day's events. But it had been a good day. An exciting day. I pictured William in his own bed, and wondered if he missed having a woman there beside him. He surely must. I smiled, closing my eyes, imagining myself lying beside him.

As the candles flickered and burned, I dozed off, finally feeling safe.

***

"Elizzzabeeeth."

I moaned slightly, not ready for it to be morning. My soft feather bed felt far too good.

"Elizzzabeeeth."

My muzzy mind instantly snapped awake as I recognized the breathy, drawn-out call of my name, like someone calling to me from far away. I didn't move, telling myself it couldn't be real. That it must just be a nightmare. Lingering memories of the strange occurrences the nights before.

"Elizzzabeeeth."

This time the voice didn't sound far away at all, but very close. The tone raspy and rough, like the last rattle before death.

I kept my eyes squeezed shut. But I carefully patted around on the mattress, until my fingers found the gris gris bag. It was still looped to my wrist. I curled my fingers around the bag itself, holding it tight, willing its powers to protect me.

The room remained silent as I prayed for the magic of the bag to work. Finally, after several deathly quiet moments, I dared to open my eyes and look around. The candles still burned on either side of my bed, casting dancing shadows on the walls. Slowly I sat up. The gris gris had worked. The room was empty. I started as a movement caught my eye from beside the open window. Only the curtain fluttering in the night breeze. A small, slightly hysterical laugh escaped my lips. I had been dreaming. I was alone. I was safe.

Then I saw it. The dark figure, squatting in the corner, its shape hardly human. But in the candlelight, I could see its eyes, evil and glittering. And I could see its smile, unnaturally wide, white teeth flashing in the flickering light. A sinister, deadly smile.

"Elizzzabeeth," the evil thing said, its voice ragged, breathy, filled with hate. "You cannot escape me. Like I could not escape you."

Suddenly the thing moved, crawling across my floor as fast as a giant spider.

I screamed, screamed and screamed, sure that this time the witch, the hag, whatever it was would scurry onto my bed and finally kill me. But instead my bedroom door flew open and William rushed in. I leapt off the bed and straight into his arms, sobbing in utter panic.

This time, I didn't hesitate to tell William what I had seen and heard. He ushered me out of my dreadful room and to the parlor, where he sat with me as Bessie hurried to the kitchen to make me a cup of hot tea.

"Lizzie, it was nothing but a nightmare," he assured me, holding my trembling body close to his side. "We are all shaken by the loss of Anna. I'm sure that was what triggered such a vivid dream."

I shook my head, but I knew he wouldn't listen. He wouldn't believe. But behind him, Joseph and Cecelia stood in the doorway, their dark eyes filled with fear and pity. They believed. They knew.

***

I slept on the sofa in the parlor that night. William and Joseph stayed with me, sleeping in chairs close by. Although exhausted, we were all happy to see the sunlight the next morning.

"I hate to leave you today," William said, accepting a large mug of chicory coffee from Bessie. "I have to meet with my captains about carrying my sugar crop up north." He took a swallow of his coffee. "I may be home late, but I will leave Joseph here to look after you."

Joseph nodded, accepting William's order, but for the first time I could see wariness in the older slave's eyes. He didn't trust me. I wasn't sure why, but I didn't suppose after what he'd heard last night that I blamed him. There was no denying I was cursed. But by who? And why?

Still, in the full light of day, I could keep myself calm. After William left, I told Joseph I would be fine to go tidy myself up and get dressed. He nodded, but assured me he'd be nearby if I needed him.

I will admit, I had to force myself to enter my room. In the bright light of day, the space looked safe enough. The candles had burned down to stubs and my bedding was a shambles, but I ignored both, focusing instead on pouring water into my washbasin and pressing a cool, damp rag on my puffy, tear-streaked face.

After brushing my hair, I left my room again to look for Cecelia. She was probably with the baby, but I needed her to help me dress. I walked down the hallway to the nursery, searching for her. As I reached the small room, I noticed something on the hallway floor.

Red dust sprinkled across the entrance of the baby's room. I paused, studying it. Then I spotted more in a thick line in front of the door beside the nursery. Cecelia's room. I spun around, looking at the other doorways along the hall. Another stripe of the strange dust was spread in front of William's doorway. Slowly, I crouched down to touch it, my fingers coming back covered in red, almost like flakes of dried blood.

I stared at the dust there, remembering I had seen the very same thing on my skirt when I entered Mme. Lucrece's home. What was this? What did it do?

I stood, calling out for Cecelia. I waited, but she didn't come bustling down the hallway like she usually did when beckoned. She didn't even answer. That was strange, very strange. And frankly insolent.

But rather than shout again, I made my way to the kitchen. Surely Bessie would know where she was. Perhaps I was reacting too quickly, utterly frazzled by the events of the previous night. Maybe she had taken the baby outside for some sun. Or maybe it was laundry day. What day was it, anyway? I wasn't even sure, my mind was so distraught.

However, when I entered the kitchen, many of the slaves were assembled there. Several returned to their chores when they saw me, but Bessie, Cecelia and Joseph remained behind. David slept in his basket near the window, his downy hair fluttering in the breeze. I noticed Cecelia moved close to the sleeping child, although I didn't think much of it. She had a sincere fondness of the child.

"What is this?" I asked, far more concerned with the powder on my fingers. I held up my hand, giving them all a clear view.

Bessie looked away, returning her attention to cutting up vegetables. Joseph shifted slightly, but said nothing. Cecelia stepped yet closer to the sleeping baby.

I stared at them, unused to receiving no response. I had asked a question and I deserved a proper answer.

"What is this?" I asked again, this time more aggravated.

Finally Cecelia spoke, her voice quiet, just above a whisper. "It's brick dust, to keep evil away."

I looked down at the red stains on my fingertips, trying to grasp what they were saying. One of them had sprinkled this protective powder along their bedroom doorways. All of them, except my own.

Just then, David began rustling in his basket, making small noises to signal he was hungry. Cecelia turned to pick him up, holding him protectively against her bosom. I watched her, feeling dazed by her admission. Why hadn't they wanted me protected?

I continued gaping at her as she reached back into the baby's basket to retrieve a poppet, crudely sewn, one side of the doll made in blue material, the other in gold. Sewn to its chest was a silver dime. An odd toy, but then I remembered the poppets on Lucrece's altar. This toy looked just like those.

"What is that doll?" I finally asked, my tone low, angry.

"Just a doll, Miss Howard," Joseph answered for Cecelia.

No, this wasn't right. This wasn't right at all.

We all stared at each other, no one speaking. No one moving. The only sound in the kitchen was the increasingly desperate caterwauls of David demanding to be fed. All three sets of the eyes looking at me were filled with apprehension. With fear.

They had cursed me. I'd wondered who could have done it, and now I knew. One or all of them had created this horrible curse. But why? What did they know? They couldn't know anything. I'd been very careful no one would know. But what mattered now was how to make this curse stop.

Suddenly I knew what I had to do. I had to get back to Lucrece Dumas. She was the only one who could help me. Surely her magic had to be more powerful than that of these uneducated slaves. I turned to Joseph, all the friendliness between us yesterday gone.

"Ready the carriage. You are taking me to the city."

"Miss, I do not think Master William would want me to do that."

I glared at him. No one was going to stop me from getting the help I needed. "Ready the carriage."

I left the kitchen, going back to my room. I threw open my wardrobe and I pulled out a simple linsey-woolsey skirt, one I only used for cleaning, and a blouse that was for the same purpose. I knew I looked ragged, disheveled, but I did not care. I would not ask these traitors for help. I could go back to being the proper Southern lady once I was free of this evil spell. Now, all I cared about was getting to Lucrece Dumas.

I went to my jewelry box and took out a ring that my mother

had given to my sister upon her wedding. William had given it to me after Anna's death. I put it in my reticule, along with some other coins I had saved and the gris gris. Now I couldn't feel the magic, the power that it had yesterday. But maybe Lucrece had forgotten to include something. Maybe the gris gris could be made more powerful.

To my surprise, Joseph had the carriage waiting when I stepped outside. The day was very warm, the air thick with moisture. I didn't mind. I loved the sun. The sun was the only thing keeping me truly safe. For now.

I didn't bother with Joseph's assistance, pulling myself up into the carriage. He followed me, settling onto his seat, then he clucked and we started toward New Orleans, and hopefully my salvation.

The already long trip into town seemed all the more arduous with my mind racing, but we finally arrived and this time I directed Joseph to take me directly to 122 St. Peter. After all, there was no need to be discreet about where I was going. He knew. I didn't have time to waste. And today, I didn't hesitate to go to her front door. No debating, no fear. Of her, at least.

The same huge man answered my emphatic knock. This time, his unreadable stare now showed a hint of curiosity. I was sure my frantic appearance startled him. Gone was the woman I was yesterday, who, while frightened, had looked like a presentable lady. I knew I looked a disaster with my hair wild and barely combed, my clothing wrinkled and disheveled with no stays or petticoats. But I didn't have time to worry about such things. I needed help. And I needed it now. Darkness would be here all too soon.

"I need to see Mme. Dumas immediately."

The giant didn't step aside to allow me in. I knew he was debating whether I had gone mad.

I was going mad. Hysteria rose up in me like a tide, taking me over, stealing my breath, my reason.

"Now!"

The lovely voodoo priestess must have heard my panicked voice, because she appeared behind the large man, striding down the hallway toward us. She nodded to him and he stepped aside, although I could see he still watched me intently.

"Ma cherie," she said as she approached, her voice calm. "What dis the matter?"

I stumbled into the front hallway, desperate to get to her. "The hag. It came back. Worse than ever."

Lucrece studied me for a moment, then waved her fingers. "Come back wit me."

I gladly followed, trying to compose myself. Trying to simply breathe.

Again she took a seat on her throne and I collapsed onto the small hassock. The huge man stood sentry beside Lucrece. Now I could fully understand why he was there. Many desperate people must come to this woman. This voodoo queen. And desperate people did desperate things.

I didn't want to be like that. I had come too far to lose everything now. Pulling in a deep breath, I straightened my spine and pushed a tangle of loose hair from my face.

Lucrece smiled, seeing my attempt to collect myself. "So tell me what happened?"

I pulled in another breath, then spoke, my voice steadier, although I knew I still teetered on hysterics. "I did everything you told me. I lit the candles, two on either side of my bed. I let them burn as I fell asleep. I kept the gris gris bag on my wrist, never letting it away from me. But still the hag came."

She nodded, pondering my words. "I do not understand. The conjure bag is very strong. One of my strongest."

My panic rose. I fumbled to open my purse, digging to get the gris gris out. I placed it on the table and pushed it toward her. "Maybe it needs more. Maybe you forgot to add something."

She shook her head, still looking puzzled. "Non."

"I also know who placed this curse on me. That could make the spell even stronger, right?"

Her confusion vanished and she met my gaze directly, her dark eyes intense.

"You know?"

I nodded. "Yes, it was a slave girl on my plantation. Cecelia."

"You are sure?"

I nodded again. I was certain. On the ride, I'd realized she had to be the one who did this. She'd reacted so strangely when I'd told her about coming here. She'd seemed scared. Terrified, in fact. She had to have been so scared because she'd been worried Mme. Lucrece might have told me who caused this curse. I knew it had to

120

be her.

"How do you know dis?" Lucrece asked, her eyes still holding mine in their dark grasp.

I told her about the brick dust and the doll.

After I finished speaking, she remained silent, considering what I had shared.

Finally, she shook her head. "Des are not spells to cross you or bring you harm. Des are spells to protect herself."

She didn't believe me.

She shook her head, clearly confounded. "Dis gris gris should have worked." She pushed the bag back toward me.

I stared at it, feeling my panic bubbling up inside me like a pan of water about to boil over. She couldn't be telling me there was nothing more she could do. She was Madame Lucrece Dumas, the most powerful voodoo priestess in New Orleans.

This time I shook my head, unwilling to accept her words. I began to fumble with my reticule again, pulling out the coins. "I can pay more." I practically threw them on the table in my desperation. "I can get more too."

She stared at the money, then back to me. I could see pity in her dark eyes. But I couldn't accept it. I jammed my hand back into the purse, pulling out my mother's ring. Anna's ring. I placed it amid the scattered coins. "It was my mother's, but it is yours if you help me."

Her dark gaze locked on the ring, the ruby glinting in the candlelight. Slowly she reached out and picked up the expensive piece, but rather than inspect it further, she placed the ring in her hand, cupping her other palm over it. She lowered her head and remained that way for several moments.

Finally, when I thought I could take her silence no more, she lifted her head, her eyes meeting mine. Like before, when she'd been making the gris gris, her eyes looked completely black.

"Dis hag comes to you because of deed. Not curse. I cannot help."

She carefully set the ring back onto the table.

No. No. This wasn't all that could be done.

"Please. Please, you said you could help," I said again, my voice high, hysterical.

She shook her head. Her eyes once more normal, and again

filled with pity.

"Sometimes the only one who can help is God."

I didn't understand.

"I can pay anything. Anything you ask."

She smiled then, shaking her head once more, although I didn't know if she was denying my offer or simply showing regret over my begging.

"Sometimes the only payment God will take is justice."

She bowed her head and then rose. Without looking back, she left the room.

I stared at the now empty doorway. Behind me I heard the giant moving and knew he'd come to my side to escort me from Mme. Dumas's house. My body felt weak, my soul empty. I reached out with a shaky hand and retrieved the gris gris and the ring, leaving the money strewn over the table. Then I stood. It was over. Everything was over.

***

Like the day before, the sun was setting as Joseph pulled up to the front of the house. But unlike yesterday, William did not wait on the porch for me. And I felt no hopefulness or pleasure. I felt nothing.

I accepted Joseph's offered arm as I stepped down from the carriage, feeling like my knees might buckle from underneath me. Once on the ground, I stood looking at Chadwick Plantation for a long time. I loved this place from the very first time I saw it. Those majestic columns, that beautiful second-floor gallery where I could see myself drinking sweet tea and enjoying the evening breeze. My children playing hide and seek among the magnolia trees. William at my side.

I had seen this glorious place and I had wanted it. All of it.

I stood there for a long time. How long I was not sure. Until the light faded and the evening air was filled with sounds of crickets and frogs and other night creatures. Finally I stumbled into the house, heading up the stairs and straight into my bedroom.

I undressed, getting myself into my nightgown. Then I crawled into bed, my knees pulled tight to my chest. My forehead resting on them, I prayed. Prayed for forgiveness. Prayed for redemption.

I must have fallen asleep, or maybe I'd fallen into some sort of trance, but when I became aware again, I heard my name.

"Elizzzabeeeth."

I lifted my head and saw her standing there. The room was dark, but the light of the moon through my open window allowed me to see her. She stood beside the same window. I could see her long, dark hair, caked with dirt, hanging in her face. I could see her gown, once beautiful, now tattered and stained. She tilted her head at an angle, studying me back. Her eyes, once so blue, shone glittering black in the moonlight. And her smile, once her prettiest feature, was spread unusually wide, her white teeth jagged.

"Elizzzabeeeth."

I didn't move. I didn't scream.

She moved toward me, this time not swiftly, but in stiff, jerky movements. I could hear her bare feet on the floor, dragging, shuffling.

Fear made it impossible to breathe, but still I did not move, aside to clutch the object in my hand tighter. Not the gris gris this time. But the ring. My mother's ring. Anna's ring.

She continued her shuddering walk until she was beside my bed. Beside me. Her eyes empty and black. That eerie smile pasted on her once perfect lips.

I forced myself to remain rooted to the bed. Then I mustered the courage to lift my hand toward her and uncurl my fingers. The ring twinkled in the moonlight.

Her dead stare left me and moved to the ring. With icy-cold fingers, darkened with dirt and mud, she took the ring out of my palm.

"I'm sorry," I whispered, the terrified words coming out as nothing more than croak. "I'm sorry for wanting your life."

She looked up from the ring and back at me. Then that horrible smile changed, her mouth opening into a huge, gaping hole, and she screamed. The sound was the most horrific and deafening thing I'd ever heard, filled with rage and pain and despair. I struggled to breathe, remembering how she'd fought to breathe as she lay dying. Then I felt terrible pain in my stomach, and curled forward, groaning out in agony. I remembered her excruciating groans as the poison racked her body.

"It's so dark."

I remembered her mumbling those words, her last before she spoke no more. And I too felt the darkness falling down around me, taking me away, and I knew nothing could stop it. I could feel my body slowing down, dying. Madame Dumas had been right. Sometimes the only payment was justice. I'd taken her life and now I had to pay her back with my own.

I'm sorry, Anna. I'm sorry.

The Agent

Michael Koogler

It was a dark and stormy night.

"Bloody hell, can I get any more cliché than that?" the man grumbled, slamming the lid down on his laptop. The snapping sound of plastic or glass only soured his already dark mood. If he just broke his laptop, he was going to go ballistic.

Andre Rossell was a writer. At least, he liked to think of himself as a writer. In truth, he was unemployed, as of earlier in the day when his boss at McNeil Transportation had finally fired him after Andre had yet another pissing match with one of their long-time drivers. His boss had told him he needed to get into counseling and learn how to control his anger. Andre knew he'd actually had the last word when he told his boss that he hadn't heard the last of him!

"Just wait!" Andre had practically screamed at him, spittle flying from his mouth. "You just wait! I'll be lining them up at book stores all over the world in no time at all! Just watch! I'll be the next Stephen King!"

Yes, Andre Rossell was a horror novelist. Unfortunately, he hadn't written anything yet.

Lightning flashed outside his window as he stood up and went to the fridge. He didn't want to look at his laptop yet; didn't figure he'd be able to handle it when he saw the damage. Swinging open the refrigerator door, he pushed aside a couple of old cartons of Cantonese take-out—he didn't even want to know what kind of scientific experiments were growing in those soggy, grease-stained cardboard boxes—and grabbed a beer.

He twisted off the bottle cap and tossed it against the wall, before swigging down half of the beer as he walked back into his grimy living room. Taking a deep breath, he collapsed back onto the couch and then reached over and popped open his laptop again and looked at the screen. It was spider-webbed with cracks. Any idea that he might be able to work around it was dashed when he tried powering it back on and only got a small spot of light in the center of the screen. Everything else was black and dead.

Shaking his head, he sucked down the rest of his beer and slammed the bottle down on the table next to his ruined laptop. He was truly screwed now and he knew it. How much more could go wrong in his life? Something simply had to give and he swore silently to himself that no price was too great for his success. The first chance he got to make it big, he would be all over it.

Thunder rolled through the night again as Andre kicked his feet up on the battered coffee table and leaned his head back. He sighed and closed his eyes. He just wanted to sleep. He needed to get away from reality and just let his dreams take hold. Maybe in the morning, he could figure out what to do before he got kicked out of his apartment. He drifted off into a blissfully ignorant, but far from restful, slumber.

***

The first thing he heard the next morning was the strains of his Phil Collins "In the Air Tonight" ringtone, blaring from his phone and breaking him out of the nightmare that had held him tightly in its grip. The memory of that dark dream faded quickly into nothingness as he realized where he was. He was still on his couch and his phone was still singing to him. The iPhone was lying on the floor under the table where he'd tossed it a few days ago when AT&T had suspended his service for non-payment. Reaching down, he picked it up and looked at the screen. He didn't recognize the number and almost didn't answer. But the fact that his phone was suddenly operational again was somewhat intriguing. Besides, one never knew when opportunity might be calling. He thumbed the answer button.

"Yeah?"

"Andre, baby!" an unfamiliar voice sounded from the other end. "What's shakin', my friend? Did you get my email?"

"Your…uh, what?" Andre stammered, trying to place the voice. Something about the man's tone clicked within his brain. He just couldn't figure out where he'd heard it before.

"My email, brother! Good news, good news! But we've got a ton of work to do now!"

"Um, who is this?" Andre demanded.

"Andre, baby, no time for joking," the voice went on. "I've got hits all over the place. They are absolutely in love with the story! Details are in the email!"

"Look, I don't…"

"E… MAIL," the voice enunciated slowly.

"But… but, my laptop is broken," Andre hesitated.

"Broken? Brother, it's brand new! How the hell can it be broken?"

Andre reached down to pick up his old Lenova only to discover that it wasn't on the coffee table. Instead, he was looking the sleek case of an Alienware 18 – matte black with blood red stenciling on the lid showing a hand throwing up classic devil horns.

"What the hell is this?" he asked in shock, flipping open the top.

"Say again, buddy, I didn't catch that," the voice said and then quickly added. "But hey, never mind. Read the email. You're going places, my friend! Big places! I gotta jet!"

"Wait a sec… who is this?" He stared at the open desktop. It was loaded with files. Along with some kick-ass games that he had always wanted to play, there were a number of Microsoft Word documents in a row down the right side of his desktop. Seven of them. Each one had a different title.

"Never change, Andre baby," the voice laughed. "Gotta run. Courier will be by shortly with the contract. Standard fare. Sign it and cash the check, brother! I'm out!"

The call ended and Andre could do nothing more than stare at the laptop's display. It invited him and he ran a finger over the mouse touchpad and moved the pointer over the first Microsoft Word document. It was titled 'Hotel Hell.' He moved to the second one. 'Blood at Home.' He clicked it open and the file sprang up on screen. The first page displayed the title of the file. Underneath that, in smaller lettering was 'By Andre Rossell.'

Down in the bottom left hand corner, he noticed the word count. It was just shy of 91,000 words. Right in the sweet spot.

Mesmerized, he started reading.

He had nearly completed the first chapter when his doorbell rang, startling him. Setting the laptop carefully on the table, he hustled to the door. A courier was standing there, a young woman looking at him in wide-eyed fascination. She was smartly dressed in a black uniform with a black ball cap and a satchel over her shoulder. There were no other identifying marks on her uniform.

"Wow, you're really him?" she said, holding out a document folder, stamped 'official'.

"Him who?" Andre said absently, reaching out and taking it from her.

"Andre Rossell!" she said excitedly. "Dude, I love your stuff!"

"My stuff?"

"Oh, hey," she said, shaking her head as if she had been in a stupor. "I'm supposed to wait."

"Wait? For what?"

"For you to sign the paperwork," she replied, reaching into her bag and producing another document folder, this one unsealed and empty. It was already pre-addressed and Andre caught himself looking at the address. It was going to a firm called Krypteia Publishing located in New York City.

"What the hell is all this?" Andre asked, trying to find his mental footing.

"Dunno," came the honest reply. "This is how you've always done it, I'm told. I just got lucky and drew the assignment this time. So, what's it about?"

"The what?"

"The book!" she said excitedly. "What's this new one going to be about?"

"Um...well, I'd tell you but then I'd have to kill you," Andre replied, trying to force a smile. As he did, some dark part of his mind pictured doing just that. It would make a good story. Shocked at the sudden violent urge that seemed to rise up within him, Andre pushed the thoughts back and ripped open the document envelope. Inside, there was a packet of papers, stapled together. A yellow sticky note was attached to the back one, with a hastily scribbled "sign here!" on it. He quickly flipped to the last page and there, nestled between the papers was a cashier's check. It had a lot of zeros on it.

Andre could barely contain himself as he looked up at the courier. This had to be a joke. HAD to be!

"Big payday?" she asked excitedly, mistaking the reason for his look of shock. "Oh, I can't wait to read it!"

He looked at her dumbly for a moment, before shaking his

head and gathering his wits about him. "Yeah, pretty standard," he suddenly found himself able to play it up. What else could he do? He glanced at her, noticing for the first time that she was pretty cute for a courier – long blonde hair, blue eyes, flawless complexion, sexy figure. "Look," he went on, deciding to lay it on heavy. "I've been working pretty hard lately and thinking I need to take a break. Care to join me for a drink tonight?"

"Oh really?" she breathed. "Are you serious? Oh, Mister Rossell, that would be a dream of mine! 'Hotel Hell' is one of my all-time favorite novels. I'd love to have you sign it, if that's okay?"

"Sure thing," he answered smoothly. "Jot down your address and I'll swing by tonight to pick you up about eight."

As the young woman quickly scratched her information on a piece of paper, Andre signed the contract and slipped it into the empty document folder she had provided. He tucked the check into his pocket. Sealing up the packet, he gave it back to her, taking her piece of paper at the same time.

"This is going to be so great!" she breathed. "I can't wait to tell everyone that I'm having drinks with Andre Rossell!"

"Yeah, it'll be a great time, uh…," he said and then hesitated, looking at her expectantly.

"Oh, it's Dani," she replied, blushing. "Danielle, actually, but my friends all call me Dani."

"Okay, Dani," he said with a wink. "Pick you up at eight."

He closed the door and then turned and leaned back up against it, blowing out a long sigh. The weirdness of the morning was forgotten and he was already thinking about what the night would bring. He even had a title for the book.

'FED sEX: Delivery to Hell.'

***

Three years later, Andre Rossell watched the stretch limousine pull up to the curb of the Hyatt Regency, where he currently had the penthouse suite. The driver immediately came around to open the door for him, offering him a huge smile.

"Exciting time for you, sir?" he drawled with a bit of a southern twang.

Andre ignored the comment and slid into the back seat. He

wasn't about to tell the man that he really was excited about tonight. 'FED sEX' had been his third book, following 'Hotel Hell' and 'Blood at Home.' Of course, he hadn't written it. It had already been on his desktop, a startlingly accurate depiction of the bloody night he and the courier, Dani, had shared. He wasn't worried about anyone finding her body. To be honest, he wasn't even sure where it was. But it made for a helluva story and he had submitted it to Krypteia Publishing the next day, no questions asked. The email had come 48 hours later, same as the first two. They wanted full rights and would be shopping this one to Hollywood. Three years later, here he was, getting ready to step out for the red carpet premier of 'FED sEX', starring Jillian Reed, one of the hottest young actresses in Hollywood. She was the very same Jillian Reed who he had married a year ago after a whirlwind romance on the set.

Andre Rossell had made it. Everyone knew his name. In the past three years, he had put out seven horror novels, his latest, Highway of the Dead, debuting just this morning to world-wide applause. Seven best-selling novels all attributed to him and his writing brilliance. And he hadn't written a single one of them. All seven novels had been pre-written and were on his laptop when he woke up that fateful morning. Two of them had already been published, establishing him as the premier name in horror. And after seeing that first royalty check, he had never asked questions and he never looked back.

Oh, he had occasionally wondered where the books had come from, but the money took care of any lingering questions he had. The fame took care of the rest. His fans glorified him as one of the greatest horror novelists of all time. His critics called him crass, vile, and even evil. He cared for none of that, though. He only cared for the life he was living. And Jillian, of course. Somewhere in that whirlwind journey, he had truly fallen in love with her. And somewhere in that love affair, the quest for fame and fortune had fallen back a notch on his personal list of requirements.

That wasn't a bad thing, he knew. It wouldn't hurt him to step back out of the limelight. He had Jillian. And they had a baby on the way. Jillian had told him that wonderful news just two weeks ago. And besides, there were no more files on his desktop to submit. If he couldn't think of anything himself, he could easily just hang it up.

Yes, life was pretty darn sweet for Andre Rossell.

The idea that his world could come crashing down on him, though, had never once occurred to him.

$$***$$

It was later that night and while the after-party was still in full swing in the Hyatt Regency's ballroom, Andre decided that it was time to call it a night. Jillian had already retired and he was anxious to join her for festivities of their own before getting a much-needed night's sleep.

The premiere of 'FED sEX' had been a rousing success, but even he had watched the blood-soaked movie with some degree of trepidation. It was raw and disturbing and had garnered an NC-17 rating that the producers had loudly trumpeted instead of shy away from. And the rating hadn't hurt the project, not in the least. The book had been a screaming success and the monster's career that it launched would rival that of Freddy Krueger and Hannibal Lecter. The movie had been anticipated almost as soon as the book was released, with fans clamoring to see it on the big screen from day one and most entertainment rags pegging it for a mid 8-digit opening weekend, something unheard of for the genre.

All of it had served to make Andre Rossell a very happy and a very rich man.

Reaching the penthouse, he swiped his card key through the slot and stepped in. The room was dark. As a matter of fact, the whole apartment was dark. He walked to the wall plate and ran his hand over the sensor that would activate the sunken living room's lights. Nothing happened.

He tried several more times with the same lack of success and was about to call out for Jillian when a match flared to life from the other side of the room, hissing in the dark silence of the apartment. Andre froze, the blood draining from his face as the flame was touched to the end of a cigar. It glowed brightly in the shadows, illuminating a face for just a brief moment. Then the intruder shook out the match and the image faded into the darkness until Andre could only see the tip of the burning cigar.

"Andre, baby," a voice came out of the darkness. "What's shakin'?"

Andre froze. He had heard that voice only one other time

over the past three years and that was on the morning that he met Dani, the courier, the young lady who had died to give him and 'FED sEX' the golden ticket to the Hollywood big screen. After that one instance, he had never heard the voice again, communicating with his benefactor only by email. The contracts showed up via courier when promised and the checks always cleared. He never thought any more of it.

Until now.

"Andre, baby," the stranger repeated, the slow deep roll of a business man that never lost. "Come have a seat."

"Where's Jillian?" he asked, his heart racing. Terror threatened to drown him and he found his footsteps wooden and slow. "Who are you?"

"It's time to settle," the voice said easily, ignoring his question. "Seven up means time is up. It's time to reset the game clock."

"Who are you?" Andre demanded again, struggling to find his courage and finding it completely lacking.

"I'm your agent, Andre," the man replied, shifting against the plush leather chair he was seated in. To Andre, it sounded like fire hissing in the background. "You're a rousing success in the entertainment world with nothing but more fame and fortune still to come. It can be unending, if you want it to. I've simply come to collect my commission for this round. Agents don't work for free, you know."

"Your... commission?" he asked shakily. "Wait a sec... I don't understand."

"I said...sit," the voice commanded and suddenly, Andre found himself sprawled on the floor in front of the shadowy figure, thrown by a force he could not see. The man, however, had not moved and leisurely drew in a lung full of smoke as Andre scrambled to his knees. The brightened tip of the cigar cast just enough illumination that Andre could see two massive booted feet and black jeans. The light faded before he could take in any more of his visitor and darkness once again claimed the room.

Shaking in fear, Andre pulled himself to his feet and then sat down meekly on the edge of the couch, facing the speaker, or at least his cigar. "Okay," he stammered, trying to maintain control of the panic threatening to send him screaming from the room. "I'm in the dark, here. Can you please tell me what this is about? I'm sure we can work something out."

"We've already worked it out," the voice stated calmly. "It's all in the contract. Surely you knew we had an appointment today, right?"

"What contract? What appointment? I swear I don't know what you mean! I don't know about any of this!"

"Andre," the man laughed. "How do you think all this came to be? You don't believe it all just happened, do you?"

"I don't understand," he pleaded, desperately trying to find a way out. "I signed contracts for books, yes, but…"

"Books that you never wrote," the voice interrupted. "But books that would bring you the wildest of success and fame beyond even your own lofty dreams."

"But…but I…" Andre stammered, completely at a loss.

The man—at least Andre thought it was a man—leaned forward in the darkness and sucked in another long drag of cigar smoke. The end flared to life and for a moment, Andre could see his face. Dark skin and eyes rimmed with red, his features could have been carved out of stone.

"A deal's a deal," the intruder said and stood. He towered over Andre and the faux author shrank away in terror. The man smoothed out a long black trench coat and then reached inside. He pulled out a sheaf of papers and presented them to Andre. There were seven of them, each of them the signature page of a standard contract – contracts that he'd never bothered to read. He had simply signed them when the couriers brought them, always more interested in the money that had accompanied them.

Now, as he stared at the papers, each of them bearing his signature below the written legal statement pertaining to his agent's fee, he felt himself go cold inside. Looking up, he felt a tear form at the corner of his eye and roll down his cheek. "Are you saying…I sold my soul? To you? To Satan?"

The man threw back his head and laughed, a deep rough sound that reminded Andre of an avalanche. "Lord, no," he laughed. "Selling your soul to the devil is so passé. Not to mention, it's been way overdone. Not a lot of people are willing to consign themselves to an eternity of damnation for a few years of prosperity, despite what the movies might say."

"Then…then…"

"Then what?" the man mocked. "We still deal in souls, Andre, if that's your question. Oh, that will never change. But we deal in the souls of your loved ones. People are so much more willing to sign on the dotted line when it's not their own soul they're gambling with."

"Are you saying…?"

"Jillian will make a fine addition to my museum," the man answered, cutting Andre off. "And in this case, I get a twofer. 'Bout time I got a baby bonus. I was wondering if you were going to come through one of these times."

Horror dawned on Andre and anger and rage roared up inside of him, pushing back the terror. "Wait a minute!" he shouted. "No! You can't!" He felt himself lunging out of his chair, hands reaching for the man. He didn't care how big he was or even *what* he was. He couldn't lose Jillian. He couldn't lose their baby! He couldn't! Not now! Not ever!

But the man was as solid as granite and Andre ricocheted off him and tumbled to the floor. He towered over him, dragging on his cigar, clearly unconcerned with the attack. From his position on the floor, Andre could swear that the smoke wreathing the man's head made him look like the devil himself.

He reached down and picked up the scattered papers. "As per our agreement, Andre, I'll be taking Jillian," he said matter-of-factly. "We have a nice room all made up for her and the baby. As a matter of fact, we'll keep it as close to your blockbuster hit as possible. 'FED sEX,'" he chuckled. "Have to give myself credit there. That was a good one. People in today's world just eat that stuff up."

"NO!" Andre screamed and lunged for the man again, only to find a huge hand closing about his throat.

The man drew him close, so that Andre could see his features clearly now. The red in his eyes seemed to flicker and glow in the light of the burning cigar. "Do we have to do this every time I have to collect?" he asked dangerously, before casually tossing him back to the floor.

Andre wheezed as the breath was driven from his lungs from the impact. "Wha… wha… what do… you mean?" he gasped, rubbing his throat.

"Every time I come to collect, it's the same old song and

dance," the man rumbled. "You whine and cry about what's due to me. First it was Sarah. Then it was Autumn. Then Shelby... her, I really like, by the way. She's a lively one. Then there was Dawn, then Thomas..." he paused and snickered. "You caught me by surprise with that one. Have to admit, I didn't know you had it in you, but Hollywood sure ate it up."

"I don't... I don't understand," Andre cried, the tears coming freely now.

"Oh, that's right, I forget sometimes that you never read the fine print," the man said, snapping his fingers as if remembering something. "Part of the deal is the reset. That's back on page 3 of the contract, by the way. Maybe you should get a lawyer next time."

"The... reset?"

"Right. The deal is for seven books and unlimited fame, my boy," he said. "Per the contract stipulations, however, as soon as the seventh book is released, it's time to pay the piper. 'Highway of the Dead' debuted as a number one best-seller on the New York Times list this morning. You should be thrilled. However, that's number seven and signifies the end of the contract, so it's time to pay up. Terms are non-negotiable. I get your loved one's soul, you get a few minutes of pure abject horror in knowing what you've done, and then we reset the project and you get to do it all over again. You get to live forever in your very own real-life version of 'Groundhog Day.'"

"Wait... this has happened before?" Andre was shaken to his very core. It had to be a dream. This could not be happening. It could not be real!

"Right you are," the man said, tapping the side of his head and making a very real thumping sound. "Jillian makes this the sixth time we've done this."

"You...you mean..." he trailed off, his thoughts scattering. To think that he had done this before, that he had spent the souls of loved ones, sent his mind reeling in shock.

"Right-o, Andre, baby," he chuckled. "Six times now, you've lived this lifestyle. Six times, you've had to pay up. This will be the sixth time we've pushed the reset button."

"But there has to be a way," he begged. "This has to stop!"

"Andre, bubby! It *can* stop! Page 5 of the contract states: The contracted—that's you—has the legal authority to void this agreement in the beginning, by refusing to answer the call."

"Refusing… er… what?" He was a mess. "What are you talking about?!"

"All you have to do is not answer the phone," the man said, leaning down and leering at him. "Every time we reset you, we kick it off with the phone call and two books in the hopper to jumpstart your success. Don't answer your phone and the deal's off. You never get the contract, the books never get published under your name, and you're free and clear to go about your life as…well, a loser. Simple as that."

"Don't answer the phone? I don't get it. What do you mean?"

From the back bedroom, Jillian began to scream, starting low as she transitioned from sleep to wakefulness and quickly rising into high-pitched terror.

"Jillian!" Andre shrieked, trying to jump to his feet.

But the man caught him by the throat again and this time lifted him high into the air, squeezing with his massive hand. Andre hung there, hearing his wife's horrified scream, as his world closed around him. The man—his agent—drew him close one last time. Andre could see his own image trapped within the dark orbs of the man's hellish eyes, flames dancing around him, burning him for eternity. Then with Jillian's screams resounding in his ears, blackness took him.

"See you tomorrow," his agent sneered.

***

The first thing he heard the next morning was the strains of his Phil Collins "In the Air Tonight" ringtone, blaring from his phone and breaking him out of the nightmare that had held him tightly in its grip. The memory of that dark dream faded quickly into nothingness as he realized where he was. He was still on his couch and his phone was still singing to him. The iPhone was lying on the floor under the table where he'd tossed it a few days ago when AT&T had suspended his service for non-payment. Reaching down, he picked it up and looked at the screen. He didn't recognize the number and almost didn't answer. But the fact that his phone was suddenly operational again was somewhat intriguing. Besides, one never knew when opportunity might be calling. He thumbed the answer button.

"Yeah?"

"Andre, baby!" an unfamiliar voice sounded from the other end. "What's shakin', my friend?"

The Girl Next Door

E. McCarthy

"Did you hear that?" Nick asked, lifting his head up and cocking it to the side.

The only thing Sadie heard was their mutual ragged breathing and the pounding of her heart in her ears. She listened to gauge if her roommate was returning to their dorm room, but the hallway was silent. Just her and Nick and disheveled clothing, legs entangled with each other on her twin bed. She'd been crushing on him all semester and there was no way she was going to let him sit up now, right when she was on the verge of victory.

"I don't hear anything." She ran her fingers down his chest and below his waist. Right before she could really get down to business, he grabbed her wrist.

"What does this go to anyway?" He nodded in the dim light toward the door her bed was shoved up against, preventing its use.

"It's an empty dorm room." Sadie fought the urge to sigh, more than a little irritated. He'd been in her room before and now was when he decided to notice the oddity? Worst timing ever. "This door is painted shut and there's no door to it in the hallway."

"Why would there be an empty room?" He was already sitting back on his knees, making a fist and knocking on the wood. "It sounds hollow."

"Because it's an empty room. We hear mice or whatever in there all the time. Maybe that's what you heard." Sadie fought the urge to smack him with a pillow. Her social skills weren't the best, but even she knew that was inappropriate for the situation. Then again, what he was doing was inappropriate for the situation as well. The therapist always said she needed to learn to read cues from people. But in this case, Nick should be reading the cue that she wanted a little more action, a lot less talk.

Maybe if she explained he'd let it go. "This used to be the yellow fever ward. That's why these six rooms are separate from the rest of the dorm. They sent students who were dying to live in these rooms."

He looked back at her in horror. "Are you shitting me? So people *died* in this room?"

She shrugged. "I guess."

"And that doesn't bother you?" Even in the dim light she could see his frown, his eyebrows furrowing.

"It bothers me that I have such a sucky closet. Apparently you didn't need a full wardrobe if you were about to kick, but it's totally not fair. All the other rooms have closets four times as big."

It seemed that was the wrong thing to say.

Nick ran his hands through his hair and reached for his shirt. "Okay, that's just wrong. I can't do this. Not in this room. It's creeping me out."

Alarmed, Sadie sat up, her bra dangling forward in front of her exposed breasts. "That was well over a hundred years ago. Do you know how many girls have lived in this room since then? And nothing bad has ever happened. I mean, those girls weren't murdered, they didn't put some kind of curse on these rooms. They just died of disease. Naturally." She silently cursed herself for saying anything. Why did she do that? Screw up every chance with a guy she ever had? "You can look through the keyhole of the room next door. It's just empty, with a school chair in it."

Sometimes, in the morning, she rolled onto her side and she stared through that perfectly arched keyhole into the dust-filled room on the other side of the wall and imagined passing through the hole and having the space entirely to herself. No more annoying as hell roommate who came home drunk every weekend, usually with some mouth-breathing guy, who then both summarily ignored her. The aggressive New Orleans sun penetrated the darkness of the room whenever she glanced through at daybreak, displaying dancing dust motes, mouse droppings, the disintegrating curtain on the window, and the chair.

The single, solitary chair that waited for someone to sit on it.

She liked to think it beckoned her, and only her. Her roommate had refused to take this bed on move-in day because it abutted the unexplained door, with the chair beyond. It sat like an electric chair. A chair for torture. A porno prop. She could picture them all. Shoving her roommate onto it. Duct taping her there.

Sending jolts of electricity through her. Or having Nick sit there while she gave him a lap dance. Oh, yeah. She could picture it.

"I'm not looking in there. That's freaky as hell," Nick said. He slid down off her bed. "I'm going to head out. I'll text you later."

He was leaving. That pissed her off. "Are you scared?" she demanded. He couldn't seriously be afraid of a chair and the idea of people croaking a hundred years ago.

Nick shuffled and he didn't look nearly as hot as he had before. So tough guy football player with his badass tattoos was afraid of the dark. "What's scary is that you're not scared," he said. He leaned over and gave her a lame kiss. "Night."

Sadie stared at his parting back and didn't bother to respond. When he opened the door to the hallway, light flooded into the room. She saw her roommate Hannah giggling, shoving groping hands off her chest. "Oh! Hi, Nick," she said as he exited the room.

"Hey, Hannah. Hey, Tim." His voice faded as he moved down the hallway.

"So Sadie's there?" Tim said, in an exaggerated drunk dude whisper. "You told me she was gone tonight, Hannah. She gives me the creeps. Let's go to my room."

"Shh," Hannah said fiercely. "Don't be a dick. Just because she's not a flirt doesn't mean she's weird."

Sadie decided she would ease up on the mental duct taping of her roommate. Maybe Hannah wasn't so bad. Pulling back on her abandoned tank top, she reached for her cell phone on her nightstand, no longer interested in them. What had Nick heard? The light from the cracked open door wasn't substantial enough to illuminate the gloom beyond, so she hit the flashlight feature on her phone and aimed it at the keyhole.

She promptly dropped it on her comforter, her heart racing. Holy…

The chair wasn't empty. Shining the light again with shaking fingers, she leaned in close, squeezing her left eye shut for better visibility. There was a doll sitting on the chair. A Victorian era doll, looking small and lonely on the human-sized chair. She had dark hair that stuck straight out in either direction, her porcelain face gleaming in the glow of the flashlight. One eye looked normal, one was obscured. Her dress was ivory, and she wore little boots. It looked like there was soot or something on the fabric. None of which mattered.

What mattered was she hadn't been there before.

It was November. For three months Sadie had been staring through the keyhole and for three months the room had been empty. With this door the only entrance. Someone must have gone through the window and put the doll there. That was what Nick had heard. Someone moving around in there. She tried to splash light around the rest of the room but she couldn't see anything else.

Lying back on her bed, she turned her flashlight feature off and stared at the ceiling, thinking. She could hear Hannah and Tim making out on her roommate's bed a few feet away and their sloppy wet sounds rose and fell, getting louder and louder, until it crowded out her thoughts, driving her insane. She tried to ignore it but she fixated on the slurp and slop, her body growing tense. Poe had his tell-tale heart and she had Tim Johnson's tongue.

Sitting up, she slid off her bed and pulled on a sweatshirt. She shoved her feet into her boots and grabbed her keys off her desk.

"Where are you going?" Hannah asked when she yanked open the door and light flooded their room.

Sadie glanced back at Hannah and Tim, both squinting against the sudden pupil-dilating fluorescent light. "I'm just checking on something. I'll be back."

Hannah grinned. "Tell Nick I said hi," she said in a sing-song voice.

She didn't bother to explain she wasn't going to Nick's room. He lived in Butler on the other side of campus and she couldn't be bothered. She had other things to think about. Running down the stairs that kept her little wing separate from the rest of the building, she ran her fingers along the brick wall. She'd chosen this dorm because it was the oldest dorm, with primarily freshman residents. Her parents had approved because it was the only all-female dorm on campus. But she had liked that it wasn't a high-rise, that it was surrounded by huge oak trees, and gave the sense that she was both in New Orleans and on a college campus. It felt traditional, like a place where girls hung out together and where she could belong.

That had been a bit naïve, but as she nodded to the front desk attendant and ran down the exterior stairs to the grassy lawn out front, she still liked the vibe, even if she wasn't exactly in demand as anyone's BFF. She went around the side, walking towards Broadway

Street, then on around back where her room was. She knew which window was hers, because it was directly across from the day care center, in perfect alignment with a street light. The night was quiet except for an occasional car driving down, or a random yell from the direction of the fraternity houses. It wasn't hot and it wasn't cold. Just… nothing. The kind of night where you aren't even aware of the temperature, as opposed to August when the heat came at you like a stumbling drunk, invading your space and robbing you of breathable air.

There was her room. But she narrowed her eyes, frowning. There should be more one window between her room and the end of the building for the empty room. Yet there was no window.

That made no freaking sense. She'd seen that window every time she glanced in that room. It was an exterior window, she was sure of it. It let in light.

"What the hell?" she murmured, walking back and forth twice. Counting windows. She could see lights and shadows behind the blinds of other rooms, and she could see the sticker on the glass of her room, some political sticker Hannah had stuck on there without having any clue what it actually meant. Her roommate, the social activist. Not.

No window.

It didn't exist.

She glanced around, suddenly conscious of being alone, of having goose bumps crawl up her skin like a stealthy spider. Fear tickled her for the first time. She ran. Not the careening blast of pure terror, but a healthy jog, wanting back inside. She wanted to look through the keyhole again. But when she got back in and tried to use her flashlight, Hannah protested loudly.

"OMG, turn that off. You're burning my pupils."

"I think you mean your retinas," she said, but she obliged and turned the light back off, lying on her back, fingers trembling. She was more curious than scared.

But even though she turned it around and around in her head, she couldn't find an answer. No window. But a window. Empty chair. Mysterious doll on chair. Around and around her thoughts turned, the dark eye of the doll dancing behind her lids. In her head she imagined the doll crawling through the keyhole and beating Tim and Hannah into silence with her tiny glossy fist. Bam. And blood would spatter over her ivory ruffled dress.

After Tim started snoring and Hannah's mewls of pleasure went silent, Sadie rolled slowly toward the door so as not to cause the mattress to creak, resting her hand on it as if she could feel something on the other side. The door was cool, and despite the paint clogging the seam between door and frame, she could feel a wisp of air. Angling her phone so the beam would go straight through the keyhole, she leaned in.

And was met with the blank stare of the doll, inches from her own face.

A perfect porcelain face, one eye cold and glassy, with soft lustrous eyelashes, the other orb looking like an angry child had taken a black marker and colored it in rapidly with vicious strokes. Beauty defiled. Evil meets innocence.

Sadie fell back, dropping her phone. A sudden blinding headache gripped her skull and she grabbed her ears, pressed her temples. The pressure grew and grew and when she tried to lean over, it felt like her head was going to burst. Blow apart like a confetti popper on New Year's Eve.

Letting out a cry, she half climbed, half fell out of bed.

Tim jerked awake. "What the hell is wrong with you?"

Sadie didn't bother to answer but stumbled down the hall to the common bathroom and splashed water on her face, gritting her teeth against the pain. When she stared into the mirror her eyes were red. Like someone had put a gel over them, or backlit them. Reaching out, she poked one, just to see if it would feel like liquid, like the sticky warmth of blood. It just felt squishy, like her eyeball. Head still pounding, she lay on the cool tiles of the bathroom floor inside a shower stall and licked the wet drain. She was dizzy and nauseated and the cool water remnants felt refreshing.

Somewhere in the back of her mind it struck her as strange, that she was flicking her tongue where dozens of feet had stood, scraping off their skin cells and shredding sock lint and sweat and toenail-captured dirt. But she couldn't stop herself. She licked like a cat with a bowl of cream. Flick, flick. Her little lizard tongue.

She spent the whole night on the floor, dozing in and out of sleep.

Dreaming of the pretty little creepy doll cutting Nick's uneasy eyes out with a miniature scalpel. And eating them.

***

When Sadie woke up, stiff and cold, her cheek damp and shriveled from the hours of water exposure, a girl with thick brown hair was staring down at her.

"Wow, rough night?" she asked, her voice sympathetic. "Been there, done that." She was wearing a towel, obviously intending to shower. "But that floor is yuck. You're going to need to bleach your face."

Sadie hauled herself upright, fighting the urge to roll her eyes. Bleach on her face. That was a fabulous idea. Was everyone here an idiot? Then again, she was told she was too literal. "Sorry, I'll be out of here in a second."

"It's okay." The girl held her hand out. "Tequila does that to me."

Sadie took the help she was offered and hauled herself to her feet. She was still wearing her boots from her walk around the dorm the night before. "Thanks."

After washing her face and rinsing out her mouth, she went down to the front desk and tried to act casual. "Hey, uh, who lived in my room last year? I found something in the closet and I thought they might want it back."

The RA, a senior, just stared at Sadie blankly. "No one lived in that room last year. Or the year before. Or the year before. They're only used if the dorms are overcrowded, like overflow. I think this is the first time that wing has been used since the fifties."

That made no sense. That made no fucking sense at all. Or maybe it did. Sadie's head still hurt, the pain alive, pulsing out of her temples through her veins. Like an alien creature seeking an escape. "Okay, thanks."

As she wandered away the RA asked, "What did you find?"

"Just a fake ID," she lied.

"Weird."

"Totally." Sadie paused for a second, thinking, then went back up and to her room. The door was locked and she'd left the night before without her key. Pounding on the door, she bounced on the heels of her feet, impatient. Her phone was still in the room too so she couldn't text Hannah to let her in.

Tim opened the door in his underwear, looking sleepy and pissed off. She brushed past him and started to dig around in her bed for her cell phone. There was a text from Nick, which she ignored. Going to the bottom of her bed she started to yank the whole thing away from the wall as it screeched and protested on the wooden floor.

Hannah's head lifted from her pillow. She had makeup smeared under her eyes and her nose was swollen. "What are you doing? Oh, my God, just kill me now."

"I want in that room next door," she said, dragging the bed as far to the left as she could, penning Hannah in.

Tim was leaning on the door to the hallway, scratching his chest. "When you get the door open can you move in there? Because this is bullshit. It's Saturday fucking morning, Sadie."

"Sure," she told him, not really giving a shit that she had interrupted his sleep. He'd kept her up half the night with his groans as he banged her roommate four feet away from her. That wasn't exactly the top of her list of ways she wanted to be woken up. She visualized dragging Tim by his chest hairs into the room, slamming the door behind her, and sealing it shut again. She'd eat ice cream and pizza while she listened to him scream, clawing at the door...

In her desk drawer was a pocketknife her father had given her when she'd decided to go to school in New Orleans. He'd thought she could shiv the criminal element around town if she were attacked. Instead, she went at the tacky paint sealing the door to the frame. She sawed at it up and down, her arm burning from the strain, paint flecks flying all over the floor and the top of her floral comforter.

"That's probably lead paint," Tim said, crawling back into bed with Hannah.

It wasn't like it could make him any dumber, she thought meanly.

An hour later she was out of breath and decided she needed to take a break. She changed her dirty clothes inside her microscopic closet and went for coffee and a muffin. Nick was in the cafeteria eating eggs and cereal.

"Hey. You never texted me back. Are you pissed?" he asked.

"No." She was distracted though. She wanted to get back to her room. Her head still hurt and the muffin was making her stomach cramp.

Nick was standing next to her, ready to toss his trash. He

frowned at her. "Look, uh, I just had a weird moment. Can I see you tonight? There's a party off campus."

"Sure." She was startled to realize that she didn't care that much one way or the other. For months he'd been all she could think about. Now he was crowded out by thoughts of the perfect porcelain doll and her blank, sightless eye, staring at Sadie.

When he bent over and kissed her, in front of everyone in the cafeteria, she was surprised. He'd never really acknowledged her like that in public before. It made her body warm. She felt the tightening of arousal, and satisfaction. She smiled up at him.

"Later." He smiled back.

Back in her room she felt less rabid, less intense. She melodically kept at the door, but she took breaks. She cleaned up her mess. She felt less driven, less insane. It had scared her, that feeling of desperation. The doll and the room didn't scare her. But losing control did. She fixated on things, she knew that. So now she listened to music and worked steadily on the door, but without the tension she'd felt earlier.

She hadn't looked though the keyhole, wanting it to be a present she unwrapped. A Christmas gift. Lift the lid on the box and get exactly what you want. That's what was going to happen. She was going to open the door and find her doll, sitting on the chair, and the window pouring light down onto the dust choked floor. It would prove she wasn't crazy.

But when she finally pried the door open at the bottom with Tim's help, the wood groaning in protest, there was nothing there. Just the chair. And undisturbed dust. There was no window. No doll.

She sat back on her ass, stunned, fear tightening her throat, the hairs on the back of her neck teasingly rising up one by one. There should be a window.

"Dude. This room is creeptacular." Tim leaned his head in. "I can't believe you sleep next to this every night."

"What's in there?" Hannah asked from behind them.

"Nothing." Sadie crawled into the room on her hands and knees, checking the shadowy corners one by one. Nothing. She stood up and went for the closet. But yanking it open revealed nothing except for the corpse of a cockroach on its back, dry and brittle. She stomped on it, listening to the crunch, dust rising on either side of her foot.

Backing up, she rubbed her face, the panic making her itch. She spun in a circle, taking in the room in its entirety. It was just a twin dorm room to hers. Identical in size and materials.

But missing a window.

And a doll.

***

Sadie drank three beers at the party. Enough for a buzz, but not enough to get loaded. She wanted to take the edge off, to forget what she'd seen the night before. How she'd felt. After he did two shots she and Nick started making out in the foliage crowded courtyard of the duplex hosting the party. Wind whipped around them and it felt brisk, refreshing. She felt alive. His kisses stoked the flames of her desire, and she opened her mouth for his hot, thrusting tongue.

What if she bit his tongue off? Just sank her teeth right into that plump, moist organ. Would she choke on it? Then she could jam her fingers into his ears drilling into them until she reached his innermost thoughts. Until she swallowed them and all his thoughts and words.

Jerking back, Sadie breathed hard, staring at Nick. She was losing her mind. It was skittering away from her, like dropping a jar of marbles. Rational thought rolling away, leaving chaos in its wake. She needed to focus. Be in control.

"Let's go back to my room," she said.

He grinned. "Finish what we started? I like the sound of that." He kissed her neck and swatted her butt. "You like it kinky, don't you? I can tell."

Could he tell that she wanted to sweep his feet out from under him and watch him tumble to the sidewalk, scraping up his pretty boy face?

Given his smile, he couldn't. Nick held her hand and led her out of the courtyard onto the side street. He had a beer in his other hand and he passed it to her. They walked and finished off the liquid with big swallows, and occasionally he would lean over and kiss her. She felt normal. She even felt happy. Excited.

Part of her wanted to explain to him about the doll. To share her. But Nick wasn't special enough. The doll was hers. Sadie wasn't stupid. She knew that Nick just wanted to get laid. He didn't want to be together-together with her. Which was fine. Except that meant she couldn't share the secret with him.

Especially because she wasn't even sure exactly what the secret was.

She just knew it was important. Windows and doors and dolls and that little knife...

"I can't believe you opened that door," Nick said an hour later, his voice sounding amused. "You're intense."

He was leaning out her open window smoking.

Sadie stretched and pulled a pair of yoga pants and a T-shirt on. She strode towards him, feeling satisfied and smug. "Want to go in there? Round two? There's a chair in there I can bend over."

His eyebrows rose. "Can I spank you?"

Why not? She was feeling elated. Almost high. "Sure." Leaning over she pulled his hand to her mouth and took a drag on his cigarette. "Smoking will kill you."

"So could you. Got to die of something."

Interesting. Did he know? Sadie grinned back at him and pulled her bed away from the wall again. "Come into my secret lair." She hooked her finger at him.

He laughed and took another drag. He lounged against the window, beautifully naked. Such a great body. It was so strong. So full of life.

"Give me a minute. I need recovery time."

She slipped her pocketknife off the nightstand and tucked it into the waistband of her yoga pants when he turned to blow smoke out the window. She felt... delicious. But when she opened the door with a hard yank and went to walk in, she drew up short.

The doll was there again, perched on the chair.

"Fuck," she breathed, a sweat breaking out on her forehead, above her lip. In the palm of her hands, an instant oil slick of anxiety. How was that possible?

"What's wrong?" Nick moved in beside her. "Whoa. This is a dark little room from hell, isn't it? I know I heard mice in here last night. I don't know if this is such a good idea, Sadie. What if the door blows shut behind us or something?"

Such a whiny-ass baby. Maybe he'd like a bottle of milk too. "It's fine. But we need to move the doll."

She didn't want Nick touching her doll though. She wasn't for his hands. As she moved closer to the chair, Sadie stared at that black eye, getting drawn into it like a whirlpool. Around and around it drew her down, tugged at her, held her. She forced herself to look away, down at that little ivory dress, which was smudged with dirt and blood spatters. There was a tiny knife in her hand, remarkably similar to the knife Sadie held in her own hand. When had she pulled that out?

"What doll?"

That made her halt her progress. She looked back at Nick. "What do you mean, what doll? This doll." She gestured to the chair.

His jaw dropped. "There's nothing there, Sadie." He started to shift backwards toward the door. "Uh…"

"You have to see it! Why don't you see it?" There was no fucking way he didn't see that doll. He was messing with her. Bile rose in her gut, and her stomach convulsed. Without warning, she shot a stream of vomit out of her mouth. It splashed all over the floor and onto her feet.

Nick paused. "Shit, you're trashed. Come here, baby." He reached out and took her by the hand, pulling her into the dorm room.

She fought him, though she wasn't sure why, and the knife tumbled out of her hand. It was only when she crossed the threshold she remembered it was because she was supposed to kill him. Stab him repeatedly until his blood soaked her dress.

When they got into the light of the room, Hannah's colorful posters on the walls, Nick blanched. "Holy shit, you're puking up blood! It's all over you."

She was. She glanced down at her shirt, at the vibrant red spatter.

It was beautiful.

***

"Thanks for helping me," Hannah told Tim, super happy that he was willing to lug boxes for her. It meant their relationship was totally moving in the right direction. "I'm so glad Housing is letting me change rooms. It's seriously creepy being in here now after everything."

Maintenance had painted the door shut again, but whenever Tim didn't spend the night and she was alone all she could think about was that empty room, the chair, Nick's description of Sadie puking blood. She'd started sleeping in the room across the hall with a couple of friends.

"It's creepy that your roommate has yellow fever. I mean, who gets that?" Tim picked up a box and glanced over at Sadie's empty bed.

Sadie's parents were due to come in a few days before winter break started to collect all of her stuff. She was in the hospital or whatever. Hannah wasn't really sure. "She went to Malaria or something like that over the summer. They said that's where she got it."

"Malaria is a disease, not a country."

His words ticked Hannah off. She frowned at him. "You sound just like Sadie always correcting me. God! Who cares what it's called?"

"Probably a lot of people. The Center for Disease Control, for one." Tim wasn't even looking at her. He was picking through the box she'd filled up with her bras and panties. He touched lace, rubbing his fingers over it.

What a douche. She suddenly felt like taking his head and smashing it into the brick wall behind him. He shouldn't talk to her like that… but then the thought trailed off and she mentally laughed at herself. Overreacting. Geez. She would never hurt his cute little head.

"I don't think she has yellow fever. I just think she went schizo. She was always weird."

"I'm sure the doctors know what it is."

"I just hope I don't get it." Though maybe if she got a disease, she could tell her parents that was why her grades sucked so hard. She was in over her head, even when she studied, which admittedly wasn't often.

"It's been a month. I think you're good." Tim set the box down and went over to Hannah's bed. He climbed on it and rapped on the door. "Did you ever look in here?"

"No." She shivered. "Did you put something in there?" She wasn't falling for that.

He snorted. "The door is painted shut. How could I put

anything in there?"

Annoyed with him, she got onto the bed next to him. "If I look what do I get?"

"Anything you want." He pretended to shove her head towards the door.

She laughed and pawed at him. "Stop!" But then curious, more curious than she had ever been before, she peered into the keyhole, squinting one eye.

The face of a doll stared back at her, one beautiful glass eye, the other solid black, as matte as Hannah's favorite Marc Jacobs lipstick. The doll's hair spilled out in all directions and even though her mouth didn't move she whispered under her breath.

Hannah cocked her head and listened.

She nodded.

Then turned and smiled at Tim.

Maybe she could crush his pretty little head after all.

Forward Base Fourteen

Patrick Freivald

A warning blip chimed, and a green dot turned red in Sarah DeSouza's vision.

Droplets streaked her visor, fogged opaque in the New Phoenix humidity so that only her HUD gave any useful information—temperature, vitals, team position, the seventeen rounds left in her magazine, and an endless stream of data from the track drones stationed around Forward Base 14. Sweat matted her hair under the helmet, the pungent tang of wet dog and body odor an unwelcome reminder that their last supply drop came too long ago, and with too little.

"DeSouza, status?" Sergeant Brett Jackson's voice in her ear carried a razor's edge buried under gravel, both harder and more fragile than months past.

"Track nine went offline." She punched directions into the keyboard and fine-tuned them through the neural link. "I'm shifting eight and ten to cover the sweep."

"Battery?"

"Likely. It's been leaking H-gel since the last attack." Their most vital and scarcest resource, hydrogen stabilized in a fire-retardant gel ran the microfusion reactors that powered everything from their rail guns to the track drones to the AC units and refrigerators, to the massive terraformers that loomed in skies a thousand miles to the south.

Not that they had any AC or refrigerators, or more than a dozen track drones left.

She licked her lips. "When do you think they'll hit us, Sergeant?"

"Server's offline, private. Predictive models—"

"When do *you* think, Sergeant?"

Jackson sighed. "Any time. They're wearing us down before the headshot." He paused, then, "And we're about as worn down as we can get."

Her heart skipped. "You think we have a chance?"

He said nothing for far too long. "No. Do your duty, private. It's all that's left."

Jackson and DeSouza, the last of twenty-eight personnel sent to relieve FB14, had survived the past few weeks by blind luck. The Takers had broken their line too many times, carried off too many bodies, or worse, infected them with biomechanical parasites and left them behind. Bodies that came back, armed and augmented with biomechanical appendages a generation ahead of United States technology.

A technician, DeSouza managed the sixty-eight track drones slaved to her neural link, so she did more good inside HQ than out in the thick of the fighting.

Eleven. Not sixty-eight. Eight months prior they'd had sixty-eight well-armed and spit-polished track drones, and another two dozen wingers patrolling the sky. Seven months of boredom, patrols through the endless forests, defending the supply routes from an enemy that never came.

Then the sky lit up over the horizon, too far to see the mushroom cloud, too far to hear the roar, or smell the burning concrete and bodies. That light severed contact from New Houston and from orbital command. Two weeks later the satlink went down for good, and the attacks had started.

"Private?" Jackson's voice startled her out of the reverie.

"Yes, sergeant?"

"You can gather wool when you're dead. Stay alert."

"Yes, sergeant."

***

Static scrabbled across the network, and scattered through it fragments of words.

Eyes wide, Sarah cranked the volume and patched it through the PA system. "Sergeant, you getting this?"

Voices. Human voices, the first they'd heard in weeks and in snippets too short to make out. A sob escaped her throat, unbidden and unwanted, and she choked down those that followed.

"I read. Triangulate?"

Her harsh chuckle held no mirth. "I'm not signals. Do you know how?"

He appeared in the doorway, soft brown eyes glistening over tear-streaked cheeks, a pistol forgotten in one hand, a crumpled photograph in the other. He rushed the console, dropping the weapon on a chair on the way by, and fiddled with knobs, dark muscles bulging under his tight white t-shirt.

The rich, burnt-wood smell of bourbon filled the room, with oniony human odor beneath. *Thanks for sharing, jerk.* She frowned at the uncharitable thought, and the smell.

Behind Sergeant Jackson's back, Sarah picked up his weapon. One round chambered, nothing in the magazine, the grip clammy with sweat from being held too long. She plucked the picture from the console and smoothed it out. A chocolate-skinned woman cradled a black-haired baby to her breast while Jackson beamed with a father's pride.

A woman's voice filled the room. "Forward Base Twelve, do you copy?"

Jackson leaned in and pressed the COM button. "This is Forward Base Fourteen. We are low on supplies and expecting attack. Do you read me?"

"Forward Base Twelve, this is Eagle Command, do you copy?" she repeated.

Leaning in, he raised his voice. "Eagle Command, this is Forward Base *Fourteen* requesting immediate evac."

"Forward Base Twelve, this is Eagle Co—" Her voice exploded in a burst of static.

"Fuck!" Jackson slammed his fist on the table. "EAGLE COMMAND, DO YOU COPY?"

He tried for hours, in turn broadcasting a distress signal and sweeping for replies. None came. Night fell, and with it the track drones switched to thermal imaging in her mind.

A ragged moan erupted from Jackson's throat, followed by rasping hyperventilation.

Sarah stood and backed away, tucking the pistol into the back of her pants. "Tomorrow, Sergeant. They'll find us tomorrow. We're going to be okay."

He lifted his face from his hands and stared at her with bloodshot eyes devoid of hope. "Give me my weapon."

She shook her head. "I think it's best I hold onto it, at least for tonight."

"Private, give me my weapon."

"No, sergeant. You can court martial me when we—"

The chair flipped as he came out of it in a bull's charge. She spun but not fast enough.

Air blasted from her lungs as he checked her into the wall. Strong hands crushed around her throat. She clawed at his wrists, gaping and gasping and pleading with unseen eyes. Face twisted in hatred and despair, he screamed at her, hot spittle spraying her face, burnt wood and ethanol and unbrushed teeth. "GIVE ME MY GUN!"

Her knee glanced off his thigh.

Pain shredded her thoughts as he slammed his forehead down on the bridge of her nose. Eyes rolling back, she balled one hand into a fist. She punched, but with no leverage it bounced off of his muscled abdomen. He screamed, slamming her head into the wall with each word. "GIVE. ME. MY. GUN. YOU. FUCKING. CUNT."

The world hazed to a muddy red as she groped back. Hot agony shrieked up her arm as her fingers crushed between the pistol and the wall. It slipped free and she brought it around. Rail weapons make no sound as they fire, save for the click of the trigger.

The recoil ripped the gun from her hand, and in the deafening silence Brett fell back. She gasped precious air into her lungs and dropped to her hands and knees. Her pointer and middle fingers bent at unnatural angles, but she couldn't feel them through the consuming fire in her chest.

Slumping to the side, she rolled her eyes up to her assailant.

Brett lay back on her cot, only his legs visible over the side, but hot gore steamed on the wall behind him.

Gagging, she rolled back up to her hands and knees, then stayed there, light-headed, to regain her equilibrium. Thick tendrils of bloody snot streamed from her mouth and nose. She coughed, spat, coughed again.

And as the world slowed its spinning, she stood, and looked down at Sergeant Jackson.

The bullet had entered just under his sternum and traveled upward, tearing a gaping hole that left pieces of ribs and shoulder behind him on the bed. A pungent mix of blood and fresh shit filled the room. Her gorge rose, then chunky red-and-brown vomit erupted from her mouth to join the sticky mess.

Bile burning her throat, she grabbed the cot one-handed and dragged it into the hall. That done, she sat back down at her desk to monitor the drones.

Drone two died at three a.m., and drone seven an hour later. They hadn't been damaged.

She fanned the rest out to cover her escape route and grabbed what she could before the Takers breached the perimeter.

***

Boots crunching across generations of leaves that choked out any undergrowth, Sarah carried everything she could manage toward the rising sun and Forward Base Twelve: two bladder canteens—one of clean water, the other the remnants of the bourbon taken from the small shrine in his room where Jackson had planned to kill himself—a drone power core and six feet of heavy wire, one microfusion antipersonnel mine, and a pistol with four rounds. The rifle had more ammo, but she couldn't manage it as well with broken fingers. Firing a pistol left-handed might work. Might.

The world rocked as Forward Base Fourteen's power core detonated. A scaled-up version of the drone cores, her training at scuttling the small equipment translated exactly to the larger machine. She stumbled on, one foot in front of the next, her HUD displaying GPS information and highlighting obstacles in her path.

Three days to Forward Base Twelve, and possible rescue.

One foot in front of the next. One foot in front of the next.

***

Her HUD blinked red, once: enemy signature detected. Ducking behind a tree, she scanned left and right. A double triangle, red on red, highlighted a dark shape under a fallen log. She staggered toward a stream babbling to the left, not having to feign her exhaustion or thirst.

Kneeling, she put the pistol on the ground and winced as she lowered to take a drink, eyes closed to track the stealthy shuffling behind her. Her right hand throbbed in time with her racing heart, and the cool water held a metallic hint of blood.

The rustle turned into a charge. She rolled left and choked up the pistol, firing twice at the humanoid shape flying toward her. The double-tap took it center-of-mass at point-blank range. Puffs of black-red hydraulic fluid sprayed the trees behind the Taker, and it shrieked with a voice not its own.

Corporal Nedel's body collapsed and writhed as the Taker's biomechanical dendrites and hydraulic muscle writhed and squirmed to repair the damage to its host. She rolled to her feet, stepped forward, and put her foot on its back to force it still.

As she shot the neural cortex embedded into his lower spine, a tendril stabbed from between its ribs, an icy lance that punctured straight through her boot and the foot inside. Grunting at the sudden pain, she reached down and pulled out the ropy black mass. It came free with a slippery, wet feeling, but no blood leaked from the wound.

She looked around, using the HUD to highlight any further danger. The woods stood quiet under a blue sky, a beauty she hadn't noticed in her determined run toward Forward Base Twelve. She sat next to the body and pulled off her boot and sock.

And gasped.

Tiny black filaments writhed around the wound.

"Oh, fuck you," she snarled. She looked up at the sky and laughed, a mirthless despair given voice. Her eyes fell to the pistol, a single round left. She sighed and murmured, "You can't have me you sons of bitches, but I'm not going out like that either."

A quick search of Nedel's body told her what she didn't want to know: he carried no food, no painkillers, and no knife.

It took more effort than she'd imagined to remove a belt with two broken fingers, and more still to loop it and twist a long stick through it. Working methodically, she hummed a lullaby her mother used to sing, something to distract her from the gruesome task at hand.

She worked a single strand of copper wire into a loop, one end twisted around an oblong rock, a cave man electrician's garrote. She took off her pants, tightened the belt tourniquet above her knee and the makeshift cutter below it, then clenched a stout stick between her teeth, and took a deep breath.

She rolled her weight onto the stick to hold it in place, grabbed the rock with her left hand, and lay back so she wouldn't have to look. Eyes squeezed shut, she bit down on the stick and mumbled around it.

"I'm not becoming one of you motherfuckers. I'm not."

She twisted and slid the rock back and forth. Her skin parted in a line of hot fire. Another twist, another slide, another jolt of crippling madness and pain. And another, and another. Blinded by tears, she tried not to hyperventilate, but passed out multiple times. She'd wake, crying, and grab the rock. And twist, and slide. Twist, and slide. Even as the circle tightened through the tendons and ligaments of her knee. She couldn't give up; she had work to do. Twist, and slide.

An eternity later the leg came off, a relief that brought no relief. She sighed and forced her cramped fingers to open, dropping the makeshift saw. She drank the whiskey, three whole swallows of soothing heat, and didn't bother to pour any on her wound. No point in disinfecting a dead woman.

She pulled the antipersonnel mine to her and removed the cover. Wires snaked from the fusion core to a customizable trigger mechanism next to a sticker that boasted a kill radius of sixty meters. Left-handed, she discarded the button and tripwire, and instead attached the pressure switch. The sun crested and crept toward the horizon. "Come and get it, you bastards."

Fever burned through her. She struggled to think, to move, to remember her last act of patriotism and bravery: take as many of those bastards as she could on her way out.

As twilight darkened the woods it took all of her effort to roll sideways, slide the mine and pressure switch under her back, and roll on top of them. The switch primed with a dull snap.

Nothing to do now but live. Takers would ignore a corpse, but injured humans drew them like flies to honey.

Her eyes closed despite her protests.

***

She woke to flashes of light. Biomechanical shrieks in the distance answered dull clicks above her, Takers using human throats to voice their pain and outrage. One eye flickered open, the most she could manage.

Two men in forest camo and helmets stood over her, rail rifles barking silent death into the surrounding woods with casual, brutal efficiency.

"Confirmed alive and uninfected," one said. "Send medevac ASAP."

"We're moving out. Fall back on my position," the other said. A chorus of acknowledgments slithered through her neural link.

"No, you can't," she said. But nothing came out of her dry mouth. She tried to force her tongue through cracked lips, but the thick, desiccated muscle wouldn't respond. A knot in her lower back pulsed with the gunfire, a shrieking reminder of the death waiting beneath her.

The first man knelt, fired two shots, and looked down at her. Her own face, wan and wasted, stared back out of his mirrored visor. "Ma'am, you're going to be okay." She tried to swat his hand away as he pressed a narcopatch to her neck.

The world swam, soft and warm. Her eyes fluttered as more men backed to stand over her, weapons chattering, a full squad of soldiers in tactical response gear.

"Back!" she tried, but only a giggle came out, a narcotic-fueled manic amusement.

If they heard they didn't react. A Brightsky-pattern transport swooped low above them, chrome steel wings blanketing the sky thirty feet above the treetops, propellers blasting them with a downward wash of air. Two squads of men hung from their deployment pods, weapons flashing as they fired through the canopy.

She slapped at the soldiers as they knelt and reached for her. "You can't...."

"It's okay, ma'am. You're safe now. We've got them on the run all across the sector. You're a hero."

She shook her head. "No!" It came out clear and strong.

"Yeah. You are."

The medic smiled and lifted her.

Snapped!

Rich Devin

It started unannounced, unnoticed, unseen… and then spread.

"Look at that." A shooting star silently streamed through the night sky above the naked couple. "That looked like it was so close."

"Uh-huh." Jarred said without looking up. He continued to kiss the sides of her neck and shoulders.

"Really?" Amaya pushed his head away from her neck.

Jarred rolled to his side, pulling Amaya with him. "Oh, now that's better."

"You like it when I'm on top?"

"I like it when you're everywhere," he said, wrapping his legs around her, pulling her in tight to his body. "And I like it when you're trapped." He locked his arms around her back. "Now you're mine. All mine."

She bit lightly on his ear then caressed it with soft kisses, brushing her lips along the side of his face, trailing down to his neck and onto his chest. "You think you have me trapped," she said. "But I have ways of escaping." Amaya giggled as she tenderly took his nipple into her mouth, allowing her teeth to grab onto it and pull.

Jarred groaned, unlocking his arms from around her, giving her free access to his body.

Amaya looked up, glanced into his eyes, and smiled. "See? I'm free." She quickly took his other nipple into her mouth and bit down. She could feel him hard and raging between her legs, while she moved slowly, kissing and licking his chest, then onto his stomach, circling around his navel as she made her way down his body.

He placed his hands on top of her head, pushing her gently toward his engorged penis.

She obliged him by allowing him to move her head freely to the tip of his cock, and she took him fully into her mouth.

He sucked in a breath, heaving it out with a gasp and groan.

Amaya released him, pulling her head up and looking again into his eyes. "Everything all right?" She allowed a sly smile to settle on her face.

He didn't respond with words, instead pushed her head back onto him.

Amaya again took him fully into her mouth. Her tongue circled him, then licked up and down the shaft.

He arched his back, pushing deeper into her mouth, pulling her head down farther onto him. He could feel her lips brushing up against his pubic hairs, accompanied by a slight breeze that blew across his skin. He heard the rustling leaves on the branches above him. Jarred closed his eyes, giving himself over to the ecstasy.

Amaya's mouth pushed down on him, pausing, holding there. Then she drew herself up the hard shaft, then down again, and up, this time dragging her teeth slightly along Jarred's full length.

He was near to bursting, and heaved with shivers of pleasure.

Amaya pulled her head up, allowing him to slip completely out of her mouth. She looked up at him, wanting to meet his eyes.

He met her sexy gaze and groaned, "Don't stop."

She smiled at him, then again took him fully into her mouth.

He could not hold back any longer. Arching his back, he let go. Throbbing and pulsing, he poured into her. Chills cascaded up, then down his body.

He groaned long and low.

Then screamed.

Amaya bit down onto the bottom of his shaft clamping her teeth together as hard as she could, and like a dog on prey, shook her head from side to side, grinding her teeth, until she had bitten completely through the hard shaft.

Jarred tried to push her off as adrenaline and pain surged through his body, giving him momentary strength, that quickly began to fade as the blood loss from the wound, that was once his penis, drained him.

Amaya pulled her head up, and watched as he slowly faded from life. Blood seeped from her mouth, onto her breasts and down her flat stomach. She allowed a distorted smile to spread across her face. She had a glint in her eye... and Jarred's penis still clenched between her teeth.

No one knew where or when or how… it just happened. They Snapped. That's what people said. They Snapped. There wasn't any single sign, like you might expect there to be. No twitching or dying or convulsing. No outbreak of flu or some wide-spread contagious disease. Snap. They were human … and then … they were not.

"Duffin?" Correctional Officer, Sergeant Gordy Barajas shouted as he banged his fist on the green-gray metal door of the solitary confinement cell. "Duffin? Acknowledge."

"Where could I possibly be, you asshole?" The muffled voice of prisoner number 24601, Clyde Duffin, could be heard from the other side of the cell door.

"Coming in." Sergeant Barajas opened the viewing slot and peered in. "Stand at the head of the cell, Duffin." He watched as Clyde Duffin sat up from the bunk built into the wall of the cell, pulled his faded pink, standard-issue jumpsuit up and walked the few feet to the head of the cell. "Hope we didn't disturb anything?" Barajas laughed.

"Nope. Just rubbing one out. I got plenty of time to do that."

"That you do. Now turn around, hands on your head. Come on, you know the drill," Barajas shouted.

"That I do." Duffin turned, placed his hands on top of his head, spread his legs slightly apart, and waited.

The well-oiled door swung almost silently open. Barajas leaned into the microphone clipped to his shoulder epaulet and spoke, "Control. Barajas. Cell 1021 open. Awaiting backup."

"Roger that, Barajas. On the way," Control radioed back.

"What, the big bad officer can't come in on his own?" Duffin said, turning his head slightly. "Or aren't you rent-a-cops allowed to be brave?"

"Not happening. Not going to work." Barajas closed the cell door, relocking it.

"Almost had you didn't I? Officer?"

"Not nearly. Now shut the fuck up."

"Sure thing, Officer."

A moment later, three back-up officers arrived. The lead officer, Sipple, called out, "Barajas, your ass is now covered. Let's get this done. I've got dinner and a hot date waiting to cover my ass when I'm done." He laughed at his own pun.

"I'm sure you do." Barajas turned the key and again pulled open the cell door.

Duffin stood as he had before, hands on his head, feet spread apart. "Remain in the position."

The two other back-up officers moved around Sipple and Barajas, then moved into the cell. One took hold of Duffin's hands and quickly shackled them, while the other patted him down. "Clear." They stepped to the side and spun Duffin around.

"Come on, Duffin," Barajas said. "Let's move."

Duffin stood firm. Not speaking. Not moving. Not blinking.

"Duffin? You heard the sergeant. Get a move on it."

The prisoner did not move.

"Move it." One of the backup officers pulled on Duffin's arm. He was met with stiff, still resistance.

Then in a burst of rushed movement, the prisoner lurched toward the guard on his right, smashing a shoulder into the guard's chin. The guard fell back hitting his head on the steel rack bolted into the cement flooring of the cell. The guard to the left grabbed at Duffin's shackled arms, pulling him back. Duffin turned, teeth bared, aiming for the guard's jugular.

"Get out of there," Barajas screamed at the guards.

Recovering from the fall, the guard pulled himself up, wiped away the blood dripping down the side of his face, and, together with the other guard, pushed, pulled and shoved Duffin to the corner of the cell, detaining him barely long enough for them to be able to head for the cell door.

Barajas held the door open, just wide enough for the guards to pass through, then slammed it shut as Duffin rushed forward, jaws gaping open.

A thud and groan commingled with metal hitting metal as the lock on the door slid into place. Duffin's mouth hit the cold steel.

"What the fuck?" one of the guard's said as he inspected his arms and hands. "Did that fucker bite me? That fucker tried to bit me!" He turned around so the others could see. "What the fuck?"

Barajas grabbed the guard's arms and inspected them. "Don't see anything."

From inside the cell, a primeval, guttural sound emitted and echoed throughout the prison complex.

"What the fuck?" the guard repeated, turning to Barajas.

Barajas looked to Sipple, waited for a confirmation signal. It came in the form of a quick nod. Barajas nodded back, then popped open the tray slot in the cell door. He jumped back quickly, followed by the others. When the anticipated flinging of piss or spit didn't occur, he squatted down a safe distance from the cell door and peered in. He leaned to the left then to the right, attempting to get a good sight line into the cell. From his vantage point, he could only see Duffin's faint shadow on the cell's back wall.

Remaining in his crouched position, he moved a foot closer... then another, until he was just a few inches from the cell door. He glanced down, saw Duffin's legs, and followed them with his eyes up to the prone body of the prisoner. "What the fuck?" This time it was Barajas' turn to say it. He fell back. "What the fuck?" Then righted himself and looked back into the cell.

Duffin was on the floor, legs spread out before him, back resting against the steel cot that had once served as his bed. He looked up at Barajas, blood dripping from his mouth and from the bits of flesh that hung caught in his teeth. Duffin's lips were gone-- chewed off. A large section of his forearm and biceps on both arms had been ripped away as well. Barajas glanced at Duffin's hands. Most of his fingers had been eaten away. Duffin tried to lift an arm, but the missing muscle and tendons made it impossible for him to move them. In a convulsive movement, he fell to his side, his body slipped on the blood-covered floor. He flopped and wriggled, teeth clamping down on air in a vain attempt to reach his legs. His teeth clattered as he stretched to reach the flesh. He lurched, missed, but in the process his arm flopped nearer and he bit into the remaining flesh and muscle greedily, chewing the bits and pieces until only sinew and bone remained.

Barajas slammed the tray slot shut, then pushed himself back from the cell as far as he could, slamming into the opposite wall. The guards looked to Barajas who was now pale and sweating. His eyes were wide and held a vacant look of horror. The guards warily approached the door. Barajas thrust himself back at the cell, barring it from the men. "Don't," is all Barajas could manage before his stomach lurched up his remaining bits of breakfast.

People said that it was happening everywhere, and there was no telling when someone Snapped. At first there was only anecdotal evidence, no video or pictures, only eye-witness accounts. Not many believed them. Perhaps they didn't want to. Imagine if the person you were with suddenly--Snapped.

"This is freakin' awesome." Ed wrapped his arms around Lily, pulling her in closer to him, feeling her warmth.

She leaned back into him. "I understand why this used to be the honeymoon place to go back in the fifties." Lily said, allowing Ed to engulf her in his arms.

"My parents loved it here. Spent three days of their honeymoon here, and they only lived an hour-and-a-half away."

Lily turned around to face him. "And now it's our turn." She kissed him. "Very sweet of you to plan this for me."

"I thought you'd like it." He kissed her back. "Retracing my parents honeymoon and the years of "happily ever after" too, I hope."

"How did you know which motel they stayed in?"

Ed pulled a creased Polaroid picture out of his jacket pocket and showed it to Lily.

She took it from him, held it up and squinted with one eye closed. "Well, the sign is still there, faded a bit, but you can still see the wording: Seneca Motel and Motor Lodge Welcomes You to Niagara Falls, The Honeymoon Capital of the World," she read the faint words captured in the picture aloud.

"I promise that we'll do a real honeymoon as soon as we get settled and have some bucks coming in."

"I'm perfectly happy with this." She kissed Ed long and hard. "Come on, let's get better view of the falls."

Ed took the Polaroid from her and returned it to his pocket. "Let's start over there and then make our way around the entire American side. Then the Cave of the Winds… before it gets too dark. Tomorrow we can hit the Canadian side."

"Sounds like a plan." Lily took hold of his hand as they made their way across the street and headed toward the park and the falls.

"Awesome," Ed said, as he leaned over the slick, wet, metal guardrail, keeping him just a few feet from the raging current of the Niagara River. "The water looks so calm right here and the falls are not but twenty yards away."

"The current must be incredible."

"I couldn't imagine falling in and being so helpless, knowing those falls are just ahead."

"Can we change the subject and maybe talk about something else?" Lily took hold of his hand. "You're not being very romantic with talk about being swept over the falls."

Ed smiled. "I'm not?"

Lily kissed him on the cheek. "Uh, not really. No."

Ed returned the kiss, lightly brushing his lips against hers. "Is that better?" He didn't let her answer, kissing her again. He pulled her in close to him, wrapping his arms around her. He moved from her lips to her neck, kissing her as he moved. He caught her earlobe, first between his lips, then his teeth. He could hear her groan and he bit down harder. Then he slid slowly down the back of her neck to her shoulder then around to the front of her neck.

Lily arched her back, pushing into Ed and leaning her head back, giving him full access to her neck.

She shuddered as he used his teeth to scrape against the soft skin of her neck. He could feel the pulsing of her veins just below the surface. He kissed up and down her neck, then paused and sucked hard on the spot where her shoulder merged into her throat.

"Ed, no." She tried to push him away.

He resisted, sucking harder.

"You're going to leave a mark."

"I know," he said. "I want to."

Lily gave herself to him.

Ed felt her body relax, going limp in his arms. He dragged his teeth lightly across her skin. He opened his mouth and bit down hard, piercing her skin.

She screamed as she pushed at his head.

Too late.

Ed held fast and sank his teeth deeper into her neck. Her veins. And ripped. Blood spurted in a stream from the gaping wound in Lily's neck, puddling at the edge of the Niagara River before it dripped into the water and headed toward the falls.

Lily collapsed in Ed's arms.

He grabbed her, not letting her fall to the ground. Holding tightly on to Lily's limp body, he pulled himself up, with Lily clutched in his arms, and over the slick wet railing of the guardrail and into the deceivingly calm waters. Immediately, both he and Lily were carried downstream toward the falls by the raging undercurrent. Seconds later, he and Lily, locked in a fatal embrace, were swept over the falls, their bodies lost to the thundering cascade of white foaming water and the rocks below.

Then, video evidence began to show up. A closed-circuit security system in a prison captured some footage of a prisoner who Snapped, and a park surveillance camera at Niagara Falls showed what appeared to be a murder-suicide. It wasn't long after, that YouTube listings of reported cases caught on cell phone video began appearing in droves.

"This is ridiculous," Kaylin said, stomping her foot. "Let's just go, Mommy."

"You're being a brat, "Kaylin's mother said. "Two more people ahead of us, and we'll be out of here."

Kaylin looked up at her mother, eyes filling with tears. "But it's been so long already."

"Baby, I'm sorry. We're not getting out of the line, and I have to get these things so we'll have food to eat." She glanced back to the long line of people behind her. "Only two more, and then we'll be through the checkout and on our way home."

"Maybe I could have a snack?"

"Maybe you could." Kaylin's mother laughed. "Why don't you pick something out from the rack behind you, and then you can have it as soon as we get in the car."

"Okay." Kaylin turned to the rack of toys, gum, candy, magazines and other impulse products placed right before the checkout registers and began to peruse the items, slowly mulling over each one.

"Next in line, please," a cashier shouted to those waiting in the now rapidly growing line.

"See honey, just one more to go."

Kaylin picked up a candy bar, inspected it, then set it back on the rack and reached for another. "Mommy, we might need to let people go ahead of us."

"Oh no we won't. You need to hurry up and make a choice."

"Not the most proficient parenting I've ever witnessed." The statement was followed by an audible "tsk."

Kaylin's mother turned to face the curt-speaking blond woman standing behind her.

"Perhaps it's not my place, but bribing your child with sweets and toys is not the best way to prepare your little girl for the real world."

"I'm sorry…" She paused for a moment. "I didn't catch your name."

"Carolyn."

"How nice to meet you, Carolyn. I'm Maggie and this is my daughter, Kaylin."

"Hello," Kaylin said without turning away from the task at hand.

Maggie gently placed her hand on Kaylin's head in an unconscious move of parental protection. "Well, Carolyn, should you have any children …" She paused. "Do you have any children?"

"No. I don't."

"I thought not." Maggie tousled Kaylin's hair. "Well, should you ever, you'll be able to parent the way you'd like."

"Next in line, please," a cashier at the far end of the store checkouts shouted, as she waved a hand-held sign reading, "I'm ready to serve you."

"Come on, honey. Make your choice quickly. We're next."

Another audible "tsk" from Carolyn accompanied the mother and daughter as they hurried toward the check out.

"Next, please." The cashier's voice had a hint of pleasant impatience to it, and she held the sign higher.

"We're on our way." Maggie took Kaylin's hand and urged her forward.

With the shopping cart securely in the checkout lane, Maggie began to empty the contents onto the conveyor belt.

"Don't forget my lemon drops," Kaylin said, peering through the boxes and bags of groceries on the way to the cashier.

"Right here." Maggie held up the small bag of lemon drops.

A scream echoed around the big-box store.

Maggie turned, taking a quick look back at the waiting line of shoppers.

Another scream rang out, followed by a parting of the waiting crowd… like the waters of the Red Sea. Shoppers left their carts, dropping the handfuls of packages that had been bundled in arms. Bottles broke as they hit the tile floor of the store. Aisle end caps turned over, spilling the contents of boxes and jars to the already wet, slippery floor. People scattered in all directions… except a few.

A body lay prone on the cold tile, a stream of blood gurgled out of the jugular vein like the water from a drinking fountain, first strong, then in an arch, then subsiding, followed by a strong steam again. Each heartbeat pumped more blood into the gaping wound and out of the woman's body.

Maggie noticed at once that it was Carolyn. Her instincts were to go to the woman, whom she had just met, and help, but the cry of Kaylin brought her back.

The cashiers, and those not immediately in line, stood nearly frozen watching a spectral hand. A man dressed in army fatigues and tan T-shirt, clung to the back of another man, his arms wrapped around the man in a bear hug. He was biting into the man's shoulders and the back of his neck.

The man screamed while backing up into a shelf in a vain attempt to dislodge the fatigue-wearing grunt. The shelf crashed to the floor, sending bags of tortilla chips and bottles of con queso to the floor. The man slipped in the mixture of bags, chips and cheese sauce and took a hard fall to the floor.

The army grunt stood and turned.

Maggie stared at the man. The thought that he was very attractive, with broad shoulders, well-muscled arms and chest, struck her as an odd and disturbing as she took in the site of blood dripping from his mouth.

The grunt turned again and set off after an elderly woman a few feet away.

The woman raised her hands in a protective posture, but was quickly overwhelmed by the grunt. Her screams were muffled by his own as he tore her lips from her mouth with his teeth, spit them out, then sunk his teeth into the old thin flesh of her face easily ripping it from the muscle underneath.

The grunt left the woman and took off for the back of the store. Screams came from all directions, screams of fear and terror mixed with those of pain and death, as the grunt ran by some and attacked others in a random game of tag.

Maggie grabbed Kaylin swinging her up into her arms and dashed for the doors.

"My candy, Mommy. My candy," Kaylin whined.

Before Maggie could make it through the doors, a woman

fleeing a goth-dressed teenage boy, smashed into Maggie, slamming her into the wall.

The goth-boy chased after the other woman tackling her and immediately began to bite into her arms and legs. Her screams were muffled by the mouth of the attacker as he went after her face.

Maggie watched, frozen in fear as the goth-boy was then attacked by a well-dressed, suit-wearing man. The goth and suit growled while they rolled about the floor of the store, ripping flesh and muscle from each other and themselves, like sharks in a feeding frenzy.

Maggie pulled on Kaylin, sliding her across the floor and into a small office. She slammed the door shut, locked it, pushed a small chair in front of it, and leaned back against the wall as the adrenalin-fueled panic subsided.

"Mommy, my candy," Kaylin said, sniffling.

"Yes, honey, we'll have to..." Maggie's words were cut short, replaced instead with a scream, as she looked at her little girl.

Kaylin Snapped.

Then it was everywhere. Every state, city, town and village in the U.S. was reporting incidence of people Snapping. News crews were out in force to capture the processes in action. Vigilante groups roamed the streets, shooting people randomly who appeared to them to be on the brink of Snapping. Chaos ruled for weeks, decimating populations and communities, families and friends clung together, but were never fully trusting. Churches filled with believers and nonbelievers. Parishioners refused to leave the perceived safety of the church sanctuary and set up communal communities within the walls of the church. Still others turned against those that they knew and once loved, now fearing them instead.

There was no law.

No order.

No trust.

And then, as quickly as it had appeared... it vanished. The spell, the curse, the act of nature, the wrath of God--stopped. No one Snapped for a day... then a few days... a week... and more.

It was as it was in the beginning... and yet everything had changed.

Where Billy Monasco Lay

Paul Mannering

We were on the north bank of the Rio Penasco, about a hundred miles up from the New Mexico-Mexican border, when Billy Monasco came back. I'd been out gathering some wood for the fire, nights get cold out here in the desert and I figured we were far enough ahead of pursuit that keeping warm wouldn't get us killed. The horses were huddled together on their line, cropping the bit of grass they could reach.

Tabasco Pete squatted next to the fire, burning beans and the last of our salt beef. Squatting there like a toad with a hairy ass he let out a thunderous fart that rolled across the desert.

"Yer gonna fart in the fire one of these days Pete, fart and blow yourself to Kingdom Come!" I dropped the load of firewood and helped myself to the coffee. Thick as tar and bitter as the pretty girl I left in Tuscon. I prefer it with sugar myself, but I ain't seen sugar in a long while. The girl in Tuscon promised me plenty of sugar, but she wanted to be married first.

Pete slopped beans into a plate and sat himself down with a contented sigh. "Get yerself a plate full boss, ain't nothing to be done till mornin'."

We ate beans, Pete grunting like a pig, me eatin' with a spoon and one eye and one ear open to any change in the night around us.

"Grady'll be coming," I said to Pete, though I may have been speaking to myself for all the intelligent conversation I got in reply.

"They gurn be right along," Pete said, nodding and spitting beans and gravy down his chin.

"If he met up with Sam like he was told, then we'll be right to lit out for Mexico," I stirred the beans in my plate. The Albuquerque job shoulda been simple. The plan was good, we rob the bank and we ride like hell for Mexico. No one gets hurt, no one got dragged out of there as a shield when the goddamn sheriff and a bunch of deputies turn up and start shooting. Yeah a real simple plan, and it all turned to buffalo chips. I used the saddle bags as a pillow. My count came to eight thousand dollars in paper and silver, it weren't soft to rest my head on, but I slept okay and dreamed of the sweet life south of the border.

Billy Monasco turned up in my dreams, walking through the shallows of the Penasco River and raising his hands to wave hello. He had red hands, dripping with blood. I tried to tell him how sorry I was but my tongue wouldn't move. When I woke up I knowed I'm not sorry at all.

There's no reason in Hell that boy's death was my fault. We didn't start shooting. We just took the lead they threw at us and sent it back.

The gun smoke blew out thick and white that day, the stink of it seared my nose. Smoke got so thick we couldn't see. We could hear plenty though. Could hear the screams of the dying and the roar of the posse's guns.

We'd ducked under the window sills, reloading and coming up again to shoot some more. Two deputies went down, and we made a break for it, running through a thunderstorm of bullets to get to the horses.

Brown didn't make it, they had a shooter on the roof of the General Store across the way, one shot and Bad Boy Brown's bearded head came apart like a crushed tomato. 'Fore I ran outta the bank, I'd grabbed the nearest warm body, a skinny lad of teenage years. With him in front of me I lead the charge out to the horses. Screaming the whole time that he would die and his blood would be on the bastard sheriff's hands if they squeezed off another round.

We got out of there, me, Tabasco Pete, Skinny Grady, and Willy's boy Sam. I sent Grady and Sam south and west, told them to ride for a day and then swing round and meet us. Me and Pete we road south and east. We had the spot marked out on the river. Three days, if you ain't there in three days, then you lose your share and we go to Mexico without you.

I woke up shivering, the stars above glittering like ice, memories of the bank robbery echoing like the screams of the folk we left inside.

I needed a piss like I needed to breathe. Tossing my blanket aside I stood up and did a quick shuffle to the edge of camp. Pete snored in his bedroll as I stood there pissing my soul out and breathing fog into the cold night. The crack of two rocks knocking together had me reaching for my gun belt. I'd left it in my blanket. Buttoning up I scampered back and snatched my 45 from its holster. The fire'd died down, only a few red embers remained.

I listened to the night, the owls, and the wind in the bushes. Then I heard it, a splashing sound, and then a foot sliding off a rock and hitting the water. Keeping my back to the fire I moved around to the river side of our camp. Crouching low I crept forward, gun steady, ready to plug the first son of a bitch that showed his face.

The moon was a crescent slice in the sky, only a little light shining down on the water, but it was enough to let me see.

Billy Monasco stood there staring south across the river, the water flowing over his boots, washing the mud from his trousers. I didn't recognize him, even when he turned round I thought it had to be some farm boy out shootin' for supper or maybe runnin' away from home. Billy started walking towards me, one casual step at a time, like he was asleep, or'd been drinking corn liquor. His eyes on the silted water flowing over his boots.

I stood up, pulling the hammer back on my Colt.

"Hey there," I said softly. The boy looked up and I nearly shit. Billy Monasco, he'd died right here on the sand and we'd buried him. Now he was standing in front of me, stained in blood and mud and looking sour. "Billy?"

We'd ridden hard out of Albuquerque, bullets zipping past our ears like angry bees. Pete had a hand on his hat and was leaning over his chestnut mare whooping and hollering. You'd think he was in a horse race at a county fair. I had Billy Monasco in front of me, one arm wrapped around him and holding the reins. The other hand held my Colt up to Billy's chin. We ran like rabbits and we got away free. Or so I thought.

By the third night the horses near quit under us, at least Billy had quit crying and moaning. We slept cold under the stars and Pete took first watch. I heard the shot, and thought the sheriff's posse had found us. I sprang up, Billy had Pete's gun and his shot had gone wide, putting a hole in the fat bastard's hat.

"Stay back!" Billy yelled, waving Pete's gun around like he was trying to shake a booger off his finger.

"Easy boy. Just calm down. Ain't no reason to get riled up," I'd slept with my gun belt on, though my iron still lay snug in its boot.

"Yeh, just lay the gun down boy, we'll let you go," Pete sounded even less trustworthy when he tried to be sincere.

"Stay back!" Billy hollered again and now he started crying like the girl back in Tuscon did when I slapped her till her thighs opened.

Pete's gun fired again, Billy was shaking so hard the second shot missed Pete and almost laid me out.

"Goddamnit!" I drew and fired. My shot hit the kid in gut. He coughed, the gun tilting towards the sand. "Momma…" he said and slowly toppled forward. Me and Pete watched him die, his blood soaking into the desert sand as we listened to his moaning cries for his momma. Before dawn we buried him, digging into the soft, wet river sand with sticks and our hands. We dropped the dead boy in a wet hole about three feet deep and covered him up.

Now the dead boy stood before me, face pale as milk and eyes as dark as the river stones. "Billy?" I said. He didn't respond with words, he raised his hand and pointed at me. I knew I was being marked by God. *You see Lord,* Billy was saying with that white finger. *You see this no-good murdering dog, you mark him Lord. You mark him in your ledger for Hell.*

I shot Billy again, this time through the eye. The shot punched out the back of his head. He staggered and fell, toppling over with a splash into the river. From the camp behind me I heard Pete give a snort and stumble awake.

Holstering my pistol I dragged Billy out of the water by his boots. He was dead now, that was for sure. Pete arrived and I laughed then made some joke about how you can't keep a good man down. We took an ankle each and dragged the boy back to his grave. Scooping out the mud and sand we laid him in it again.

"Rest in peace," I said.

Pete built up the fire and made fresh coffee. The sun was coming up when we heard the sound of hoof beats. Guns ready we waited to see who would come through the brush.

Grady and Sam came in to view. They were sharing a horse and Grady's arm lay in a blood stained sling. He looked half dead and Sam held him upright in the saddle.

"Howdy boys!" I stood up grinning.

"Mornin' boss," Sam touched his hat brim.

"You look beat, Grady. Coffee's hot," I indicated the fire. Sam and Pete got Grady off the horse then they laid him down on Pete's bedroll.

"Now, how about you tell me what the Hell happened?" I asked Sam.

"We lit out and I rode a day like you said. Then I went looking for Grady. I found him, his horse had tripped, busted its leg in some damn hole. Grady's arm took the worst of the fall. Bone's sticking out of it." Sam spat in the dust.

"Pete," I called. "How's Grady doin'? " Pete came over and rubbed his hairy jaw.

"He's got a fever and the wound smells bad. He's gonna die," he said.

"Want me to shoot him boss?" Sam's hand dropped to his pistol.

"Nah, we'll give him till tomorrow. If Grady comes through, then we take him with us. If he dies, then we split his share."

"How much did we get?" Sam asked.

"Around eight thousand," I said. Sam and Pete both grinned.

"Goddamn! I say goddamn!" Sam swept his hat off and beat the dust out of it on his thigh. "How much is that each?" he said, his eyes shining.

"It's two thousand each for you and Pete," I said.

"Goddamn! I say goddamn!" Sam didn't have a lot else to say. Pete's eyes narrowed, but he didn't say nothin'

I spent the day catching up on my sleep, dreaming of Billy Monasco and the rest of them in the Albuquerque bank. The screams and the smoke.

Sitting up I scratched the sand from my neck and the memories from my eyes. Drinking coffee I watched the sunset, my eyes drawn to the mound in the river beach where Billy Monasco lay buried.

"Grady's dyin'," Pete spoke up from behind me.

"It happens," I said.

"Want us to put him down?" Pete asked.

"Make it quick and easy. Grady was a good man," I said. I kept watching the river and that mound in the mud until a shot rang out from the camp.

Sam came running over, "Pete shot Grady, right in the damn

head!" he squawked.

"On my orders," I said. Yesterday Sam'd been offering to end Grady himself, now he was having a tizzy about it.

"Goddamn…" Sam whispered.

"You knew he was dyin'," I said. "Easier this way."

Sam just pointed; the grave of Billy Monasco was opening. A pale white hand pushed out of the mud and after a moment the soft earth split open and the rest of him birthed out of the ground.

"Goddamn…" Sam whispered again, his voice hoarse with shock.

"Fuck it," I swore. I drew my pistol and shot at the crawling boy. The first bullet splattered the mud. The second shot hit him in the shoulder. Bill Monasco clawed his way to his feet. "You're dead goddamnit!" I shouted at him and fired again. This bullet Billy in the chest. He didn't bleed and he didn't stop neither.

I heard Sam laughing, a high pitched whining sound, as if the humor was squeezing its way out of a throat choked in terror.

"Sam, put that fucker down," I ordered and opened my pistol to reload. Sam walked past me, shooting with each step. Billy kept coming at us with his slow shuffling steps. He came right up to Sam and put his hands around the man's neck. I would have fired again, except bullets weren't working and Sam was in the way.

Billy's fingers dug into the soft, warm flesh of Sam's throat and he started choking and gurgling. Blood began to gush as the dead boy ripped Sam's throat out. I turned around and walked back to camp. Some things no man should witness.

"Where's Sam? What'n Hell were you all shootin' at?" Pete said looking up from the pan of beans he stirred over the fire.

"He's dead," I said. Sitting down and staring into the flames I opened my Colt and emptied out the cartridges.

"The Hell you say?" Pete asked.

Slotting each bullet back into my gun belt I holstered my pistol.

"We done wrong Pete. We done real wrong." I could hear the screams of the people in the bank echoing in the flames of the fire. The flames of the bank burnin'. The sound of their prayers. Beggin' God for mercy and an end to their sufferin'. The heat of the fire forced us out of the bank, under cover of the smoke, with Billy Monasco shielding me from the sheriff's bullets. We left his ma and his pa burning. We left all the folks doin' their business to die in the flames. Locked behind the steel gate of the bank vault.

"Who in the Hell is that?" Pete rose to his feet. I didn't look. Billy was on God's business, lookin' him in the eye wouldn't change a damn thing.

I heard Pete yellin', his gun fired, again and again. I heard each shot hit. I heard Pete swearing, callin' out to God and then I heard him dyin' with the steady click, click, click of the hammer dropping on empty cylinders.

Billy's hand fell on my shoulder. I twisted away, not ready to die without facing him. Standin' up I backed around the fire. The dead boy swayed slightly, congealed blood and gore dripping off his face. Bits of Sam and Pete were smeared over his hands and teeth like raw gravy. His dead hand pointed at me. I stared at him, slowly unbucklin' my gun belt and letting it drop. My killin' days were done.

I bolted for the horses. One was dead, the other two had run off, maybe it was them I heard screamin' and not Pete. I headed towards the river, runnin' now, my spurs jinglin' as I jumped over rocks and bushes. Splashin' into the water I waded out into the current. I didn't look back, I knew Billy Monasco would be followin' me. I could bury him every dawn and every night he would come back. The river took me, pushin' me off my feet and forcin' me to swim. I made it to the other side.

I'd left the saddle-bags of money, the last of our food, and my gun. Ahead of me was a hundred miles of desert and sage brush. Somewhere out there was Mexico, if I ran far enough maybe God would lose interest.

I'm tellin' this to a priest, a Father Pedro in a one burro town called San Miguel. He's writin' it down. My confession, it ain't gonna be enough. I can hear the slow shuffling steps of Billy Monasco coming up the aisle of the church. I'm too tired to run anymore. The priest is prayin', cleansin' me of my sins. There's no way he can know there'll be no forgiveness for me.

Not till Gabriel blows his trumpet.

The Barrens

F. Paul Wilson

1.
In Search of a Devil

I shot my answering machine today. Took out the old twelve gauge my father left me, and blew it to pieces. A silly, futile gesture, I know, but it illustrates my present state of mind, I think.

And it felt good. If not for an answering machine, my life would be completely different now. I would have missed Jonathan Creighton's call. I'd be less wise but far, far happier. And I'd still have some semblance of order and meaning in my life.

He left an innocent enough message:

"'The office of Kathleen McKelston and Associates!' Sounds like Big Business! How's it going, Mac? This is Jon Creighton calling. I'm going to be in the area later this week and I'd like to see you. Lunch or dinner – whatever's better. Give me a buzz." And he left a number with a 212 area code.

So simple, so forthright, giving no hint of where it would lead.

You work your way through life day by day, learning how to play the game, carving out your niche, making a place for yourself. You have some good luck, some bad luck, sometimes you make your own luck, and along the way you begin to think that you've figured out some of the answers – not all of them, of course, but enough to make you feel that you've learned something, that you've got a handle on life and just might be able to get a decent ride out of it. You start to think you're in control. Then along comes someone like Jonathan Creighton and he smashes everything. Not just your plans, your hopes, your dreams, but *everything*, up to and including your sense of what is real and what is not.

I'd heard nothing from or about him since college, and had thought of him only occasionally until that day in early August when he called my office. Intrigued, I returned his call and set a date for lunch.

That was my first mistake. If I'd had the slightest inkling of where that simple lunch with an old college lover would lead, I'd have slammed down the phone and fled to Europe, or the Orient, anywhere where Jonathan Creighton wasn't.

We'd met at a freshmen mixer at Rutgers University. Maybe we each picked up subliminal cues – we called them "vibes" in those days – that told us we shared a rural upbringing. We didn't dress like it, act like it, or feel like it, but we were a couple of Jersey hicks. I came from the Pemberton area, Jon came from another rural zone, but in North Jersey, near a place called Gilead. Despite that link, we were polar opposites in most other ways. I'm still amazed we hit it off. I was career oriented while Jon was…well, he was a flake. He earned the name Crazy Creighton and he lived up to it every day. He never stayed with one thing long enough to allow anyone to pin him down. Always on to the Next New Thing before the crowd had tuned into it, *always* into the exotic and esoteric. Looking for the Truth, he'd say.

And as so often happens with people who are incompatible in so many ways, we found each other irresistible and fell madly in love.

Sophomore year we found an apartment off campus and moved in together. It was my first affair, and not at all a tranquil one. I read the strange books he'd find and I kept up with his strange hours, but I put my foot down when it came to the Pickman prints. There was something deeply disturbing about those paintings that went beyond their gruesome subject matter. Jon didn't fight me on it. He just smiled sadly in his condescending way, as if disappointed that I had missed the point, and rolled them up and put them away.

The thing that kept us together – at least for the year we were together – was our devotion to personal autonomy. We spent weeks of nights talking about how we had to take complete control of our own lives, and brainstorming how we were going to go about it. It seems so silly now, but that was the Sixties, and we really discussed those sorts of things back then.

We lasted sophomore year and then we fell apart. It might

have gone on longer if Creighton hadn't got in with the druggies. That was the path toward loss of *all* autonomy as far as I was concerned, but Creighton said you can't be free until you know what's real. And if drugs might reveal the Truth, he had to try them. Which was hippie bullshit as far as I was concerned. After that, we rarely ran into each other. He wound up living alone off campus in his senior year. Somehow he managed to graduate, with a degree in anthropology, and that was the last I'd heard of him.

But that doesn't mean he hadn't left his mark.

I suppose I'm what you might call a feminist. I don't belong to NOW and I don't march in the streets, but I don't let anyone leave footprints on my back simply because I'm a woman. I believe in myself and I guess I owe some of that to Jonanthan Creighton. He always treated me as an equal. He never made an issue of it – it was simply implicit in his attitude that I was intelligent, competent, worthy of respect, able to stand on my own. It helped shape me. And I'll always revere him for that.

Lunch. I chose Rosario's on the Point Pleasant Beach side of the Manasquan Inlet, not so much for its food as for the view. Creighton was late and that didn't terribly surprise me. I didn't mind. I sipped a Chablis spritzer and watched the party boats roll in from their half-day runs of bottom fishing. Then a voice with echoes of familiarity broke through my thoughts.

"Well, Mac, I see you haven't changed much."

I turned and was shocked at what I saw. I barely recognized Creighton. He'd always been thin to the point of emaciation. Could the plump, bearded, almost cherubic figure standing before me now be–?

"Jon? Is that you?"

"The one and only," he said and spread his arms.

We embraced briefly, then took our seats in a booth by the window. As he squeezed into the far side of the table, he called the waitress over and pointed to my glass.

"Two Lites for me and another of those for her."

At first glance I'd thought that Creighton's extra poundage made him look healthy for the first time in his life. His hair was still thick and dark brown, but despite his round, rosy cheeks, his eyes were sunken and too bright. He seemed jovial but I sensed a grim undertone. I wondered if he was still into drugs.

"Almost a quarter century since we were together," he said. "Hard to believe it's been that long. The years look as if they've been kind to you."

As far as looks go, I suppose that's true. I don't dye my hair, so there's a little gray tucked in with the red. But I've always had a young face. I don't wear make-p – with my high coloring and freckles, I don't need it.

"And you."

Which wasn't actually true. His open shirt collar was frayed and looked as if this might be the third time he'd worn it since it was last washed. His tweed sport coat was worn at the elbows and a good two sizes too small for him.

We spent the drinks, appetizers, and most of the entrees catching up on each other's lives. I told him about my small accounting firm, my marriage, my recent divorce.

"No children?"

I shook my head. The marriage had gone sour, the divorce had been a nightmare. I wanted off the subject.

"But enough about me," I said. "What have you been up to?"

"Would you believe clinical psychology?"

"No," I said, too shocked to lie. "I wouldn't"

The Jonathan Creighton I'd known had been so eccentric, so out of step, so self-absorbed, I couldn't imagine him as a psychotherapist. Jonathan Creighton helping other people get their lives together – it was almost laughable.

He was the one laughing, however – good-naturedly, too.

"Yeah. It *is* hard to believe, but I went on to get a masters, and then a Ph.D. Actually went into practice."

His voice trailed off.

"You're using the past tense," I said.

"Right. It didn't work out. The practice never got off the ground. But the problem was really within myself. I was using a form of reality therapy but it never worked as it should. And finally I realized why: I don't know – really *know* – what reality is. Nobody does."

This had an all-too-familiar ring to it. I tried to lighten things up before they got too heavy.

"Didn't someone once say that reality is what trips you up whenever you walk around with your eyes closed?"

Creighton's smile showed a touch of the old condescension that so infuriated some people.

"Yes, I suppose someone would say something like that. Anyway, I decided to go off and see if I could find out what reality really was. Did a lot of traveling. Wound up in a place called Miskatonic University. Ever heard of it?"

"In Massachusetts, isn't it?"

"That's the one. In a small town called Arkham. I hooked up with the anthropology department there – that was my undergraduate major, after all. But now I've left academe to write a book."

"A book?"

This was beginning to sound like a pretty disjointed life. But that shouldn't have surprised me.

"What a deal!" he said, his eyes sparkling. "I've got grants from Rutgers, Princeton, the American Folklore Society, the New Jersey Historical Society, and half a dozen others, just to write a book!"

"What's it about?"

"The origins of folk tales. I'm going to select a few and trace them back to their roots. That's where you come in."

"Oh?"

"I'm going to devote a significant chapter to the Jersey Devil."

"There've been whole books written about the Jersey Devil. Why don't you–"

"I want real sources for this, Mac. Primary all the way. Nothing second-hand. This is going to be definitive."

"What can I do for you?"

"You're a Piney, aren't you?"

Resentment flashed through me. Even though people nowadays described themselves as "Piney" with a certain amount of pride, and I'd even seen bumper stickers touting "Piney Power," some of us still couldn't help bristling when an outsider said it. When I was a kid it was always used as a pejorative. Like "clam digger" here on the coast. Fighting words. Officially it referred to the multigenerational natives of the great Pine Barrens that ran south from Route 70 all the way down to the lower end of the state. I've always hated the term. To me it was the equivalent of calling someone a redneck.

Which, to be honest, wasn't so far from the truth. The true Pineys are poor rural folk, often working truck farms and doing menial labor in the berry fields and cranberry bogs – a lot of them do indeed have red necks. Many are uneducated, or at best undereducated. Those who can afford wheels drive the prototypical battered pick-up with the gun rack in the rear window. They even speak with an accent that sounds southern. They're Jersey hillbillies. Country bumpkins in the very heart of the industrial Northeast. Anachronisms.

Pineys.

"Who told you that?" I said as levelly as I could.

"You did. Back in school."

"Did I?"

It shook me to see how far I'd traveled from my roots. As a scared, naive, self-deprecating frosh at Rutgers I probably had indeed referred to myself as a Piney. Now I never mentioned the word, not in reference to myself or anyone else. I was a college educated woman; I was a respected professional who spoke with a colorless northeast accent. No one in his right mind would consider me a Piney.

"Well, that was just a gag," I said. "My family roots are back in the Pine Barrens, but I am by no stretch of the imagination a Piney. So I doubt I can help you."

"Oh, but you can! The McKelston name is big in the Barrens. Everybody knows it. You've got plenty of relatives there."

"Really? How do you know?"

Suddenly he looked sheepish.

"Because I've been into the Barrens a few times now. No one will open up to me. I'm an outsider. They don't trust me. Instead of answering my questions, they play games with me. They say they don't know what I'm talking about but they know someone who might, then they send me driving in circles. I was lost out there for two solid days last month. And believe me, I was getting scared. I thought I'd never find my way out."

"You wouldn't be the first. Plenty of people, many of them experienced hunters, have gone into the Barrens and never been seen again. You'd better stay out."

His hand darted across the table and clutched mine.

"You've got to help me, Kathy. My whole future hinges on

this."

I was shocked. He'd always called me "Mac." Even in bed back in our college days he'd never called me "Kathy." Gently, I pulled my hand free, saying.

"Come on, Jon—"

He leaned back and stared out the window at the circling gulls.

"If I do this right, do something really definitive, it may get me back into Miskatonic where I can finish my doctoral thesis."

I was immediately suspicious.

"I thought you said you 'left' Miskatonic, Jon. Why can't you get back in without it?"

"'Irregularities,'" he said, still not looking at me. "The old farts in the antiquities department didn't like where my research was leading me."

"This 'reality' business?"

"Yes."

"They told you that?"

Now he looked at me.

"Not in so many words, but I could tell." He leaned forward. His eyes were brighter than ever. "They've got books and manuscripts locked in huge safes there, one-of-a-kind volumes from times most scholars think of as pre-history. I managed to get a pass, a forgery that got me into the vaults. It's incredible what they have there, Mac. *Incredible!* I've got to get back there. Will you help me?"

His intensity was startling. And tantalizing.

"What would I have to do?"

"Just accompany me into the Pine Barrens. Just for a few trips. If I can use you as a reference, I know they'll talk to me about the Jersey Devil. After that, I can take it on my own. All I need is some straight answers from these people and I'll have my primary sources. I may be able to track a folk myth to its very roots! I'll give you credit in the book, I'll pay you, anything, Mac, just don't leave we twisting in the wind!"

He was positively frantic by the time he finished speaking.

"Easy, Jon. Easy. Let me think."

Tax season was over and I had a loose schedule for the summer. And even if I was looking ahead to a tight schedule, so what? Frankly, the job wasn't anywhere near as satisfying as it once had been. The challenge of overcoming the business community's prejudice and doubts about a woman accountant, the thrill of building a string of clients, that was all over. Everything was mostly routine now. Plus, I no longer had a husband. No children to usher toward adulthood. I had to admit that my life was pretty empty at that moment. And so was I. Why not take a little time to inspect my roots and help Crazy Creighton put his life on track, if such a thing was possible? In the bargain maybe I could gain a little perspective on my own life.

"All right, Jon," I said. "I'll do it."

Creighton's eyes lit with true pleasure, a glow distinct from the feverish intensity since he'd sat down. He thrust both his hands toward me.

"I could kiss you, Mac! I can't tell you how much this means to me! You have no idea how important this is!"

He was right about that. No idea at all.

2.

The Pine Barrens

Two days later we were ready to make our first foray into the woods.

Creighton was wearing a safari jacket when he picked me up in a slightly battered four-wheel drive Jeep Wrangler.

"This isn't Africa we're headed for," I told him.

"I know. I like the pockets. They hold all sorts of things."

I glanced in the rear compartment. He was surprisingly well equipped. I noticed a water cooler, a food chest, back packs, and what looked like sleeping bags. I hoped he wasn't harboring any romantic ideas. I'd just split from one man and I wasn't looking for another, especially not Jonathan Creighton.

"I promised to help you look around. I didn't say anything about camping out."

He laughed. "I'm with you. Holiday Inn is my idea of roughing it. I was never a Boy Scout, but I do believe in being prepared. I've already been lost once in there."

"And we can do without that happening again. Got a compass?"

He nodded. "And maps. Even have a sextant."

"You actually know how to use one?"

"I learned."

I dimly remember being bothered then by his having a

sextant, and not being quite sure why. Before I could say anything else, he tossed me the keys.

"You're the Piney. You drive."

"Still Mr. Macho, I see."

He laughed. I drove.

It's easy to get into the Pine Barrens from northern Ocean County. You just get on Route 70 and head west. About half way between the Atlantic Ocean and Philadelphia, say, near a place known as Ongs Hat, you turn left. And wave bye-bye to the Twentieth Century, and civilization as you know it.

How do I describe the Pine Barrens to someone who's never been through them? First of all, it's big. You have to fly over it in a small plane to appreciate just how big. It runs through seven counties, takes up one fourth of the state, but since Jersey's not a big state, that doesn't tell the story. How does 2,000 square miles sound? Or a million acres? Almost the size of Yosemite National Park. Does that give you an idea of its vastness?

How do I describe what a wilderness this is? Maps will give you a clue. Look at a road map of New Jersey. If you don't happen to have one handy, imagine an oblong platter of spaghetti; now imagine what it looks like after someone's devoured most of the spaghetti out of the middle of the lower half, leaving only a few strands crossing the exposed plate. Same thing with a population density map – a big gaping hole in the southern half where the Pine Barrens sits. New Jersey is the most densely populated state in the U.S., averaging a thousand bodies per square mile. But the New York City suburbs in north Jersey teem with forty thousand per square mile. After you account for the crowds along the coast and in the cities and towns along the western interstate corridor, there aren't too many people left over when you get to the Pine Barrens. I've heard of an area of over a hundred thousand acres – that's in the neighborhood of 160 square miles – in the south-central Barrens with twenty-one known inhabitants. *Twenty-one.* One human being per eight square miles in an area that lies on the route between Boston, New York, Philadelphia, Baltimore, and D.C.

Even when you take a turn off one of the state or federal roads that cut through the Barrens, you feel the isolation almost immediately. The forty-foot scrub pines close in behind you and quietly but oh so effectively cut you off from the rest of the world.

I'll bet there are people who've lived to ripe old ages in the Barrens who have never seen a paved road. Conversely, there are no complete topographical maps of the Barrens because there are vast areas that no human eyes have ever seen.

Are you getting the picture?

"Where do we start?" Creighton asked as we crawled past the retirement villages along Route 70. This had been an empty stretch of road when I was a kid. Now it was Wrinkle City.

"We start at the capitol."

"Trenton? I don't want to go to Trenton."

"Not the state capital. The capital of the pines. Used to be called Shamong Station. Now it's known as Chatsworth."

He pulled out his map and squinted through the index.

"Oh, right. I see it. Right smack in the middle of the Barrens. How big is it?"

"A veritable Piney megalopolis, my friend. Three hundred souls."

Creighton smiled, and for a second or two he seemed almost...innocent.

"Think we can get there before rush hour?"

3.
Jasper Mulliner

I stuck to the main roads, taking 70 to 72 to 563, and we were there in no time.

"You'll see something here you won't see in anyplace else in the Barrens," I said as I drove down Chatsworth's main street.

"Electricity?" Creighton said.

He didn't look up from the clutter of maps on his lap. He'd been following our progress on paper, mile by mile.

"No. Lawns. Years ago a number of families decided they wanted grass in their front yards. There's no topsoil to speak of out here; the ground's mostly sand. So they trucked in loads of topsoil and seeded themselves some lawns. Now they've got to cut them."

I drove past the general store and its three gas pumps out on the sidewalk.

"*Esso,*" Creighton said, staring at the sign over the pumps. "That says it all, doesn't it."

"That it do."

We continued on until we came to a sandy lot occupied by a single trailer. No lawn here.

"Who's this?" Creighton said, folding up his maps as I hopped out of the wrangler.

"An old friend of the family."

This was Jasper Mulliner's place. He was some sort of an uncle – on my mother's side, I think. But distant blood relationships are nothing special in the Barrens. An awful lot of people are related in one way or another. Some said he was a descendant of the notorious bandit of the pines, Joseph Mulliner. Jasper had never confirmed that, but he'd never denied it, either.

I knocked on the door, wondering who would answer. I wasn't even sure Jasper was still alive. But when the door opened, I immediately recognized the grizzled old head that poked through the opening.

"You're not sellin' anything, are you?" he said.

"Nothing, Mr. Mulliner," I said. "I'm Kathleen McKelston. I don't know if you remember me, but–"

His eyes lit as his face broke into a toothless grin.

"Danny's girl? The one who got the college scholarship? Sure I remember you! Come on in!"

Jasper was wearing khaki shorts, a sleeveless orange tee shirt, and duck boots – no socks. His white hair was neatly combed and he was freshly shaved. He'd been a salt hay farmer in his younger days and his hands were still callused from it. He'd moved on to overseeing a cranberry bog in his later years. His skin was a weathered brown and looked tougher than saddle leather. The inside of the trailer reminded me more of a low ceilinged freight car than a home, but it was clean. The presence of the television set told me he had electricity but I saw no phone sign or running water.

I introduced him to Creighton and we settled onto a three-legged stool and a pair of ladderback chairs as I spent the better part of half an hour telling him about my life since leaving the Barrens and answering questions about my mother and how she was doing since my father died. Then he went into a soliloquy about what a great man my father was. I let him run on, pretending to be listening, but turning my mind to other things. Not because I disagreed with him, but because it had been barely a year since Dad had dropped dead and I was still hurting.

Dad had not been your typical Piney. Although he loved the Barrens as much as anyone else who grew up here, he'd known there was a bigger though not necessarily better life beyond them. That bigger world didn't interest him in the least, but just because he was content with where he was didn't mean that I'd be. He wanted to allow his only child a choice. He knew I'd need a decent education if that choice was to be meaningful. And to provide that education for me, he did what few Pineys like to do: he took a steady job.

That's not to say that Pineys are afraid of hard work. Far from it. They'll break their backs at any job they're doing. It's simply that they don't like to be tied down to the same job day after day, month after month. Most of them have grown up flowing with the cycle of the Barrens. Spring is for gathering sphagnum moss to sell to the florists and nurseries. In June and July they work the blueberry and huckleberry fields. In the fall they move into the bogs for the cranberry harvest. And in the cold of winter they cut cordwood, or cut holly and mistletoe, or go "pineballing"–collecting pine cones to sell. None of this is easy work. But it's not the same work. And that's what matters.

The Piney attitude toward jobs is the most laid back you'll ever encounter. That's because they're in such close harmony with their surroundings. They know that with all the pure water all around them and flowing beneath their feet, they'll never go thirsty. With all the wild vegetation around them, they'll never lack for fruit and vegetables. And whenever the meat supply gets low, they pick up a rifle and head into the brush for squirrel, rabbit, or venison, whatever the season.

When I neared fourteen, my father bit the bullet and moved us close to Pemberton where he took a job with a well-drilling crew. It was steady work, with benefits, and I got to go to Pemberton High. He pushed me to take my school work seriously, and I did. My high grades coupled with my gender and low socioeconomic status earned me a full ride – room, board, and tuition – at Rutgers. As soon as that was settled, he was ready to move back into the Barrens. But my mother had become used to the conveniences and amenities of town living. She wanted to stay in Pemberton. So they stayed.

I still can't help but wonder whether Dad might have lived longer if he'd moved back into the woods. I've never mentioned that to my mother, of course.

When Jasper paused, I jumped in: "My friend Jon's doing a book and he's devoting a chapter to the Jersey Devil."

"Is that so?" Jasper said. "And you brought him to me, did you?"

"Well, Dad always told me there weren't many folks in the

Pines you didn't know, and not much that went on that you didn't know about."

The old man beamed and did what many Pineys do: he repeated a phrase three times.

"Did he now? Did he now? Did he really now? Ain't that somethin'! I do believe that calls for a little jack."

As Jasper turned and reached into his cupboard, Creighton threw me a questioning look.

"Applejack," I told him.

He smiled. "Ah. Jersey lightning."

Jasper turned back with three glasses and a brown quart jug. With a practiced hand he poured two fingers' worth into each and handed them to us. The tumblers were smudged and maybe a little crusty, but I wasn't worried about germs. There's never been a germ that could stand up to straight jack from Jasper Mulliner's still. I remember siphoning some off from my father's jug and sneaking off into the brush at night to meet a couple of my girlfriends from high school, and we'd sit around and sing and get plastered.

I could tell by the way the vapor singed my nasal membranes that this was from a potent batch. I neglected to tell Creighton to go slow. As I took a respectful sip, he tossed his off. I watched him wince as he swallowed, saw his face grow red and his eyes begin to water.

"Whoa!" he said hoarsely. "You could etch glass with that stuff!" He caught Jasper looking at him sideways and held out his glass. "But delicious! Could I have just a drop more?"

"Help yourself," Jasper said, pouring him another couple of fingers. "Plenty more where this came from. But down it slow. This here's sippin' whiskey. You go puttin' too much of it down like that and you'll get apple palsy. Slow and leisurely does it when you're drinking Gus Sooy's best."

"This isn't yours?" I said.

"Naw! I stopped that long time ago. Too much trouble and gettin' too civilized 'round here. Besides, Gus's jack is as good as mine ever was. Maybe better."

He set the jug on the floor between us.

"About that Jersey Devil," I said, prompting him before he got off on another tangent.

"Right. The ol' Devil. He used to be known as the Leeds'

Devil. I'm sure you've heard various versions of the story, but I'll tell you the real one. That ol' devil's been around a spell, better'n two and a half centuries. All started back around seventeen-thirty or so. That was when Mrs. Leeds of Estellville found herself in the family way for the thirteenth time. Now she was so fed up and angry about this that she cried out, 'I hope this time it's the Devil!' Well now, someone must've been listenin' that night, because she got her wish. When that thirteenth baby was born, it was an ugly-faced thing, born with teeth like no one'd ever seen before, and it had a curly, sharp-pointed tail, and leathery wings like a bat. It bit its mother and flew out through the window. It grew up out in the pine wilds, stealing and eating chickens and small piglets at first, then graduating to cows, children, even growed men. All they ever found of its victims was their bones, and they was chipped and nicked by powerful sharp teeth. Some say it's dead now, some say it'll never die. Every so often someone says he shot and killed it, but most folks think it can't be killed. It gets blamed for every missing chicken and every pig or cow that wanders off, and so after a while you think it's just an ol' Piney folk tale. But it's out there. It's out there. It's surely out there."

"Have you ever seen it?" Creighton asked. He was sipping his jack with respect this time around.

"Saw its shadow. It was up on Apple Pie Hill, up at the top, in the days before they put up the fire tower. Before you was born, Kathleen. I'd been out doing some summer hunting, tracking a big ol' stag. You know what a climb Apple Pie is, dontcha?"

I nodded. "Sure do."

It didn't look like much of a hill. No cliffs or precipices, just a slow incline that seemed to go on forever. You didn't have to do much more than walk to get to the top, but you were bushed when you finally reached it.

"Anyways, I was about three-quarters the way up when it got too dark to do any more tracking. Well, I was tired and it was a warm summer night so's I just settled down on the pine needles and decided I'd spend the night. I had some jerky and some pone and my jug." He pointed to the floor. "Just like that one. You two be sure to help yourselves, hear me?"

"I'm fine," I said.

I saw Creighton reach for the jug. He always could handle a lot. I was already feeling my two sips. It was getting warmer in here by the minute.

"Anyways," Jasper went on, "I was sitting there chewing and sipping when I saw some pine lights."

Creighton started in mid-pour and spilled some applejack over his hand. He was suddenly very alert, almost tense.

"Pine lights?" he said. "You saw pine lights? Where were they?"

"So you've heard of the pine lights, have you?"

"I sure have. I've been doing my homework. Where did you see them? Were they moving?"

"They were streaming across the crest of Apple Pie Hill, just skirting the tops of the trees."

Creighton put his tumbler down and began fumbling with his map.

"Apple Pie Hill... I remember seeing that somewhere. Here it is." He jabbed his finger down on the map as if he were driving a spike into the hill. "Okay. So you were on Apple Pie Hill when you saw the pine lights. How many were there?"

"A whole town's worth of them, maybe a hunnert, more than I've ever seen before or since."

"How fast were they going?"

"Different speeds. Different sizes. Some gliding peacefully, some zipping along, moving past the slower ones. Looked like the Turnpike on a summer weekend."

Creighton leaned forward, his eyes brighter than ever.

"Tell me about it."

Something about Creighton's intensity disturbed me. All of a sudden he'd become an avid listener. He'd been listening politely to Jasper's retelling of the Jersey Devil story, but he'd seemed more interested in the applejack than in the tale. He hadn't bothered to check the location of Apple Pie Hill when Jasper had said he'd seen the Jersey Devil there, but he'd been in a rush to find it at the first mention of the pine lights.

The pine lights. I'd heard of them but I'd never seen one. People tended to catch sight of them on summer nights, mostly toward the end of the season. Some said it was ball lightning or some form of St. Elmo's fire, some called it swamp gas, and some said it was the souls of dead Pineys coming back for periodic visits. Why was Creighton so interested?

"Well," Jasper said, "I spotted one or two moving along the crest of the hill and didn't think too much of it. I spot a couple just about every summer. Then I saw a few more. And then a few more. I got a little excited and decided to get up to the top of Apple Pie and see what was going on. I was breathing hard by the time I got there. I stopped and looked up and there they was, flowing along the tree tops forty feet above me, pale yellow, some ping-pong sized and some big as beach balls, all moving in the same direction."

"What direction?" Creighton said. If he leaned forward any farther, he was going to fall off his stool. "Which way were they going?"

"I'm getting to that, son," Jasper said. "Just hold your horses. So as I was saying, I was standing there watching them flow against the clear night sky, and I was feeling this strange tightness in my chest, like I was witnessing something I shouldn't. But I couldn't tear my eyes away. And then they thinned out and was gone. They'd all passed. So I did something crazy. I climbed a tree to see where they was going. Something in my gut told me not to, but I was filled with this wonder, almost like holy rapture. So I climbed as far as I could, until the tree started to bend with my weight and the branches got too thin to hold me. And I watched them go. They was strung out in long trail, dipping down when the land dipped down, and moving up when the land rose, moving just above the tops of the pines, like they was being pulled along strings." He looked at Creighton. "And they was heading southwest."

"You're sure of that?"

Jasper looked insulted. "Course I'm sure of that. Bear Swamp Hill was behind my left shoulder, and everybody knows Bear Swamp is east of Apple Pie. Those lights was on their way southwest."

"And this was the summer?"

"Nigh on to Labor Day, if I 'member correct."

"And you were on the crest of Apple Pie Hill?"

"The tippy top."

"Great!" He began folding his map.

"I thought you wanted to hear about the Jersey Devil."

"I do, I do."

"Then how come you're asking me all these questions about the lights and not asking me about my meeting with the Devil?"

I hid a smile. Jasper was as sharp as ever.

Creighton looked confused for a moment. An expression darted across his face. It was only there for a second, but I caught it. Furtiveness. Then he leaned forward and spoke to Jasper is a confidential tone.

"Don't tell anybody this, but I think they're connected. The pine lights and the Jersey Devil. Connected."

Jasper leaned back. "You know, you might have something there. Cause it was while I was up that tree that I spotted the ol' Devil himself. Or at least his shadow. I was watching the lights flow out of sight when I heard this noise in the brush. It had a slithery sound to it. I looked down and there was this dark shape moving below. And you know what? It was heading in the same direction as the lights. What do you think of that?"

Creighton's voice oozed sincerity.

"I think that's damn interesting, Jasper."

I thought they both were shoveling it, but I couldn't decide who was carrying the bigger load.

"But don't you go getting too interested in those pine lights, son. Gus Sooy says they're bad medicine."

"The guy who made this jack?" I said, holding up my empty tumbler.

"The very same. Gus says there's lots of pine light activity in his neighborhood every summer. Told me I was a fool for climbing that tree. Says he wouldn't get near one of those lights for all the tea in China."

I noticed that Creighton was tense again.

"Where's this Gus Sooy's neighborhood?" he said. "Does he live in Chatsworth?"

Jasper burst out laughing.

"Gus live in Chatsworth? That's a good un! Gus Sooy's an old Hessian who lives way out in the wildest part of the pines. Never catch him *near* a city like this!"

City? I didn't challenge him on that.

"Where do we find him then?" Creighton said, his expression like a kid who's been told there's a cache of M&M's hidden somewhere nearby.

"Not easy," Jasper said. "Gus done a good job of getting himself well away from everybody. He's well away. Yes, he's well away. But if you go down to Apple Pie Hill and head along the road there that runs along its south flank, and you follow that about two mile and turn south onto the sand road by Applegate's cranberry bog, then follow that for about ten-twelve mile till you come to the fork where you bear left, then go right again at the cripple beyond it, then it's a good ten mile down that road till you get to the big red cedar–"

Creighton was scribbling furiously.

"I'm not sure I know what a red cedar looks like," I said.

"You'll know it," Jasper said. "Its kind don't grow naturally around here. Gus planted it there a good many year ago so people could find their way to him. The *right* people," he said, eyeing Creighton. "People who want to buy his wares, if you get my meaning."

I nodded. I got his meaning: Gus made his living off his still.

"Anyways, you turn right at the red cedar and go to the end of the road. Then you've got to get out and walk about a third of the way up the hill. That's where you'll find Gus Sooy."

I tried to drive the route across a mental map in my head. I couldn't get there. My map was blank where he was sending us. But I was amazed at how far I did get. As a Piney, even a girl, you've got to develop a good sense of where you are, got to have a store of maps in your head that you can picture by reflex, otherwise you'll spend most of your time being lost. Even with a good library of mental maps, you'll still get lost occasionally. I could still travel my old maps. The skill must be like the proverbial bicycle – once you've learned, you never forget.

I had a sense that Gus Sooy's place was somewhere far down in Burlington County, near Atlantic County. But county lines don't mean much in the Pinelands.

"That's *really* in the middle of nowhere!" I said.

"That it is, Kathy, that it is. That it surely is. It's on the slope of Razorback Hill."

Creighton shuffled through his maps again.

"Razorback...Razorback...there's no Razorback Hill here."

"That's because it ain't much of a hill. But it's there all right. Just 'cause it ain't on your diddly map don't mean it ain't there. Lots of things ain't on that map."

Creighton rose to his feet.

"Maybe we can run out there now and buy some of this applejack from him. What do you say, Mac?"

"We've got time."

I had a feeling he truly did want to buy some of Sooy's jack, but I was sure some questions about the pine lights would come up during the transaction.

"Better bring your own jugs if you're goin'," Jasper said. "Gus don't carry no spares. You can buy some from the Buzbys at the general store."

"Will do," I said.

I thanked him and promised I'd say hello to my mom for him, then I joined Creighton out at the Wrangler. He had one of his maps unfolded on the hood and was drawing a line southwest from Apple Pie Hill through the emptiest part of the Barrens.

"What's that for?" I asked.

"I don't know just yet. We'll see if it comes to mean anything."

It would. Sooner than either of us realized.

4.

The Hessian

I bought a gallon-sized brown jug at the Chatsworth general store; Creighton bought two.

"I want this Sooy fellow to be *real* glad to see me!"

I drove us down 563, then off to Apple Pie Hill. We got south of it and began following Jasper's directions. Creighton read while I drove.

"What the hell's a cripple?" he said.

"That's a spong with no cedars."

"Ah! That clears up everything!"

"A spong is a low wet spot; if it's got cedars growing around it, it's a cripple. What could be clearer?"

"I'm not sure, but I know I'll think of something. By the way, why's this Sooy fellow called a Hessian? Mulliner doesn't really think he's–?"

"Of course not. Sooy's an old German name around the Pine Barrens. Comes from the Hessians who deserted the British army and fled into the woods after the battle of Trenton."

"The Revolution?"

"Sure. This sand road we're riding on now was here three hundred-odd years ago as a wagon trail. It probably hasn't changed any since. Might even have been used by the smugglers who used to unload freight in the marshes and move it overland through the Pines to avoid port taxes in New York and Philly. A lot of them settled in here. So did a good number of Tories and Loyalists who were chased from their land after the Revolution. Some of them probably arrived dressed in tar and feathers and little else. The Lenape Indians settled in here, too, so did Quakers who were kicked out of their churches for taking up arms during the Revolution."

Creighton laughed. "Sounds like Australia! Didn't anyone besides outcasts settle here?"

"Sure. Bog iron was a major industry. This was the center of the colonial iron production. Most of the cannon balls fired against the British in the Revolution and the War of 1812 were forged right here in the Pine Barrens."

"Where'd everybody go?"

"A place called Pittsburgh. There was more iron there and it was cheaper to produce. The furnaces here tried to shift over to glass production but they were running out of wood to keep them going. Each furnace consumed something like a thousand acres of pine a year. With the charcoal industry, the lumber industry, even the cedar shake industry all adding to the daily toll on the tree population, the Barrens couldn't keep up with the demand. The whole economy collapsed after the Civil War. Which probably saved the area from becoming a desert."

I noticed the underbrush between the ruts getting higher, slapping against the front bumper as we passed, a sure sign that not many people came this way. Then I spotted the red cedar. Jasper had been right – it didn't look like it belonged here. We turned right and drove until we came to a cul-de-sac at the base of a hill. Three rusting cars hugged the bushes along the perimeter.

"This must be the place," I said.

"This is not a place. This is *no*where."

We grabbed our jugs and walked up the path. About a third of the way up the slope we broke into a clearing with a slant-roofed shack in the far left corner. It looked maybe twenty feet on a side, and was covered with tar paper that was peeling away in spots, exposing the plywood beneath. Somewhere behind the shack a dog had begun to bark.

Creighton said, "Finally!" and started forward.

I laid a hand on his arm.

"Call out first," I told him. "Otherwise we may be ducking

buckshot."

He thought I was joking at first, then saw that I meant it.

"You're serious?"

"We're dressed like city folk. We could be revenuers. He'll shoot first and ask questions later."

"Hello in the house!" Creighton cried. "Jasper Mulliner sent us! Can we come up?"

A wizened figure appeared on the front step, a twelve gauge cradled in his arms.

"How'd he send you?"

"By way of the red cedar, Mr. Sooy!" I replied.

"C'mon up then!"

Where Jasper had been neat, Gus Sooy was slovenly. His white hair looked like a deranged bird had tried to nest in it; for a shirt he wore the stained top from a set of long johns and had canvas pants secured around his waist with coarse rope. His lower face was obscured by a huge white beard, stained around the mouth. An Appalachian Santa Claus, going to seed in the off-season.

We followed him into the single room of his home. The floor was covered with a mismatched assortment of throw rugs and carpet remnants. A bed sat in the far left corner, a kerosene stove was immediately to our right. Set about the room were a number of Aladdin lamps with the tall flues. Dominating the scene was a heavy legged kitchen table with an enamel top.

We introduced ourselves and Gus said he'd met my father years ago.

"So what brings you two kids out here to see Gus Sooy?"

I had to smile, not just at the way he managed to ignore the jugs we were carrying, but at being referred to as a "kid." A long time since anyone had called me that. I wouldn't let anyone call me a "girl" these days, but somehow I didn't mind "kid."

"Today we tasted some of the best applejack in the world," Creighton said with convincing sincerity, "and Jasper told us you were the source." He slammed his two jugs on the table. "Fill 'em up!"

I placed my own jug next to Creighton's.

"I gotta warn you," Gus said. "It's five dollars a quart."

"Five dollars!" Creighton said.

"Yeah," Gus added quickly, "but seein' as you're buying so

much at once–"

"Don't get me wrong, Mr. Sooy. I wasn't saying the price is too high. I was just shocked that you'd be selling such high grade sipping whiskey for such a low price."

"You were?" The old man beamed with delight. "It is awful good, isn't it?"

"That it is, sir. That it is. That it surely is."

I almost burst out laughing. I don't know how Creighton managed to keep a straight face.

Gus held up a finger. "You kids stay right here. I'll dip into my stock and be back in a jiffy."

We both broke down into helpless laughter as soon as he was gone.

"You're laying it on awful thick," I said when I caught my breath.

"I know, but he's lapping up every bit."

Gus returned in a few minutes with two gallon jugs of his own.

"Hadn't we ought to test this first before you begin filling our jugs?" Creighton said.

"Not a bad idea. No, sir, not a bad idea. Not a bad idea at all."

Creighton produced some paper cups from one of the pockets in his safari jacket and placed them on the table. Gus poured. We all sipped.

"This is even smoother than what Jasper served us. How do you do it, Mr. Sooy?"

"That's a secret," he said with a wink as he brought out a funnel and began decanting from his jugs into ours.

I brought up Jon's book and Gus launched into a slightly different version of the Jersey Devil story, saying it was born in Leeds, which is at the opposite end of the Pine Barrens from Estellville. Otherwise the tales were almost identical.

"Jasper says he saw the devil once," Creighton said as Gus topped off the last of our jugs.

"If he says he did, then he did. That'll be sixty dollar."

Creighton gave him three twenties.

"And now I'd like to buy you a drink, Mr. Sooy."

"Call me Gus. And I don't mind if I do."

Creighton was overly generous, I thought, with the way he filled the three paper cups. I didn't want any more, but I felt I had to keep up appearances. I sipped while the men quaffed.

"Jasper told us about the time he saw the Jersey Devil. He mentioned seeing pine lights at the same time."

I sensed rather than saw Gus stiffen.

"Is that so?"

"Yeah. He said you see pine lights around here all the time. Is that true?"

"You interested in pine lights or the Jersey Devil, boy?"

"Both. I'm interested in all the folk tales of the pines."

"Well, don't get too interested in the pine lights.

"Why not?"

"Just don't."

I watched Creighton tip his jug and refill Gus's cup.

"A toast!" Creighton said, lifting his cup. "To the Pine Barrens!"

"I'll drink to that!" Gus said, and drained his cup.

Creighton followed suit, causing his eyes to fill with tears. I sipped while he poured another round.

"To the Jersey Devil!" Creighton cried, hoisting his cup again.

And again they both tossed off their drinks. And then another round.

"To the pine lights!"

Gus wouldn't drink to that one. I was glad. I don't think either of them would have remained standing if he had.

"Have you seen any pine lights lately, Gus," Creighton said.

"You don't give up, do you, boy," the old man said.

"It's an affliction."

"So it is. All right. Sure. I see 'em all the time. Saw some last night."

"Really? Where?"

"None of your business."

"Why not?"

"Because you'll probably try to do something stupid like catch one, and then I'll be responsible for what happens to you and this young lady here. Not on my conscience, no thank you."

"I wouldn't dream of trying to catch one of those things!" Creighton said.

"Well, if you did you wouldn't be the first. Peggy Clevenger was the first." Gus lifted his head and looked at me. "You heard of Peggy Clevenger, ain't you, Miss McKelston?"

I nodded. "Sure. The Witch of the Pines. In the old days people used to put salt over their doors to keep her away."

Creighton began scribbling.

"No kidding? This is great! What about her and the pine lights?"

"Peggy was a Hessian, like me. Lived over in Pasadena. Not the California Pasadena, the Pines Pasadena. A few mile east of Mount Misery. The town's gone now, like it never been. But she lived thereabouts by herself in a small cabin, and people said she had all sorts of strange powers, like she could change her shape and become a rabbit or a snake. I don't know about that stuff, but I heard from someone who should know that she was powerful interested in the pine lights. She told this fella one day that she had caught one of the pine lights, put a spell on it and brought it down."

Creighton had stopped writing. He was staring at Gus.

"How could she ...?"

"Don't know," Gus said, draining his cup and shaking his head. "But that very night her cabin burned to the ground. They found her blackened and burned body among the ashes the next morning. So I tell you, kids, it ain't a good idea to get too interested in the pine lights."

"I don't want to capture one," Creighton said. "I don't even want to see one. I just want to know where other people have seen them. How can that be dangerous?"

Gus thought about that. And while he was thinking, Creighton poured him another cupful.

"Don't s'pose it would do any harm to show you where they was," he said after a long slow sip.

"Then it's settled. Let's go."

We gathered up the jugs and headed out into the late afternoon sunshine. The fresh air was like a tonic. It perked me up but didn't dissipate the effects of all the jack I'd consumed.

When we reached the Wrangler, Creighton pulled out his sextant and compass.

"Before we go, there's something I've got to do."

Gus and I watched in silence as he took his sightings and

scribbled in his notebook. Then he spread his map out on the hood again.

"What's up?" I said.

"I'm putting Razorback Hill on the map," he said.

He jotted his readings on the map and drew a circle. Before he folded everything up, I glanced over his shoulder and noticed that the line he had drawn from Apple Pie Hill ran right by the circle that was Razorback Hill.

"You through dawdlin'?" Gus said.

"Sure am. You want to ride in front?"

"No thanks," Gus said, heading for the rusty DeSoto. "I'll drive myself and you kids follow."

I said, "Won't it be easier if we all go together?"

"Hell no! You kids have been drinkin'!"

When we stopped laughing, we pulled ourselves into the Wrangler and followed the old Hessian back up his private sand road.

5.

The Firing Place

"I used to make charcoal here when I was young," Gus said.

We were standing in a small clearing surrounded by young pines. Before us was a shallow sandy depression, choked with weeds.

"This used to be my firing place. It was deeper then. I made some fine charcoal here before the big companies started selling their bags of 'brick-*etts*.'" He fairly spat the word. "Ain't no way any one of those smelly little things was ever part of a tree, I'll tell you that."

"Is this where you saw the lights, Gus?" Creighton said. "Were they moving?"

Gus said, "You got a one track mind, don't you, boy?" He glanced around. "Yeah, this is where I saw them. Saw them here last night and I saw them here fifty years ago, and I seen them near about every summer in between. Lots of memories here. I remember how while I was letting my charcoal burn I'd use the time to hunt up box turtles."

"And sell them as snail hunters?" I said.

I'd heard of box turtle hunting – another Pinelands mini-industry – but I'd never met anyone who'd actually done it.

"Sure. Folks in Philadelphia'd buy all I could find. They liked to let them loose in their cellars to keep the snails and slugs under control."

"The lights, Gus," Creighton said. "Which way were they

going?"

"They was goin' the same way they always went when I seen them here. That way."

He was pointing southeast.

"Are you sure?"

"Sure as shit, boy." Gus's tone was getting testy, but he quickly turned to me. "'Scuse me, miss," then back to Creighton. "I was standing back there right where my car is when about a half dozen of them swooped in low right overhead – not a hunting swoop, but a floaty sort of swoop – and traveled away over that pitch pine there with the split top."

"Good!" said Creighton, eying the sky.

A thick sheet of cloud was pulling up from the west, encroaching on the sinking sun. Out came the sextant and compass. Creighton took his readings, wrote his numbers, then took a bearing on the tree Gus had pointed out. A slow, satisfied smile crept over his face as he drew the latest line on his map. He folded it up before I had a chance to see where that line went. I didn't have to see. His next question told me.

"Say, Gus," he said offhandedly. "What's on the far side of Razorback Hill?"

Gus turned on Creighton like an angry bear.

"Nothing! There's nothing there! So don't you even think about going over there!"

Creighton's smile was amused. "I was only asking. No harm in a little question, is there?"

"There is. There is. Yes, there surely is! Especially when those questions is the wrong ones. And you've been asking a whole lot of wrong questions, boy. Questions that's gonna get you in a whole mess of bad trouble if you don't get smart and learn that certain things is best left alone. You hear me?"

He sounded like a character from one of those old Frankenstein movies.

"I hear you," Creighton said, "and I appreciate your concern. But can you tell me the best way to get to the other side of that hill?"

Gus threw up his hands with an angry growl.

"That's it! I'm havin' no more to do with the two of you! I've already told you too much as it is." He turned to me, his eyes blazing. "And you, Miss McKelston, you get yourself away from this boy.

He's headed straight to hell!"

With that he turned and headed for his car. He jumped in, slammed the door, and roared away with a spray of sand.

"I don't think he likes me," Creighton said.

"He seemed genuinely frightened," I told him.

Creighton shrugged and began packing away his sextant.

"Maybe he really believes in the Jersey Devil," he said. "Maybe he thinks it lives on the other side of Razorback Hill."

"I don't know about that. I got the impression he thinks the Jersey Devil is something to tell tall tales about while sitting around the stove and sipping jack. But those pine lights...he's scared of them."

"Just swamp gas, I'm sure," Creighton said.

Suddenly I was furious. Maybe it was all the jack I'd consumed, or maybe it was his attitude, but I think at that particular moment it was mostly his line of bull.

"Cut it, Jon!" I said. "If you really believe they're swamp gas, why are you tracking them on your map? You got me to guide you out here, so let's have it straight. What's going on?"

"I don't know what's going on, Mac. If I did, I wouldn't be here. Isn't that obvious? These pine lights mean something. Whether or not they're connected to the Jersey Devil, I don't know. Maybe they have an hallucinatory effect on people – after they pass overhead, people think they see things. I'm trying to establish a pattern."

"And after you've established this pattern, what do you think you'll find?"

"Maybe Truth," he said. "Reality. Who knows? Maybe the meaning – or meaninglessness – of life."

He looked at me with eyes so intense, so full of longing that my anger evaporated.

"Jon ...?"

His expression abruptly shifted back to neutral and he laughed.

"Don't worry, Mac. It's only me, Crazy Creighton, putting you on again. Let's have another snort of Gus Sooy's best and head for civilization. Okay?"

"I've had enough for the day. The *week!*"

"You don't mind if I partake, do you?"

"Help yourself."

I didn't know how he could hold so much.

While Creighton uncorked his jug, I strolled about the firing place to clear my fuzzy head. The sky was fully overcast now and the temperature was dropping to a more comfortable level.

He had everything packed away by the time I completed the circle.

"Want me to drive?" he said, tossing his paper cup onto the sand.

Normally I would have picked it up – the was something sacrilegious about leaving a Dixie cup among the pines – but I was afraid to bend over that far, afraid I'd keep on going head first into the sand and become litter myself.

"I'm okay. You'll get us lost."

We had traveled no more than a hundred feet or so when I realized that I didn't know this road. But I kept driving. I hadn't been paying close attention while following Gus here, but I was pretty sure it wouldn't be long before I'd come to a fork or a cripple or a bog that I recognized, and then we'd be home free.

It didn't quite work out that way. I drove for maybe five miles or so, winding this way and that with the roads, making my best guess when we came to a fork – and we came to plenty of those – and generally trying to keep us heading in the same general direction. I thought I was doing a pretty good job until we drove through an area of young pines that looked familiar. I stopped the Wrangler.

"Jon," I said. "Isn't this–?"

"Damn right it is!" he said, pointing to the sand beside the road. "We're back at Gus's firing place! There's my Dixie cup!"

I turned the Jeep around and headed back the way I came.

"What are you doing?" Creighton said.

"Making sure I don't make the same mistake twice!" I told him.

I didn't know how I could have driven in a circle. I usually had an excellent sense of direction. I blamed it on too much Jersey lightning and on the thickly overcast sky. Without the sun as a marker, I'd been unable to keep us on course. But that would change here and now. I'd get us out of here this time around.

Wrong.

After a good forty-five minutes of driving, I was so

embarrassed when I recognized the firing place again that I actually accelerated as we passed through, hoping Creighton wouldn't recognize the spot in the thickening dusk. But I wasn't quick enough.

"Hold it!" he cried. "Hold it just a damn minute! There's my cup again! We're right back where we started!"

"Jon," I said, "I don't understand it. Something's wrong."

"You're stewed, that's what's wrong!"

"I'm not!"

I truly believed I wasn't. I'd been feeling the effects of the jack before, true, but my head was clear now. I was sure I'd been heading due east, or at least pretty close to it. How I'd come full circle again was beyond me.

Creighton jumped out of his seat and came around the front of the Wrangler.

"Over you go, Mac. It's my turn."

I started to protest, then thought better of it. I'd blown it twice already. Maybe my sense of direction had fallen prey to the "apple palsy," as it was known. I lifted myself over the stick shift and dropped into the passenger seat.

"Be my guest."

Creighton drove like a maniac, seemingly choosing forks at random.

"Do you know where you're going?" I said.

"Yeah, Mac," he said. "I'm going whichever way you *didn't!* I think."

As darkness closed in and he turned on the headlights, I noticed that the trees were thinning out and the underbrush was closing in, rising to eight feet or better on either side of us. Creighton pulled off to the side at a widening of the road.

"You should stay on the road," I told him.

"I'm lost," he said. "We've got to think."

"Fine. But it's not as if somebody's going to be coming along and want to get by."

He laughed. "That's a fact!" He got out and looked up at the sky. "Damn! If it weren't for the clouds we could figure out where we are. Or least know where north is."

I looked around. We were surrounded by bushes. It was the Pine Barrens' equivalent of an English hedge maze. There wasn't a tree in sight. A tree can be almost as good as a compass – its moss faces north and its longest branches face south. Bushes are worse than useless for that, and the high ones only add to your confusion.

And we were confused.

"I thought Pineys never get lost," Creighton said.

"Everybody gets lost sooner or later out here."

"Well, what do Pineys do when they get lost?"

"They don't exhaust themselves or waste their gas by running around in circles. They hunker down and wait for morning."

"To hell with that!" Creighton said.

He threw the Wrangler into first and gunned it toward the road. But the vehicle didn't reach the road. It lurched forward and rocked back. He tried again and I heard the wheels spinning.

"Sugar!" I said.

Creighton looked at me and grinned.

"Stronger language is allowed and even encouraged in this sort of situation."

"I was referring to the sand."

"Don't worry. I've got four-wheel drive."

"Right. And all four wheels are spinning. We're in a patch of what's known as 'sugar sand.' "

He got out and pushed and rocked while I worked the gears and throttle, but I knew it was no use. We weren't going to get out of this superfine sand until we found some wood and piled it under the tires to give them some traction.

And we weren't going to be able to hunt up that kind of wood until morning.

I told Creighton that we'd only waste what gas we had left and that our best bet was to call it a night and pull out the sleeping bags. He seemed reluctant at first, worrying about deer ticks and catching Lyme disease, but he finally agreed.

He had no choice.

6.

The Pine Lights

"I owe you one, Jon," I said.

"How was I to know we'd get lost?" he said defensively. "I don't like this any more than you!"

"No. You don't understand. I meant that in the good sense. I'm glad you talked me into coming with you."

I'd found us a small clearing not too far from the Jeep. It surrounded the gnarled trunk of an old lone pine that towered above the dominant brush. We'd eaten the last of the sandwiches and now we sat on our respective bedrolls facing each other across the Coleman lamp sitting between us on the sand. Creighton was back to sipping his applejack. I would have killed, or at least maimed, for a cup of coffee.

I watched his face in the lamp light. His expression was puzzled.

"You must still be feeling the effects of that Jersey lightning you had this afternoon," he said.

"No. I'm perfectly sober. I've been sitting here realizing that I'm glad to be back. I've had a feeling for years that something's been missing from my life. Never had an inkling as to what it was until now. But this is it. I'm ..." My throat constricted around the word. "I'm home."

It wasn't the jack talking, it was my heart. I'd learned

something today. I'd learned that I loved the Pine Barrens. And I loved its people. So rich in history, so steeped in its own lore, somehow surviving untainted in the heart of Twentieth Century urban madness. I'd turned my back on it. Why? Too proud? Too good for it now? Maybe I'd thought I'd pulled myself up by my bootstraps and gone on to bigger and better things. I could see that I hadn't. I'd taken the girl out of the Pinelands but I hadn't taken the Pinelands out of the girl.

I promised myself to come back here again. Often. I was going to look up my many relatives, renew old ties. I wasn't ready to move back here, and perhaps I never would, but I'd never turn my back on the Pinelands again.

Creighton raised his cup to me.

"I envy anyone who's found the missing piece. I'm still looking for mine."

"You'll find it," I said, crawling into my bedroll. "You've just got to keep your eyes open. Sometimes it's right under your nose."

"Go to sleep, Mac. You're starting to sound like Dorothy from *The Wizard of Oz*."

I smiled at that. For a moment there he was very much like the Jonathan Creighton I'd fallen in love with. As I closed my eyes, I saw him pull out a pair of binoculars and begin scanning the cloud-choked sky. I knew what he was looking for, and I was fairly confident he'd never find them.

It must have been a while later when I awoke, because the sky had cleared and the stars were out when Creighton's shouts yanked me to a sitting position.

"They're coming! Look at them, Mac! My God, they're coming!"

Creighton was standing on the far side of the lamp, pointing off to my left. I followed the line of his arm and saw nothing.

"What are you talking about?"

"Stand up, damn it! They're coming! There must be a dozen of them!"

I struggled to my feet and froze.

The starlit underbrush stretched away in a gentle rise for maybe a mile or two in the direction he was pointing, broken only occasionally by the angular shadows of the few scattered trees. And coming our way over that broad expanse, skimming along at treetop level, was an oblong cluster of faintly glowing lights. *Lights*. That's what they were. Not glowing spheres. Not UFOs or any of that nonsense. They had no discernible substance. They were just light. Globules of light.

I felt my hackles rise at the sight of them. Perhaps because I'd never seen light behave that way before – it didn't seem right or natural for light to concentrate itself in a ball. Or perhaps it was the way they moved, gliding through the night with such purpose, cutting through the dark, weaving from tree to tree, floating by the topmost branches, and then forging a path toward the next. Almost as if the trees were sign posts. Or perhaps it was the silence. The awful silence. The Pine Barrens are quiet as far as civilized sounds are concerned, but there's always the noise of the living things, the hoots and cries and rustlings of the animals, the incessant insect susurration. That was all gone now. There wasn't even a breeze to rustle the bushes. Silence. More than a mere absence of noise. A holding of breath.

"Do you see them, Mac? Tell me I'm not hallucinating! Do you see them?"

"I see them, Jon."

My voice sounded funny. I realized my mouth was dry. And not just from sleep.

Creighton turned around in a quick circle, his arms spread.

"I don't have a camera! I need a picture of this!"

"You didn't bring a camera?" I said. "My God, you brought everything else!"

"I know, but I never dreamed–"

Suddenly he was running for the tree at the center of our clearing.

"Jon! You're not really–?"

"They're coming this way! If I can get close to them–!"

I was suddenly afraid for him. Something about those lights was warning me away. Why wasn't it warning Creighton? Or was he simply not listening?

I followed him at a reluctant lope.

"Don't be an idiot, Jon! You don't know what they are!"

"Exactly! It's about time somebody found out!"

He started climbing. It was a big old pitch pine with no branches to speak of for the first dozen feet or so of its trunk, but its bark was knobby and rough enough for Creighton's rubber soled boots to find purchase. He slipped off twice, but he was determined. Finally he made it to the lowest branch, and from there on it looked easy.

I can't explain the crawling sensation in my gut as I watched Jonathan Creighton climbing toward a rendezvous with the approaching pine lights. He was three-quarters of the way to the top when the trunk began to shake and sway with his weight. Then a branch broke under his foot and he almost fell. When I saw that he'd regained safe footing, I sighed with relief. The branches above him were too frail to hold him. He couldn't go any higher. He'd be safe from the lights.

And the lights were here, a good dozen of them, from baseball to basketball size, gliding across our clearing in an irregular cylindrical cluster perhaps ten feet across and twenty feet long, heading straight for Creighton's tree.

And the closer they got, the faster my insides crawled. They may have been made up of light but it was not a clean light, not the golden healthy light of day. This was a wan, sickly, anemic glow, tainted with the vaguest hint of green. But thankfully it was a glow out of Creighton's reach as the lights brushed the tree's topmost needles.

I watched their glow limn Creighton's upturned face as his body strained upward, and I wondered at his recklessness, at this obsession with finding "reality." Was he flailing and floundering about in his search, or was he actually on the trail of something? And were the pine lights part of it?

As the first light passed directly above him, not five feet beyond his outstretched hand, I heard him cry out.

"They're humming, Mac! High pitched! Can you hear it? It's almost musical! And the air up here tingles, almost as if it's charged! This is fantastic!"

I didn't hear any music or feel any tingling. All I could hear was my heart thudding in my chest, all I could feel was the cold sweat that had broken out all over my body.

Creighton spoke again, he was practically shouting now, but in a language that was not English and not like any other language I'd ever heard. He made clicks and wheezes, and the few noises that sounded like words did not seem to fit comfortably on the human tongue.

"Jon, what are you doing up there?" I cried.

He ignored me and kept up the alien gibberish, but the lights, in turn, ignored him and sailed by above him as if he didn't exist.

The cluster was almost past now, yet still I couldn't shake the dread, the dark feeling that something awful was going to happen.

And then it did.

The last light in the cluster was basketball-sized. It seemed as if it was going to trail away above Creighton just like the others, but as it approached the tree, it slowed and began to drop toward Creighton's perch.

I was panicked now.

"Jon, look out! It's coming right for you!"

"I see it!"

As the other lights flowed off toward the next treetop, this last one hung back and circled Creighton's tree at a height level with his waist.

"Get down from there!" I called.

"Are you kidding? This is more than I'd ever hoped for!"

The light suddenly stopped moving and hovered a foot or so in front of Creighton's chest.

"It's cold," he said in a more subdued tone. "Cold light."

He reached his hand toward it and I wanted to shout for him not to but my throat was locked. The tip of his index finger touched the outer edge of the glow.

"*Really* cold."

I saw his finger sink into the light to perhaps the depth of the fingernail, and then suddenly the light moved. It more than moved, it *leapt* onto Creighton's hand, engulfing it.

That's when Creighton began to scream. His words were barely intelligible but I picked out the words "cold" and "burning" again and again. I ran to the base of the tree, expecting him to lose his balance, hoping I could do something to break his fall. I saw the ball of light stretch out and slide up the length of his arm, engulfing it.

Then it disappeared.

For an instant I thought it might be over. But when Creighton clutched his chest and cried out in greater agony, I realized to my horror that the light wasn't gone – it was inside him!

And then I saw the back of his shirt begin to glow. I watched the light ooze out of him and reform itself into a globe. Then it rose and glided off to follow the other lights into the night, leaving Creighton alone in the tree, sobbing and retching.

I called up to him. "Jon! Are you all right? Do you need help?"

When he didn't answer, I grabbed hold of the tree trunk. But before I could attempt to climb, he stopped me.

"Stay there, Mac." His voice was weak, shaky. "I'm coming down."

It took him twice as long to climb down as it had to go up. His movements were slow, unsteady, and three times he had to stop to rest. Finally, he reached the lowest branch, hung from it by one hand, and made the final drop. I grabbed him immediately to keep him from collapsing into a heap, and helped him back toward the lamp and the bedrolls.

"My God, Jon! Your arm!"

In the light from the lamp his flesh seemed to be smoking. The skin on his left hand and forearm was red, almost scalded looking. Tiny blisters were already starting to form.

"It looks worse than it feels."

"We've got to get you to a doctor."

He dropped to his knees on his bedroll and hugged his injured arm against his chest with his good one.

"I'm all right. It only hurts a little now."

"It's going to get infected. Come on. I'll see if I can get us to civilization."

"Forget it," he said, and I sensed some of the strength returning to his voice. "Even if we get the Jeep free, we're still lost. We couldn't find our way out of here when it was daylight. What makes you think we'll do any better in the dark?"

He was right. But I felt I had to do something.

"Where's your first aid kit?"

"I don't have one."

I blew up then.

"Jesus Christ, Jon! You're crazy, you know that? You could have fallen out of that tree and been killed! And if you don't wind up with gangrene in that arm it'll be a miracle! What on God's earth made you do something so stupid?"

He grinned. "I knew it! You still love me!"

I was not amused.

"This is serious, Jon. You risked your life up there! For what?"

"I have to know, Mac."

"'Know?' What do you have to 'know?' Will you stop giving me this bullshit?"

"I can't. I can't stop because it's true. I have to know what's real and what's not."

"Spare me–"

"I mean it. You're sure you know what's real and so you're content and complacent with that. You can't imagine what it's like not to know. To sense there's a veil across everything, a barrier that keeps you from seeing what's really there. You don't know what it's like to spend your life searching for the edge of that veil so you can lift it and peek – just peek – at what's behind it. I know it's out there, and I can't reach it. You don't know what that's like, Mac. It makes you crazy."

"Well, that's one thing we can agree on."

He laughed – it sounded strained – and reached for his jug of applejack with his good hand.

"Haven't you had enough of that tonight?"

I hated myself for sounding like an old biddy, but what I just seen had shaken me to the core. I was still trembling.

"No. Mac. The problem is I haven't had enough. Not nearly enough."

Feeling helpless and angry, I sat down on my own bedroll and watched him take a long pull from the jug.

"What happened up there, Jon?"

"I don't know. But I don't ever want it to happen again."

"And what were you saying? It almost sounded as if you were calling to them."

He looked up sharply and stared at me.

"Did you hear what I said?"

"Not exactly. It didn't even sound like speech."

"That's because it wasn't," he said, and I was sure I detected relief in his voice. "I was trying to attract their attention."

"Well, you sure did that."

Across the top of the Coleman lamp, I thought I saw him

smile.

"Yeah. I did, didn't I?"

In the night around us, I noticed that the insects were becoming vocal again.

7.

The Shunned Place

I'd planned to stay awake the rest of the night, but somewhere along the way I must have faded into sleep. The next thing I knew there was sunlight in my eyes. I leaped up, disoriented for a moment, then I remembered where I was.

But where was Creighton? His bedroll lay stretched out on the sand, his compass, sextant, and maps upon it, but he was nowhere in sight. I called his name a couple of times. He called back from somewhere off to my left. I followed the sound of his voice through the brush and emerged on the edge of a small pond rimmed with white cedars.

Creighton was kneeling at the edge, cupping some water in his right hand.

"How'd you find this?" I said.

"Simple." He pointed out toward a group of drakes and mallards floating on the still surface. "I followed the quacking."

"You're becoming a regular Mark Trail. How's the water?"

"Polluted." He pointed to a brownish blue slick on the surface of the pond, then held up a palmful of clear, brownish water. "Look at that color. Looks like tea."

"That's not polluted," I told him. "That's the start of some bog iron floating over there. And this is cedar water. It gets brown from the iron deposits and from the cedars but it's as pure as it comes."

I scooped up double handful and took a long swallow.

"Almost sweet," I said. "Sea captains used to come into these parts to fill their water casks with cedar water before long voyages. They said it stayed fresher longer."

"Then I guess it's okay to bathe this in it," he said, twisting and showing me his left arm.

I gasped. I couldn't help it. I'd almost half-convinced myself that last night's incident with the pine light had been a nightmare. But the reddened, crusted, blistered skin on Creighton's arm said otherwise.

"We've got to get you to a doctor," I said.

"It's all right, Mac. Doesn't really hurt. Just feels hot."

He sank it past his elbow into the cool cedar water.

"Now *that* feels good!"

I looked around. The sun shone from a cloudless sky. We'd have no trouble finding our way out of here this morning. I stared out over the pond. Water. The sandy floor of the Pine Barrens was like a giant sponge that absorbed a high percentage of the rain that fell on it. It was the largest, untapped aquifer in the northeast. No rivers flowed into the Pinelands, only out. The water here was glacial in its purity. I'd read somewhere that the Barrens held an amount of water equivalent to a lake with a surface area of a thousand square miles and an average depth of 75 feet.

This little piece of wetness here was less than fifty yards across. I watched the ducks. They were quacking peacefully, tooling around, dipping their heads. Then one of them made a different sound, more like a squawk. It flapped its wings once and was gone. It happened in the blink of an eye. One second a floating duck, next second some floating bubbles.

"Did you see that?" Creighton said.

"Yeah, I did."

"What happened to that duck?" I could see the excitement starting to glow in his eyes. "What's it mean?"

"It means a snapping turtle. A big one. Fifty pounds or better, I'm sure."

Creighton pulled his arm from the pond.

"I do believe I've soaked this enough for now."

He dipped a towel in the water and wrapped it around his

scorched arm.

We walked back to the bedrolls, packed up our gear, and made our way through the brush to the Wrangler.

The Jeep was occupied.

There were people inside, and people sitting on the hood and standing on the bumpers as well. A good half dozen in all.

Only they weren't like any people I'd ever seen.

They were dressed like typical Pineys, but dirty, raggedy. The four men in jeans or canvas pants, collared shirts of various fabrics and colors or plain white tee-shirts; the two women wore cotton jumpers. But they were all deformed. Their heads were odd shapes and sizes, some way too small, others large and lopsided with bulbous protrusions. The eyes on a couple weren't lined up on the level. Everyone seemed to have one arm or leg longer than the other. Their teeth, at least in the ones who still had any, seemed to have come in at random angles.

When they spotted us, they began jabbering and pointing our way. They left the Wrangler and surrounded us. It was an intimidating group.

"Is that your car?" a young man with a lopsided head said to me.

"No." I pointed to Creighton. "It's his."

"Is that your car?" he said to Creighton.

I guessed he didn't believe me.

"It's a Jeep," Creighton said.

"Jeep! Jeep!" He laughed and kept repeating the word. The others around him took it up and chorused along.

I looked at Creighton and shrugged. We'd apparently come upon an enclave of the type of folks who'd helped turn "Piney" into a term of derision shortly before World War I. That was when Elizabeth Kite published a report titled "The Pineys" which was sensationalized by the press and led to the view that the Pinelands was a bed of alcoholism, illiteracy, degeneracy, incest, and resultant "feeblemindedness."

Unfair and untrue. But not entirely false. There has always been illiteracy and alcoholism deep in the Pinelands. Schooling here tended to be rudimentary if at all. And as for drinking? The first "drive-thru" service originated before the Revolution in the Piney jug taverns, allowing customers to ride up to a window, get their jugs topped off with applejack, pay, and move on without ever dismounting. But after the economy of the Pine Barrens faltered, and most of the workers moved on to greener pastures, much of the social structure collapsed. Those who stayed on grew a little lax as to the whys, hows, and to-whoms of marriage. The results were inevitable.

All that had supposedly changed in modern times, except in the most isolated area of the Pines. We had stumbled upon one of those areas. Except that the deformities here were extra-ordinary. I'd seen a few of the in-breds in my youth. There'd been something subtly odd about them, but nothing that terribly startling. These folk would stop you in your tracks.

"Let's head for the Jeep while they're yucking it up," I said out of the corner of my mouth.

"No. Wait. This is fascinating. Besides, we need their help."

He spoke to the group as a whole and asked their aid in freeing the Jeep.

Somebody said, "Sugar sand," and this was repeated all around. But they willingly set their shoulders against the Wrangler and we were on hard ground again in minutes.

"Where do you live?" Creighton said to anyone who was listening.

Someone said, "Town," and as one they all pointed east, toward the sun. It was also the direction the lights had been headed last night.

"Will you show me?"

They nodded and jabbered and tugged on our sleeves, anxious to show us.

"Really, Jon," I said. "We should get you to—"

"My arm can wait. This won't take long."

We followed the group in a generally uphill direction along a circuitous footpath unnavigable by any vehicle other than a motorcycle. The trees thickened and soon we were in shade. And then those trees opened up and we were in their "town."

A haze of blue wood smoke hung over a ramshackle collection of shanties made of scrap lumber and sheet metal. Garbage everywhere, and everyone coming out to look at the strangers. I'd never seen such squalor.

The fellow with the lopsided head who'd asked about the jeep before pulled Creighton toward one of the shacks.

"Hey, mister, you know about machines. How come this don't work?"

He had an old TV set inside his one room hut. He turned the knobs back and forth.

"Don't work. No pictures."

"You need electricity," Creighton told him.

"Got it. Got it. Got it."

He led us around to the back to show us the length of wire he had strung from a tree to the roof of the shack.

Creighton turned to me with stricken eyes.

"This is awful. No one should have to live like this. Can we do anything for them?"

His compassion surprised me. I'd never thought there was room for anyone else's concerns in his self-absorbed life. But then, Jonathan Creighton had always been a motherlode of surprises.

"Not much. They all look pretty content to me. Seem to have their own little community. If you bring them to the government's attention they'll be split up and most of them will probably be placed in institutions or group homes. I guess the best you can do is give them whatever you can think of to make the living easier here."

Creighton nodded, still staring around him.

"Speaking of 'here,'" he said, unshouldering his knapsack, "let's find out where we are."

The misshapen locals stared in frank awe and admiration as he took his readings. Someone asked him, "What is that thing?" a hundred times. At least. Another asked "What happened to your arm?" an equal number of times. Creighton was heroically patient with everyone. He knelt on the ground to transfer his readings to the map, then looked up at me.

"Know where we are?"

"The other side of Razorback Hill, I'd say."

"You got it."

He stood up and gathered the locals around him.

"I'm looking for a special place around here," he said.

Most of them nodded eagerly. Someone said, "We know every place there is around here, I reckon."

"Good. I'm looking for a place where nothing grows. Do you know a place like that?"

It was as if all of these people had a common plug and Creighton had just pulled it. The lights went out, the shades came down, the "Open" signs flipped to "Closed." They began to turn away.

"What'd I say?" he said, turning his anxious, bewildered eyes on me. "What'd I *say?*"

"You're starting to sound like Ray Charles," I told him. "Obviously they want nothing to do with this 'place where nothing grows' you're talking about. What's this all about, Jon?"

He ignored my question and laid his good hand on the shoulder of one of the small-headed men.

"Won't you take me there if you know where it is?"

"We know where it is," the fellow said in a squeaky voice. "But we never go there so we can't take you there. How can we take you there if we never go there?"

"You *never* go there? Why not?"

The others had stopped and were listening to the exchange. The small headed fellow looked around at his neighbors and gave them a look that asked how stupid could anyone be? Then he turned back to Creighton.

"We don't go there 'cause nobody goes there."

"What's your name?" Creighton said.

"Fred."

"Fred, my name is Jon, and I'll give you …" He patted his pockets, then tore the watch off his wrist. "I'll give you this beautiful watch that you don't have to wind – see how the numbers change with every second? – if you'll take me to a place where you *do* go and point out the place where nothing grows. How's that sound?"

Fred took the watch and held it up close to his right eye, then smiled.

"Come on! I'll show you!"

Creighton took off after Fred, and I took off after Creighton.

Again we were led along a circuitous path, this one even narrower than before, becoming less well defined as we went along. I noticed the trees becoming fewer in number and more stunted and gnarled, and the underbrush thinning out, the leaves fewer and curled on their edges. We followed Fred until he halted as abruptly as if he had run into an invisible wall. I saw why: the footpath we'd been following stopped here. He pointed ahead through what was left of the trees and underbrush.

"The bald spot's over yonder atop that there rise."

He turned and hurried back along the path.

Bald spot?

Creighton looked at me, then shrugged.

"Got your machete handy, Mac?"

"No, Bwana."

"Too bad. I guess we'll just have to bull our way through."

He rewrapped his burned arm and pushed ahead. It wasn't such rough going. The underbrush thinned out quickly and so we had an easier time of it than I'd anticipated. Soon we broke into a small field lined with scrappy weeds and occupied by the scattered, painfully gnarled trunks of dead trees. And in the center of the field was a patch of bare sand.

…a place where nothing grows …

Creighton hurried ahead. I held back, restrained by a sense of foreboding. The same something deep within me that had feared the pine lights feared this place as well. Something was wrong here, as if Nature had been careless, had made a mistake in this place and had never quite been able to rectify it. As if…

What was I thinking? It was an empty field. No eerie lights buzzing through the sky. No birds, either, for that matter. So what? The sun was up, a breeze was blowing – or at least it had been a moment ago.

Overruling my instincts, I followed Creighton. I touched the tortured trunk of one of the dead trees as I passed. It was hard and cold, like stone. A petrified tree. In the Pinelands.

I hurried ahead and caught up to Creighton at the edge of the "bald spot." He was staring at it as if in a trance. The spot was a rough oval, maybe thirty feet across. Nothing grew in that oval. Nothing.

"Look at that pristine sand," he said in a whisper. "Birds don't fly over it, insects and animals don't walk on it. Only the wind touches and shapes it. That's the way sand looked at the beginning of time."

It had always been my impression that sand wasn't yet sand at the beginning of time, but I didn't argue with him. He was on a roll. I remembered from college: You don't stop Crazy Creighton when he's on a roll.

I saw what he meant, though. The sand was rippled like water, like sand must look in areas of the Sahara far off the trade routes. I saw animal tracks leading up to it and then turning aside. Creighton was right: nothing trod this soil.

Except Creighton.

Without warning he stepped across the invisible line and walked to the center of the bald spot. He spread his arms, looked up and the sky, and whirled in dizzying circles. His eyes were aglow, his expression rapturous. He looked stoned out of his mind.

"This is it! I've found it! This is the place!"

"*What* place, Jon?"

I stood at the edge of the spot, unwilling to cross over, talking in the flat tone you might use to coax a druggie back from a bad trip, or a jumper down from a ledge.

"Where it all comes together and all comes apart! Where the Truth is revealed!"

"What the hell are you talking about, Jon?"

I was tired and uneasy and I wanted to go home. I'd had enough, and I guessed my voice showed it. The rapture faded. Abruptly, he was sober.

"Nothing, Mac. Nothing. Just let me take a few readings and we're out of here."

"That's the best news I've heard this morning."

He shot me a quick glance. I didn't know if it conveyed annoyance or disappointment. And I didn't care.

8.

Spreading Infection

I got us back to a paved road without too much difficulty. We spoke little on the way home. He dropped me off at my house and promised to see a doctor before the day was out.

"What's next for you?" I said as I closed the passenger door and looked at him through the open window.

I hoped he wouldn't ask me to guide him back into the Pines again. I was sure he hadn't been straight with me about his research. I didn't know what he was after, but I knew it wasn't the Jersey Devil. A part of me said it was better not to know, that this man was a juggernaut on a date with disaster.

"I'm not sure. I may go back and see those people, the ones on the far side of Razorback Hill. Maybe bring them some clothing, some food."

Against my will, I was touched.

"That would be nice. Just don't bring them toaster cakes or microwave dinners."

He laughed. "I won't."

"Where are you staying?"

He hesitated, looking uncertain.

"A place called the Laurelton Circle Motor Inn."

"I know it."

A tiny place. Sporting the name of a traffic circle that no

longer existed.

"I'm staying in room five if you need to get hold of me but …can you do me a favor? If anybody comes looking for me, don't tell them where I am. Don't tell them you've even seen me."

"Are you in some sort of trouble?"

"A misunderstanding, that's all."

"You wouldn't want to elaborate on that, would you?"

His expression was bleak.

"The less you know, Mac, the better."

"Like everything else these past two days, right?"

He shrugged. "Sorry."

"Me, too. Look. Stop by before you head back to Razorback. I may have a few old things I can donate to those folks."

He waved with his burnt hand, and then he was off.

***

Creighton stopped by a few days later on his way back to Razorback Hill. His left arm was heavily bandaged in gauze.

"You were right," he said. "It got infected."

I gave him some old sweaters and shirts and a couple of pairs of jeans that no longer fit the way they should.

***

The following week I bumped into him in the housewares aisle at Pathmark. He'd picked up some canned goods and was buying a couple of can openers for the Razorback folks. His left arm was bandaged as before, but I was concerned to see that there was gauze on his right hand now.

"The infection spread a little, but the doctor says it's okay. He's got me on this new antibiotic. Sure to kill it off."

Looking more closely now in the supermarket's fluorescent glare, I saw that he was pale and sweaty. He seemed to have lost weight.

"Who's your doctor?"

"Guy up in Neptune. A specialist."

"In pine light burns?"

His laugh was a bit too loud, a tad too long.

"No! Infections."

I wondered. But Jon Creighton was a big boy now. I couldn't be his mother.

I picked out some canned goods myself, checked out behind Creighton, and gave the bagful to him.

"Give them my best," I told him.

He smiled wanly and hurried off.

***

At the very tail end of August I was driving down Brick Boulevard when I spotted his Wrangler idling at the Burger King drive-thru window. I pulled into the lot and walked over.

Jon!" I said through the window and saw him jump.

"Oh, Mac. Don't ever do that!"

He looked relieved, but he didn't look terribly glad to see me. His face seemed thinner, but maybe that was because of the beard he had started to grow. A fugitive's beard.

"Sorry," I said. "I was wondering if you wanted to get together for some *real* lunch."

"Oh. Well. Thanks, but I've got a lot of errands to run. Maybe some other time."

Despite the heat, he was wearing corduroy pants and a long sleeved flannel shirt. I noticed that both his hands were still wrapped in gauze. An alarm went off inside me.

"Isn't that infection cleared up yet?"

"It's coming along slowly, but it's coming."

I glanced down at his feet and noticed that his ankles looked thick. His sneakers were unlaced, their tongues lolling out as the sides stretched to accommodate his swollen feet.

"What happened to your feet?"

"A little edema. Side effect of the medicine. Look, Mac, I've got to run." He threw the Wrangler into gear. "I'll call you soon."

***

Labor Day was a couple of weeks gone and I'd been thinking about Creighton a lot. I was worried about him, and was realizing that I still harbored deeper feelings for him than I cared to admit.

Then the state trooper showed up at my office. He was big and intimidating behind his dark glasses; his haircut came within a millimeter of complete baldness. He held out a grainy photo of Jon Creighton.

"Do you know this man?" he said in a deep voice.

My mouth was dry as I wondered if he was going to ask me if I was involved in whatever Creighton had done; or worse: if I'd care to come down and identify the body.

"Sure. We went to college together."

"Have you seen him in the past month?"

I didn't hesitate. I did the stand-up thing.

"Nope. Not since graduation."

"We have reason to believe he's in the area. If you see him, contact the State Police or your local police immediately."

"What's he done, officer?"

He turned and started toward the door without deigning to answer. That brand of arrogance never failed to set something off in me.

"I asked you a question, *officer*. I expect the courtesy of a reply."

He turned and looked at me, then shrugged. Some of the Dirty Harry facade slipped away with the shrug.

"Why not?" he said. "He's wanted for grand theft."

Oh, great.

"What did he steal?"

"A book."

"A *book?*"

"Yeah. Would you believe it? We've got rapes and murders and armed robberies, but this book is given a priority. I don't care how valuable it is or how much some university in Massachusetts wants it, it's only a book. But the Massachusetts people are really hot to get it back. Their governor got to our governor and ... well, you know how it goes. We found his car abandoned out near Lakehurst a while back, so we know he's been through here."

"You think he's on foot?"

"Maybe. Or maybe he rented or stole another car. We're running it down now."

"If he shows up, I'll let you know."

"Do that. I get the impression that if he gives the book back in one piece, all will be forgiven."

"I'll tell him that if I get the chance."

As soon as he was gone, I got on the phone to Creighton's motel. His voice was thick when he said hello.

"Jon! The state cops were just here looking for you!"

He mumbled a few words I didn't understand. Something was wrong. I hung up and headed for my car.

There are only about 20 rooms in that particular motel. I spotted the Wrangler backed into a space at the far end of the tiny parking lot. Number 5 was on a corner of the first floor. A *Do Not Disturb* sign hung from the knob. I knocked on the door twice and got no answer. I tried the knob. It turned.

It was dark inside except for the daylight I'd let in. And that light revealed a disaster area. The room looked like the inside of a dumpster behind a block of fast food stores. Smelled like one, too. There were pizza boxes, hamburger wrappers, submarine sleeves, Chinese food cartons, a sampling from every place in the area that delivered. And it was hot. Either the air conditioner had quit or it hadn't been turned on.

"Jon?" I flipped on the light. "Jon, are you here?"

He was in a chair in a corner on the far side of the bed, huddled under a pile of blankets. Papers and maps were piled on the night table beside him. His face, where visible above his matted beard, was pale and drawn. He looked as if he'd lost thirty pounds. I slammed the door closed and stood there, stunned.

"My God, Jon, what's wrong?"

"Nothing. I'm fine." His hoarse, thick voice said otherwise. "What are you doing here, Mac?"

"I came to tell you that the State Police are cruising around with photos of you, but I can see that's the least of your problems! You're really sick!" I reached for the phone. "I'm calling an ambulance."

"*No!* Mac, please *don't!*"

The terror and soul-wrenching anguish in his voice stopped me. I stared at him but still kept a grip on the receiver.

"Why not?"

"Because I'm begging you not to!"

"But you're sick, you could be dying, you're out of your head!"

"No. That's one thing I'm not. Trust me when I say that no hospital in the world can help me – because I'm not dying. And if you ever loved me, if you ever had any regard for who I am and what I want from my life, then you'll put down that phone and walk out that door."

I stood there in the hot, humid squalor of that tiny room, receiver in hand, smelling the garbage, detecting the hint of another odor, a subtle sour foulness that underlay the others, and felt myself being torn apart by the choice that faced me.

"Please, Mac," he said. "You're the only person in the world who'll understand. Don't hand me over to strangers." He sobbed once. "I can't fight you. I can only beg you. Please. Put down the phone and leave."

It was the sob that did it. I slammed the receiver onto its cradle.

"Damn you!"

"Two days, Mac. In two days I'll be better. You wait and see."

"You're damn right I'll see – I'm staying here with you!"

"No! You can't! You have no right to intrude! This is *my* life! You've got to let me take it where I must! Now leave, Mac. Please."

He was right, of course. This was what we'd been all about when we'd been together. I had to back off. And it was killing me.

"All right," I said around the lump in my throat. "You win. See you in two days."

Without waiting for a reply, I opened the door and stepped out into the bright September sunlight.

"Thanks, Mac," he said. "I love you."

I didn't want to hear that. I took one last look back as I pulled the door closed. He was still swaddled from his neck to the floor in the blankets, but in the last instant before the door shut him from view, I thought I saw something white and pointed, about the circumference of a garden hose, snake out on the carpet from under the blankets and then quickly pull back under cover.

A rush of nausea slammed me against the outer wall of the motel as the door clicked closed. I leaned there, sick and dizzy, trying to catch my breath.

A trick of the light. That was what I told myself as the vertigo faded. I'd been squinting in the brightness and the light had played a trick.

236

Of course, I didn't have to settle for merely telling myself. I could simply open the door and check it out. I actually reached for the knob, but couldn't bring myself to turn it.

Two days. Creighton had said two days. I'd find out then.

***

But I didn't last two days. I was unable to concentrate the following morning and wound up canceling all my appointments. I spent the entire day pacing my office or my living room; and when I wasn't pacing, I was on the phone. I called the American Folklore Society and the New Jersey Historical Society. Not only had they not given Creighton the grants he'd told me about, they'd never heard of him.

By nightfall I'd taken all I could. I began calling Creighton's room. I got no answer. I tried few more times, but when he still hadn't picked up by eleven o'clock, I headed for the motel.

I was almost relieved to see the Wrangler gone from the parking lot. Room five was still unlocked and still a garbage dump, which meant he was still renting it – or hadn't been gone too long.

What was he up to?

I began to search the room. I found the book under the bed. It was huge, heavy, wrapped in plastic with a scrawled note taped to the front:

Please return to Miskatonic U. archives

I slipped it out of the plastic. It was leatherbound and handwritten in Latin. I could barely decipher the title – something like *Liben Damnatus*. But inside the front cover were Creighton's maps and a sheaf of notes in his back-slanted scrawl. The notes were in disarray and probably would have been disjointed even if arranged in proper order. But certain words and phrases kept recurring: *nexus point* and *equinox* and *the lumens* and *the veil*.

It took me awhile but eventually I got the drift of the jottings. Apparently a section the book Creighton had stolen concerned "nexus points" around the globe where twice a year at the vernal and autumnal equinox "the veil" that obscures reality becomes detached for a short while, allowing an intrepid soul to peek under the hem and see the true nature of the world around us, the world we are not "allowed" to see. These "nexus points" are few and widely scattered.

Of the four known, there's one near each pole, one in Tibet, and one near the east coast of North America.

I sighed. Crazy Creighton had really started living up to his name. It was sad. This was so unlike him. He'd been the ultimate cynic, and now he was risking his health and his freedom pursuing this mystical garbage.

And what was even sadder was how he had lied to me. Obviously he hadn't been searching for tales of the Jersey Devil – he'd been searching for one of these 'nexus points." And he was probably convinced he'd found one behind Razorback Hill.

I pitied him. But I read on.

According to the notes, these "nexus points" can be located by following "the lumens" to a place shunned equally by man, beast, and vegetation.

Suddenly I was uneasy. "The lumens." Could that refer to the pine lights? And the "bald spot" that Fred had showed us – that was certainly a place shunned by man, beast, and vegetation.

I found a whole sheet filled with notes about the Razorback folk. The last paragraph was especially upsetting:

The folks behind Razorback Hill aren't deformed from inbreeding, although I'm sure that's contributed its share. I believe they're misshapen as a result of living near the nexus point for generations. The semi-annual lifting of the veil must have caused genetic damage over the years.

I pulled out Creighton's maps and unfolded them on the bed. I followed the lines he had drawn from Apple Pie Hill, from Gus's firing place, and from our campsite. All three lines represented paths of pine lights, and all three intersected at a spot near the circle he had drawn and labeled as Razorback Hill. And right near the intersection of the pine light paths, almost on top of it, he had drawn another circle, a tiny one, penciled in the latitude and longitude, and labeled it, *Nexus!*

I was worried now. Even my own skepticism was beginning to waver. Everything was fitting too neatly. I looked at my watch. 11:32. The date read "21." September 21. When was the equinox? I grabbed the phone and called an old clamdigger who'd been a client since I'd opened my office. He knew the answer right off:

"The autumnal equinox. That's September twenty-second.

'Bout a half hour from now."

I dropped the phone and ran for my car. I knew exactly where to find Jon Creighton.

9.

The Hem of the Veil

I raced down the Parkway to the Bass River exit and tried to find my way back to Gus Sooy's place. What had been a difficult trip in the day proved to be several orders of magnitude more difficult in the dark. But I managed to find Gus's red cedar. It was my plan to convince him to show me a short way to the far side of Razorback Hill, figuring the fact that Creighton was already there might make him more tractable. But when I rushed up to Gus Sooy's clearing, I discovered that he wasn't alone.

The Razorback folk were there. All of them, from the looks of the crowd.

I found Gus standing on his front step, a jug dangling from his hand. He was obviously shocked to see me, and was anything but hospitable.

"What do you want?"

Before I could answer, the Razorback folks recognized me and a small horde of them crowded around.

"Why are they all here?" I asked Gus.

"Just visiting,' he said casually, but did not look me in the eye.

"It wouldn't have anything to do with what's happening at the bald spot on the other side of Razorback Hill would it?"

"Damn you! You've been snoopin' around, haven't you? You and your friend. They told me he was coming around, askin' all sorts of questions. Where's he now? Hidin' in the bushes?"

"He's over there," I said, pointing to the top of Razorback Hill. "And if my guess is correct, he's standing right in the middle of the bald spot."

Gus dropped his jug. It shattered on the boards of his front step.

"Do you know what'll happen to him?"

"No," I said. "Do you?" I looked around at the Razorback folk. "Do they?"

"I don't think anyone knows, least most them. But they're scared. They come here twice a year, when that bald spot starts acting up."

"Have you ever seen what happens there?"

"Once. Never want to see it again."

"Why haven't you ever told anyone?"

"What? And bring all sorts of pointyheads here to look and gawk and build and ruin the place. We'd all rather put up with the bald spot craziness twice a year than pointyhead craziness every day all year long."

I didn't have time to get into Creighton's theory that the bald spot was genetically damaging the Razorback folks. I had to find Creighton.

"How do I get there? What's the fastest way?"

"You can't–"

"*They* got here!" I pointed to the Razorback folks.

"All right!" he said with open hostility. "Suit yourself. There's a trail behind my cabin here. Follow it over the left flank of the hill."

"And then?"

"And then you won't need any directions. You'll know where to go."

His words had an ominous ring, but I couldn't press him. I was being propelled by a sense of enormous urgency. Time was running out. Quickly. I already had my flashlight, so I hurried to the rear of his shanty and followed the trail.

Gus was right. As I crossed the flank of the hill I saw flashes through the trees ahead, like lightning, as if a very tiny and very violent electrical storm had been brought to ground and anchored there. I increased my pace, running when the terrain would allow. The wind picked up as I neared the storm area, growing from a fitful breeze to a full scale gale by the time I broke through the brush and stumbled into the clearing that surrounded the bald spot.

Chaos. That's the only way I can describe it. A nightmare of cascading lights and roaring wind. The pine lights – or *lumens* – were there, hundreds of them, all sizes, unaffected by the rushing vortex of air as they swirled about in wild arcs, each flaring brilliantly as it looped through the space above the bald spot. And the bald spot itself – it glowed with a faint purplish light that reached thirty or forty feet into the air before fading into the night.

The stolen book, Creighton's notes – they weren't mystical madness. Something cataclysmic was happening here, something that defied all the laws of nature – if indeed those laws had any real meaning. Whether this was one of the nexus points he had described, a fleeting rent in the reality that surrounded us, only Creighton could say for sure right now.

For I could see someone in the bald spot. I couldn't make out his features from where I was, but I knew it was Jonathan Creighton.

I dashed forward until I reached the edge but slewed to a halt in the sand before actually crossing into the glow. Creighton was there, on his knees, his hands and feet buried in the sand. He was staring about him, his expression an uneasy mix of fear and wonder. I shouted his name but he didn't hear me above the roar of the wind. Twice he looked directly at me but despite my frantic shouting and waving, did not see me.

I saw no other choice. I had to step onto the bald spot … the nexus point. It wasn't easy. Every instinct I possessed screamed at me to run in the other direction, but I couldn't leave him there like that. He looked helpless, trapped like an insect on flypaper. I had to help him.

Taking a deep breath, I closed my eyes and stepped across –

–and began to stumble forward. Up and down seemed to have a slightly different orientation here. I opened my eyes and dropped to my knees, nearly landing on Creighton. I looked around and froze.

The Pine Barrens were gone. *Night* was gone. It seemed to be pre-dawn or dusk here, but the wind still howled about us and the pine lights flashed around us, appearing and disappearing above as though passing through invisible walls. We were someplace … *else*: on a huge misty plain that seemed to stretch on forever, interrupted only by clumps of vegetation and huge fog banks, one of which was nearby on my left and seemed to go on and up forever. Off in the immeasurable distance, mountains the size of the moon reached up and disappeared into the haze of the purple sky. The horizon – or what I imagined to be the horizon – didn't curve as it should. This place seemed so much *bigger* than the world – our world – that waited just a few feet away.

"My God, Jon, where are we!"

He started and turned his head. His hands and feet remained buried in the sand. His eyes went wide with shock at the sight of me.

"No! You shouldn't be here!"

His voice was thicker and more distorted than yesterday. Oddly enough, his pale skin looked almost healthy in the mauve light.

"Neither should you!"

I heard something then. Above the shriek of the wind came another sound. A rumble like an avalanche. It came from somewhere within the fog bank to our left. There was something massive, something immense moving about in there, and the fog seemed to be drifting this way.

"We've got to get out of here, Jon!"

"No! I'm staying!"

"No way! Come on!"

He was wracked with infection and obviously deranged. I didn't care what he said, I wasn't going to let him risk his life in this place. I'd pull him out of here and let him think about it for six months. *Then* if he still wanted to try this, it would be his choice. But he wasn't competent now.

I looped my arms around his chest and tried to pull him to his feet.

"Mac, please! Don't!"

His hands remained fixed in the sand. He must have been holding onto something. I grabbed his right elbow and yanked. He screamed as his hand pulled free of the sand. Then I screamed, too, and let him go and threw myself back on the sand away from him.

Because his hand wasn't a hand anymore.

It was big and white and had these long, ropey, tapered root like projections, something like an eye on a potato when it sprouts after being left under the sink too long, only these things were moving, twisting and writing like a handful of albino snakes.

"Go, Mac!" he said in that distorted voice, and I could tell from his face and eyes that he hadn't wanted me to see him like this. "You don't belong here!"

"And you do?"

"*Now* I do!"

I couldn't bring myself to touch his hand, so I reached forward and grabbed some of his shirt. I pulled.

"We can find doctors! They can fix you! You can—"

"*NO!*"

It was a shout and it was something else. Something long and white and hard as flexed muscle, much like the things protruding from his shirt sleeve, darted out of his mouth and slammed against my chest, bruising my breasts as it thrust me away. Then it whipped back into his mouth.

I snapped then. I scrambled to my feet and blindly lurched away in the direction I'd come. Suddenly I was back in the Pine Barrens, in the cool night with the lights swirling madly above my head. I stumbled for the bushes, away from the nexus point, away from Jonathan Creighton.

At the edge of the clearing, I forced myself to stop and look back. I saw Creighton. His awful transformed hand was raised. I knew he couldn't see me, but it was almost as if he was waving goodbye. Then he lowered his hand and worked the tendrils back into the sand.

The last thing I remember of that night is vomiting.

10.

Aftermath

I awoke among the Razorback folk who'd found me the next morning and watched over me until I was conscious and lucid again. They offered me food but I couldn't eat. I walked back up to the clearing, to the bald spot.

It looked exactly as it had when Creighton and I had first seen it in August. No lights, no wind, no purple glow. Just bare sand.

And no Jonathan Creighton. I could have convinced myself that last night had never happened if not for the swollen, tender, violet bruise on my chest. Would that I had. But as much as my mind shrank from it, I could not deny the truth. I'd seen the other side of the veil and my life would never be the same.

I looked around and knew that everything I saw was a sham, an elaborate illusion. Why? Why was the veil there? To protect us from harm? Or to shield us from madness? The truth had brought me no peace. Who could find comfort in the knowledge that huge, immeasurable forces beyond our comprehension were out there, moving about us, beyond the reach of our senses?

I wanted to run... but where?

I ran home. I've been home for months now. Housebound. Moving beyond my door only for groceries. My accounting clients have all left me. I'm living on my savings, learning Latin, translating Jon's stolen book. Was what I saw the true reality of our existence, or another dimension, or what? I don't know. Creighton was right: knowing that you don't know is maddening. It consumes you.

So I'm waiting for spring. Waiting for the vernal equinox. Maybe I'll leave the house before then and hunt up some pine lights – or *lumens*, as the book calls them. Maybe I'll touch one, maybe I won't. Maybe when the equinox comes, I'll return to Razorback Hill, to the bald spot. Maybe I'll look for Jon. He may be there, he may not. I may cross into the bald spot, I may not. And if I do, I may not come back. Or I may.

I don't know what I'll do. I don't know anything anymore. I've come to the point now where I'm sure of only one thing: Nothing is sure anymore.

At least on this side of the veil.

ALSO BY THE AUTHORS

Also by Elle J Rossi

The Josie Hawk Chronicles
Crimson Beat
Indigo Dawn
Midnight Masque

The Brennan Coven Series
The Luminary
The Soother

Angels of Punishment
Broken Flight

Unspun
Chasing Fate

Other Fiction
Rehab Is For Witches

Also by Patrick Freivald

The Twice Shy Series
Twice Shy
Special Dead

Matt Rowley Novels
Jade Sky
Black Tide

With Philip Freivald
Blood List

Also by Rachel Aukes

The Deadland Saga
100 Days in Deadland
Deadland's Harvest
Deadland Rising

Short Stories in the Deadland World
Fat Zombie
At Hell's Gates

Colliding Worlds Trilogy
Collision
Implosion
Explosion

Guardians of the Seven Seals
Knightfall
Hellbound

Other Fiction
Stealing Fate
Tales from the SFR Brigade, Vol. 1
Stories on the Go

Join Rachel's mailing list and get an email when a new book is released:
www.rachelaukes.com

Also by Lance Taubold

On Two Fronts

Ripper A Love Story

Zodiac Lovers Series
Zodiac Lovers Book 1: Aquarius Pisces Aries
Zodiac Lovers Book 2: Taurus Gemini Cancer
Zodiac Lovers Book 3: Leo Virgo Libra
Zodiac Lovers Book 4: Scorpio Sagittarius Capricorn

Also by Kathy Love

The Young Brother Vampire Series

Fangs for the Memories
Fangs But No Fangs
I Only Have Fangs for You
My Sister is a Werewolf

The Bourbon Street Vampire Series

Any Way You Want It
I Want You to Make Me
Demon Can't Help It
What a Demon Wants
Truth or Demon

The Devilishly Hot Series

Devilishly Hot
Devilishly Sexy
Devilishly Wicked

Also by Michael Koogler

Antivirus (May 2015)
Antivirus II – The Awakening (2016)

The Krypteia Conspiracy
Hade's Gambit
The Rise of Cain

The Earth War Chronicles
Convergence (Late 2015)
Mirror (2016)
Godfall (TBD)
Nexus (TBD)

Other Fiction
Jigsaw, a short story in Sadistic Shorts
The Summoning, a short story in Sadistic Shorts

Also by E. McCarthy

Written as Erin McCarthy

My Immortal

Fallen

The Taking

First Blood

Out of the Light, Into the Shadows

Also by Richard Devin

The Third Hour

Ripper – A Love Story

Stop Saying Yes – Negotiate: A quick reference to better negotiations

Do You Want To Be An Actor? 101 Answers to your questions on breaking into the 'biz'

Actors' Resumes – The Definitive Guidebook

Also by Paul Mannering

The Locusts
Dead! Dead! Dead!

The Tankbread Series
Tankbread
Tankbread 2: Immortal
Tankbread 3: Deadland
Tankbread 4: Black Snow (2015)

The Drakeforth Trilogy
Engines of Empathy
Pisces of Fate

Short Works and Collections
Amazon Author Page

Editor
Tales from the Bell Club
Fat Zombie: Stories of Unlikely Survivors from the Apocalypse

Audio Drama
www.brokensea.com

Also by F. Paul Wilson

The Secret History of the World

"The Barrens" is part of a history of the world that remains undiscovered, unexplored, and unknown to most of humanity. Some of this secret history has been revealed in the Adversary Cycle, some in the Repairman Jack novels, and bits and pieces in other, seemingly unconnected works. Taken together, even these millions of words barely scratch the surface of what has been going on behind the scenes, hidden from the workaday world. I've listed them below in chronological order. (NB: "Year Zero" is the end of civilization as we know it; "Year Zero Minus One" is the year preceding it, etc.)

The Past
"Demonsong" (prehistory)
"The Compendium of Srem" (1498)
"Aryans and Absinthe"** (1923-1924)
Black Wind (1926-1945)
The Keep (1941)
Reborn (February-March 1968)
"Dat Tay Vao"*** (March 1968)
Jack: Secret Histories (1983)
Jack: Secret Circles (1983)
Jack: Secret Vengeance (1983)
"Faces"* (1988)
Cold City (1990)
Dark City (1991)
Fear City (1993)

Year Zero Minus Three
Sibs (February)
The Tomb (summer)
"The Barrens"* (ends in September)
"A Day in the Life"* (October)
"The Long Way Home"+
Legacies (December)

Year Zero Minus Two
"Interlude at Duane's"** (April)
Conspiracies (April) (includes "Home Repairs"+)
All the Rage (May) (includes "The Last Rakosh"+)
Hosts (June)
The Haunted Air (August)
Gateways (September)
Crisscross (November)
Infernal (December)

Year Zero Minus One
Harbingers (January)
"Infernal Night"++ (with Heather Graham)
Bloodline (April)
By the Sword (May)
Ground Zero (July)
The Touch (ends in August)
The Peabody-Ozymandias Traveling Circus & Oddity Emporium
(ends in
September)
"Tenants"*

Year Zero
"Pelts"*
Reprisal (ends in February)
Fatal Error (February) (includes "The Wringer"+)
The Dark at the End (March)
Nightworld (May)

* available in *The Barrens and Others*
** available in *Aftershock and Others*
*** available in the 2009 reissue of *The Touch*
+ available in *Quick Fixes – Tales of Repairman Jack*
++ available in *Face Off*

The Adversary Cycle
The Keep
The Tomb
The Touch
Reborn
Reprisal
Nightworld

Repairman Jack
The Tomb
Legacies
Conspiracies
All the Rage
Hosts
The Haunted Air
Gateways
Crisscross
Infernal
Harbingers
Bloodline
By the Sword
Ground Zero
Fatal Error
The Dark at the End
Nightworld
Quick Fixes – Tales of Repairman Jack

The Teen Trilogy
Jack: Secret Histories
Jack: Secret Circles
Jack: Secret Vengeance

The Early Years Trilogy
Cold City
Dark City
Fear City

The LaNague Federation Series
Healer
Wheels Within Wheels
An Enemy of the State
Dydeetown World
The Tery

Other Novels
Black Wind
Sibs
The Select
Virgin
Implant
Deep as the Marrow
Mirage (with Matthew J. Costello)
Nightkill (with Steven Spruill)
DNA Wars (formerly *Masque* with Matthew J. Costello)
Sims
The Fifth Harmonic
Midnight Mass
The Proteus Cure (with Tracy L. Carbone)
A Necessary End (with Sarah Pinborough)
Definitely Not Kansas (with Tom Monteleone)

Short Fiction
Soft & Others
The Barrens & Others
The Christmas Thingy
Aftershock & Others
The Peabody-Ozymandias Traveling Circus & Oddity Emporium
Quick Fixes – Tales of Repairman Jack
Sex Slaves of the Dragon Tong

Editor
Freak Show
Diagnosis: Terminal
The Hogben Chronicles (with Pierce Watters)

Omnibus Editions
The Complete LaNague
Calling Dr. Death (3 medical thrillers)

www.ingramcontent.com/pod-product-compliance
Lightning Source LLC
Chambersburg PA
CBHW030123180626
46812CB00002B/529